# Home from Home

*The lives and loves of five nurses in the 1960s*

## CATH COLE

To Tracy
Thank you for your
kind attention
Cath Cole.

Published by Corazon Books
(Wyndham Media Ltd)
27, Old Gloucester Street, London WC1N 3AX
www.greatstorieswithheart.com

ISBN: 1909752169
ISBN-13: 978-1-909752-16-0

For Charlie, Oliver, Olivia, Charlotte, Zoe, James and Ron with love.

# ACKNOWLEDGMENTS

I would like to thank the following groups for their help, encouragement and support.

Skelmersdale Writers' Group,
Mike Morris and the Pulp Idol team,
Robert Sheppard, Ailsa Cox and MA (2011-2013) students,
Kearsley Girls and
Bolton NHS Foundation Trust

Thank you to individual friends who have read chapters and drafts: it is difficult to make a list for fear of inadvertently excluding someone. However, three people cannot go without a personal, heartfelt thank you.

Ian Skillicorn, for believing in the project,
Ron Cole, for always being there and
Judith Thorpe, for friendship over a life time.

# FRIDAY NIGHT

## Theresa

'Good luck Theresa, luv. We'll miss you.' The fearless Amazon of a ward auxiliary said as she reached out, grasped Theresa into her bosom, and smacked a kiss on her forehead.

*What the bugger…?*

The force of the grapple knocked Theresa's cap flying.

'You're one of the best cadets we've ever 'ad on 6C. We'll miss your lip and back chat to say nowt about yer singin.' The auxiliary nurse fastened the top button of her white overall. The embrace had threatened to release her cantilevered chest from its starched cage. 'It'll be yer last chance to annoy Shitty.'

'I'm dreading asking to go off duty. She's a miserable cow. I don't know why she has to pick on me all the time.' Using the single hairgrip she'd managed to find from rootling around on the floor, Theresa anchored the cap back on her head as best she could. 'Do you think I could sneak off while she's giving Twitchy the afternoon report?'

'Not a chance – and any road up Twitchy'll want to wish you all the best. The least you can do for the rest of us is let Shitty have another go at you. Go on, get gone and remember them of us what's bin good to you when you come back on 'ere as a know-it-all student nurse.'

'I'll miss you too, thanks for looking after me and keeping me out of trouble – well for most of the time.'

As she left the kitchen Theresa turned to look down the long ward. A student nurse was dragging a recalcitrant set of screens towards a bed. *That'll be me, next week – yeah, too bloody true it will.*

Theresa hovered at the door of the sisters' office.

'Is it all right for me to go off duty now?'

'Look after yourself, Cadet. You've worked hard for us, hasn't she, Sister Smith?' Sister Thomas, a nervy woman at the best of times, gave her senior colleague a wary look.

'Thank you, Sister Thomas,' Theresa said.

Anxious to get away, she turned and walked into the door-frame. She felt the cap sliding out of her hair.

Sister Smith turned her head and glared at Theresa.

'You need to buck your ideas up, young lady. I've already had a word with Sister Tutor Bolton about you.'

Shoulders hunched, Theresa faced her tormentor. Too late. The cap tumbled to the floor. She stooped to retrieve it.

'You need to listen to your elders and betters and keep that muck off your face. Nursing is a vocation, not any old job where you can do as you please. If you make it beyond the first year of training, Cadet Booth, I promise you I will, I will … Now for the last time, take yourself off my ward.' She shifted her head back to the report on her desk.

'Yes, Sister,' said Theresa. She turned to leave the

office, her mouth twisted, her hands balled into fists.

Bugger off, Shitty Smith, you dried-up old frog.

'Don't bother about me, Mum,' said Theresa. 'I'll get some toast and jam later.'

In the Booth household money was hard come by. Theresa's younger sisters and her youngest brother had free school meals; Theresa had free meals as a cadet. Her dad and her brother Tommy had subsidised meals at the factory. Her mum – Bernadette – and her little sister, known to them all as 'the baby', made do with whatever food was in the house. Tea was usually jam or HP sauce butties.

Making her way from the kitchen, Theresa went through the front room into the small entrance hall behind the front door, to try and hang her coat on one of the coat hooks still in place. The front door was rarely used. If a stranger called, one of the family banged on the front room window, pointed sideways and shouted 'go round t'back'. If the visitor insisted on standing at the door they would be peered at through the narrow gap left when the door was pushed back against the thick pile of cardigans, coats and other clothing that didn't have a home. On her way back to the kitchen, Theresa retrieved the pile of clothes that the baby, who was asleep on the settee, had kicked onto the floor. She looked around for somewhere to dump her armful, glanced around the front room, shrugged at the crowded surfaces of the furniture and carried the clothes through to the kitchen.

'Do you think we'll ever move to a bigger house, Mum?'

'I've stopped frettin' about it, luv. I think the council have forgotten about us. Stick that lot on the table. I'll try and get round to ironing them later.'

'Here's my wage packet.'

'Your last one as a cadet.'

Bernadette reached inside the brown envelope, took

out a pound note and a ten-shilling note and handed the money to Theresa before stuffing the envelope in her apron pocket.

'I'll be able to give you a bit more from now on. My pay goes up on Monday.'

'That'll be good, luv, but only while you're still living at home. You'll need what bit's left for clothes and other stuff.'

'I can still give you something, Mum.'

'Get your dad a packet of his smokes every now and then, he'll like that.'

Theresa took hold of her mother's bony shoulders and steered her away from the kitchen sink.

'Leave the pots, I'll do them. Go and sit down while you can.'

The bump of feet hitting a bedroom floor, followed by running, shouting and laughing soon gave way to loud wails.

Bernadette looked upwards, shook her head, took a deep breath and dragged herself toward the stairs.

'You wicked, wicked boy, look what you've done – you little bugger. I've a good mind to give your bum a good smack. The place smells bad enough as it is.' Bernadette hoisted her youngest son out of the bathroom and pushed him onto the landing. 'Go on, out of my way.'

'He's kicked the night bucket over,' Bernadette said to Theresa, who had followed her upstairs. 'Look at the mess.'

'We'll soon sort it out, Mum. You take the girls and give them a wash down in the sink. I'll clean this lot up. How she's managed to get upstairs I don't know.' Theresa shook her head at the wisp of a child cowering in the corner of the landing. 'She was fast asleep on the couch a minute ago.'

'Win was supposed to see to the bucket before she

went to school,' Bernadette said, ushering her youngest daughters downstairs.

'Bloody typical. Where is she now?'

'She was calling at the church, something to do with …'

'Mum, it's always something to do with that bleedin' church.'

Theresa was on her hands and knees soaking up the stale urine with newspaper she'd retrieved from the outside lavvy when she felt a light kick on her bum. Glancing round she saw her brother Tommy at the top of the stairs.

'Do that again, Thomas Booth, and I'll rub your ugly mug in these papers.'

She lunged to catch his foot.

'Catch me if you can, our kid.'

Tommy turned and jumped down the flight of stairs.

**Sarah**

'Co-op,' shouted the bus conductor.

Sarah joined the other passengers queuing to climb down the stairs of the moving double decker. She always made for upstairs so that she could watch life passing by. Now that the clocks had gone forward it wasn't as interesting; glimpses of families under the glow of front room lights, before the curtains were closed; tables being set, televisions turned on and children playing provided flashes of scenes from different plays. She hated net curtains; they shut her out from the families, and her mother had them at every window.

'Hello, dear, how was your last day as a cadet?' said Mrs Green as Sarah walked toward her.

'Much the same as any other Friday except the sisters gave me a box of Black Magic.'

'How very kind of them.'

Mrs Green stepped back into the hall to let Sarah pass. She made it her business to plan her day so that she could be in position to welcome Sarah home each evening. As Sarah removed her coat her mother took it from her and opening the door under the stairs took out a coat hanger. She arranged the coat around the hanger's wooden shoulders, fastened the buttons and then tucked the hanger away on its designated peg.

'It's not really kind of them, the sisters. The chocolates will be white and sugary; they always are on Jones. The patients and their relatives give them to us as a thank you and the ward clerk shoves them at the back of the office cupboard. The sisters have got a thing about us eating on the ward.'

'Don't say "shoves", dear.'

Sarah turned from her mother, bounded upstairs and locked herself in the bathroom. Eight more weeks and then there would be no more being met at the door. At least the door was better than the bus stop. She'd been in her fourth year at the grammar school before her mother had been persuaded to stay within the confines of the house, hovering on the doorstep.

'Sarah, are you all right in there?' Mrs Green said to the bathroom door. She turned the handle. The door was locked. 'I've made a nice pot of tea.'

'I won't be a tick.'

Fifty eight days to freedom, and counting, she said silently to her reflection in the bathroom cabinet. She watched herself reach over her shoulder and draw the long auburn plait forward, carefully removing the elastic band securing the end; she shook her hair free, spread out her arms and stretched.

'I thought we might go into Farnton in the morning, to the big Co-op,' said Mrs Green as she finished chewing on her fig biscuit. She much preferred a digestive but fig biscuits were good for the *bowels*. It offended Mrs Green's sensibilities to voice, out loud, certain words, particularly those associated with bodily functions, especially those below the waist. Instead she mee-mawed the offensive word usually accompanied by a slight shudder and a glance over her shoulder to make sure no one had heard.

'Why?'

Sarah had hoped to spend Saturday getting her belongings together for Monday. It wouldn't take all day but the excuse that she needed to do it would keep her in her bedroom. She would be free to read, write some long overdue letters and listen to *Saturday Club*, albeit with the sound turned down and her portable radio held to her ear. Planning to do anything on Sunday was pointless. She would bow to the inevitable and spend the day with her mother, the vicar and church.

'You need to be fitted for a new *brassiere*, dear.'

'Why can't we go to Marks and Spencer? I don't need a fitting. I've hardly got anything to put in a bra.'

At five feet and half an inch Sarah could still fit into children's clothes. That was when she had clothes that were bought. Her mother, a skilled needlewoman, made most of her own and Sarah's clothing, often cut from the same pattern and made in similar material.

'Judith has been offered a place at teacher training college.' Mrs Green daintily eased a bit of fig from between her front teeth with the little finger of her right hand. 'She's going to study at Edge Hill.'

'That's good. It's what she's always wanted to do. How do you know? Have you seen her mum?'

'You had a letter from Judith; it came this morning, in the second post. I've read it and put it on your bedside table with the *sanitary towels* for next week. I have checked in my diary and you are due for your *monthly visitor* on Tuesday.'

Fifty-eight days to go, fifty eight days, counted

Sarah.

'And,' Mrs Green paused, crossed her hand across her chest and gave a beatific smile, 'to celebrate the next, very important, step in your vocation the Reverend and Mrs Evans have invited us to tea before evensong.'

'Fifty eight days to go, fifty eight to go.'

'What did you say, dear?'

## Jenny

The four Hayes children were sitting at the kitchen table finishing the shepherd's pie left by the daily help. A key turned. The front door clicked open and shut. A briefcase thudded onto the floor and footsteps came down the hall.

'Good evening, my boys. How are we all this glorious Friday?'

The three boys mumbled responses through bulging cheeks. Jenny stayed silent, her eyes cast down, concentrating on her plate.

'Where's Mummy?'

'I'm here, my darling.'

The children's mother appeared in the kitchen doorway smelling of Chanel No 5, her tiny frame drowned in a white towelling bathrobe.

'You look stunning as you are, my darling,' her husband said, stretching his thin lips into a smile.

'I'm all ready. I just need to step into my dress. I'll clear away the children's sup–'

'You'll do no such thing. Old mop head here can earn her keep, sort out the kitchen and see the boys into bed. What do you say to that, chaps? Can you stand the sight of Ugly Mug for the evening? We must make use of her whilst she remains with us. Although, she'll soon be back from the Infirmary, bound to be, the thick lump has yet to succeed at anything. What do you say, boys?'

Jenny caught her mother's eye, willing her to say something in her defence. Her mother turned and walked out of the kitchen.

Jenny, naked, forced herself to look in the mirror of the utility issue dressing table that dwarfed her bedroom. She stood straight, her shoulders back, her arms by her side. Her eyes travelled the length of her body.

'How ugly am I?' she asked her reflection.

She ran her hands over her breasts, down her abdomen, over her hips and gripped her thighs.

'I'm not fat or thin. Do I look like an upturned mop? My friends like my hair – I don't need to put rollers in every night. Surely I can't grow any taller. I've never been snogged, on tennis trips or at parties.' She breathed, hard, onto her hand and sniffed. 'I'm not thick – I got six O levels.'

She pulled on her worn pyjamas.

'Bugger, bloody, shit, piss, fart – Theresa would be proud of me.'

Jenny marched on the spot lifting her legs higher with each step.

'Bugger, bloody, shit, piss, fart.' The words grew louder. 'I could start swearing at him or smoking cigarettes or drinking cider. Then Theresa would be even more proud of me. Eight weeks and then I'll be away from here, even if it is only down the road. Just wait, I'll show them – him.'

Snuggled in bed, Jenny set about writing her thank you letter. As always, her granny had been generous and sent her a five pound note for her birthday. Jenny had saved hard from her weekly ten shillings pocket money, and now had eighteen pounds, thirteen shillings and sixpence. She'd never been so rich. She could now afford to treat herself to a bra and knickers. Her school knickers had had it, the hand me downs from her mother were too small, and she needed pyjamas.

She had half expected to have to find the money to buy her brown uniform shoes, text books and nurse's watch that she needed for the start of her training. Jenny had been astounded at her mother's response when Miss Bennett, one of the tutors, had handed the equipment list to her mother at the cadets' parents' evening.

'Thank you, Miss Bennett,' she had said. 'Jenny and I will enjoy our shopping trip. Perhaps we will have tea at the Crown and Mitre.'

The shopping trip didn't happen, but Jenny was given nine pounds to go into Farnton.

'It is probably better if Daddy is not aware of the expense,' her mother had said.

## Maggie

Maggie's dad was, as usual, waiting in his van at the gates to pick her up as she left the hospital at five past five. The days she was at the local tech, on day release, she was allowed to walk the short distance from the college to home.

'You don't mind if we drop off these wallpaper samples do you, luv? It'll save me having to go out again in the morning.'

John Smithfield checked his wing mirrors and eased his van into the stream of traffic. He patted his daughter's leg.

'Why are we dropping samples off on our way home? Does Mum know?' Maggie crossed her arms over her chest and hunched her shoulders. She scowled at her father's profile. 'She usually has our tea on the table at half-past five.'

'Because I say so and because they're for a good customer who wants them tonight.'

Maggie watched, out of the corner of her eye, as her dad fiddled in his jacket pocket with his left hand, his other hand manipulating the steering wheel. Deliberately turning her head to wave enthusiastically to three girls waiting to use the zebra crossing, she avoided her part in the lighting up process – opening the matchbox and striking the match. Her dad lit up then sucked deeply on his *Embassy*. Maggie narrowed her eyes and altered her breathing as smoke filled the enclosed space.

'Your last day as a cadet. Big day on Monday. You know, you don't have to go through with it, if you don't want to.'

'Course I want to.'

Maggie examined her thumbnails. Giving her right thumb her full attention she gnawed at a sliver of loose skin. So her mum hadn't sorted him out after all? What she had heard him say last night, about her working in an office, her leaving the hospital, it was going to happen. She hated him. What would Theresa and the others think when she didn't turn up on Monday?

The previous night Maggie had gone to bed and, unusually for her, tossed and turned. Her thoughts played out the excitement of her birthday: the cake and presents. Her first glass of sherry (she was eighteen after all) meant she laid awake going over her day and imagining her future as a student nurse. When she heard raised voices from her mum and dad's room she knelt on her pillows and pressed her ear to the wall. They were talking about her. She slid out of bed, slowly opened her bedroom door and inched her way toward the door of her parents' room. Their door was always left ajar in case she or her sister Elizabeth needed their parents during the night.

'Why can't she work in an office or work with kiddies like our Elizabeth?'

'John, she has always wanted to be a nurse. Why are you getting yourself in a state?'

'I know what men are like. I was in the army, or had

you forgotten? She'll see their hairy arses, their pricks; surely she won't have to touch … Dear God.'

Maggie heard loud sniffing and gasping. It wasn't the same sound that went with the knocking on her bedroom wall that woke her most Sunday mornings. Her dad was crying?

'Pull yourself together John, this is ridiculous. We're talking about Farnton General not a hospital tent in the middle of Egypt.'

Maggie stepped back when she heard the click of the bedroom light and glimpsed shadows through the door of her parents' room.

'John, for goodness sake go and swill your face and I'll sort out the covers.'

Maggie scuttled back to bed and feigned sleep in anticipation of her mother glancing into her room. Her mother opened Maggie's bedroom door and for a second or two the room was lit from the landing light and then dark again as the door was pulled too. Maggie heard her mum letting her dad have it, as only she could.

'I'll tell you this for nothing, John. If you put your foot down and stop that child being a nurse you'll break her heart and I, for one, will never forgive you. Put that toilet seat down.'

Maggie heard the flush of the toilet and her parents' footsteps returning to their room. She lay on her back staring toward the ceiling. Turning over she reached for Pussy, a balding Persian cat pyjama case, and wiped her eyes on its face. When the rhythmic knocking started she snuggled down and let a blanket of sleep take her. Her mum would sort her dad out. She always did.

'Stupid bloody fool.'

The jolting of the van and her dad's shouting brought Maggie out of her reverie. A man who had leapt from a moving bus scurried along the pavement.

'Like I said, you don't have to stick it out – at the

hospital. You can always leave, if it gets too much for you. I'll find you another job. I know loads of people in Farnton.'

Maggie's head ached. She couldn't think straight. She felt sick.

'Dad, this is taking forever. Why didn't we go round the ring road?'

The van jolted backwards and forwards, stopping and starting every few yards in its progress through Farnton town centre.

'I'll miss *Crackerjack* at this rate.'

'Let's have less of your questions and back chat, our Margaret. We'll be home soon enough.'

'Thank Christ; we're home, at long last,' said Maggie as the van swung into the drive. 'What's Uncle Brian doing here?'

'We'll have less of that sort of language, if you please, mi lady.'

Maggie jerked open the van door and stomped into the house without giving her dad a backward glance. She cocked her head; something was going on in the dining room, the door was never closed. Maggie turned the handle, pushed open the door to be greeted by her family.

'Good luck, luv,' her mum said putting her arms round Maggie as she drew her into the room, 'you don't half look surprised.'

'I am, what's it ... You knew all along. Didn't you?' Maggie threw herself at her dad as he walked through the door. 'That's why we had to take our time coming home.'

John held out his arms.

The Smithfield clan – Mr and Mrs Smithfield, Elizabeth, Grandma, Uncle Brian, Aunty Miffy and their son Dave – had gathered to wish their Margaret all the best for her SRN training. The dining table was set with the traditional Smithfield feast of home-made pie, pickles, bread and butter and salad. A sherry trifle and left over birthday cake had replaced the ornaments on the sideboard. Maggie glanced at the presents on the dining chair that indicated her place at the table.

'What are these for? It was my birthday yesterday.'

'I decided, this morning, that we'd have a little party. Go on, luv, let's watch you open your presents and then I'll put the kettle on,' her mother said.

Maggie opened the present from her aunty and uncle; hand cream from Boots the chemist. She moved on to the next present. It was wrapped in crumpled brown paper haphazardly sealed with Christmas sellotape.

'Is this from you, Grandma?'

Grandma smiled.

'It is, luv. I already had it in. I've only used a bit of it, but I thought it ud be more use to you, wi' havin' to keep washin' yer 'ands when you've wiped bums and mopped up sick and that.'

'Mother!' said John as everyone else laughed.

'I didn't expect all this, a party and presents,' Maggie beamed at her parents. 'You could have given them to me yesterday.'

'We wanted to wish you all the best for Monday. Didn't we, Dad?'

'There's a lot of hand cream here,' Maggie said. 'It's lovely though and I'm sure it's all going to be useful, really useful – thanks.'

'You need to keep your hands soft, for when you meet a nice boy,' said Grandma. 'It's time we had a weddin' in t'family. Nobody seems keen on shaping 'emselves. Well, other than our Dave and the least said about that the better.'

'Thank you, for that, Grandma. Which ward will you be on?' said Dave, looking directly at Maggie.

'Yer can't say owt to anybody in this family without

gerrin yer 'ead bitten off,' Grandma said.

'We're in the School of Nursing for eight weeks before we get allocated to a ward. Come on Grandma, come and sit next to me.' Maggie held out her arm to support the old lady as the family found seats at the table.

'I wanted Theresa to be here.'

Mrs Smithfield folded the wrapping paper and pushed it in the top drawer of the sideboard.

'Aw thanks, Mum. I'm sure she'd have loved it.'

'Who's this Theresa, when she's at home?' Grandma said.

'She's my best friend from the hospital. She's a Catholic, but it's all right Grandma, she's really lovely. Isn't she, Mum?'

Her mother nodded.

'A Catholic?' Grandma snorted, twisting her face as though she'd sucked a lemon.

Maggie went on to tell her that Theresa would be living in the nurses' home when work on the wards started.

'Will you have to stop and sleep at yon hospital then, our Margaret?'

'No, she doesn't need to. I'm happy to take her,' said John before Maggie had time to speak.

## Chris

'… In conclusion, I am sure you will all join me in wishing Christine good luck as she leaves us to start her new career as a nurse.'

The senior partner finished his short speech. The two other partners and their secretaries clapped politely. Chris stepped forward and was given a small package that she knew contained a nurse's watch. The presentation had been timed to take ten minutes and finish precisely at the end of business at five o'clock.

Chris sat at her desk making an effort to look busy. She removed her few belongings from the top drawer: the Parker fountain pen her Nana had given her for her twenty-first, a pencil case, a single stocking, half a tube of Polo mints, a sanitary towel wrapped in a handkerchief and a sixpence. Heaving shopping bags over their arms, Chris's office colleagues prepared to bustle out of the office.

'Don't forget to come back and see us.'

'Be sure to come back and tell us when you meet a handsome doctor.'

'I will, I will – come back I mean,' Chris said to their departing backs.

She dallied in the ladies' lavatory, combing her hair, applying lipstick, straightening her stockings and fastening, unfastening and refastening her cardigan. It was only when she heard Madge opening the mop cupboard that Chris reached for her coat and gloves.

'Thank you for signing my leaving card, Madge.'

'Very nice of you to say so, Miss Warrington. You never know, I might get to see you when I comes t'Infirmary to see that eye doctor. My youngest lad skens like I don't know what.'

'I expect you'll be looking forward to getting home for *Coronation Street*?'

Chris stepped aside so that Madge could mop the floor around the sink.

'I am that. I'm worried about Ken Barlow's wife. That poor woman'll be worn out, what wi fetchin' up them twins. All he can think about is havin' his way wi' her – durin' t'week as well. I ask you! It's Saturday night after t'pub or not at all, at our 'ouse.'

Chris walked slowly up the deliberately quaint cobbled street, past solicitors' and accountants' offices. She made her way through the main shopping centre, gazing at window displays. A shop assistant was arranging orange cellophane over the three mannequins in Miss Gloria's Gowns. Why was she doing that on a sunless April afternoon? They were hardly likely to be bleached by the sun for a while yet. Arriving at the Hippodrome, Chris wasn't surprised to find herself at the front of the queue for the first house. She had no idea which film was showing. Inside she stared at the screen, vaguely aware that the film involved a group of schoolgirls and a train robbery. Her head, above her right eye, throbbed. Her mouth was dry, her eyes heavy. The loud shrieks and coarse laughter of the schoolgirls intensified her gloom.

*What the hell have I done? How am I going to cope, cooped up with young girls of eighteen? I don't have any other choice. Do I? Me; a nurse? I can't stand sick or snot or sh… Don't think about it. It gives me a job as well as a home. I have to get out of that house, get away. I wish I were dead. Oh God. I have to get out of here before I'm sick.*

The smell of burnt popcorn overwhelmed her as she pushed past knees, fighting her way into the aisle and out into the dazzling lights of the foyer. She stumbled into the ladies' lavatory and rifled through her handbag for her aspirins.

'Chris, we're in here.'

'I'm tired, Mum,' said Chris hanging her coat on the hall stand.

She made straight for the stairs and, once in her room, pushed a chair against the door, lodging the cross bar under the handle.

# FIRST YEAR

## CHAPTER ONE

Theresa paused mid brush stroke. *What the* ...? She let her heavy hair fall around her shoulders, pushed the elastic band from around her fingers back over her wrist, and went to investigate the noise. From the bathroom door she peered downstairs into the hall.

'Mum, what's up? Is something wrong?'

'No, luv,' Bernadette said, smiling up at Theresa. She looked for a space to hang her coat, gave up and threw it on the bottom stairs. 'I asked to finish my shift a bit earlier so that I could come home and see you off.'

Theresa leapt downstairs and threw her arms round her mother. Bernadette gently lifted her daughter's chin and bent to kiss her cheek.

'I am so proud of you – make a success of this for me and your dad.'

'I will, Mum. I really will.'

'Come on then, let's get that hair fastened back and see you on your way. You don't want to be late on your first day as a proper nurse.'

Theresa gave the brush and the elastic band to her

mother. She closed her eyes and enjoyed the sensation of the slow brush strokes. It was ages since her mother had brushed her hair.

At the front gate, Theresa turned to wave. She grinned when she saw Tommy standing at the window next to her mum. Bleary-eyed, he waved back and mouthed 'good luck, our kid.' She'd waited up to see him last night but he hadn't appeared by the time she was ready for bed. She would miss Tommy when she left home. They were only ten months apart in age and after a lifetime of friendly loathing they had, over the last few months, become closer.

We pay our way, look after ourselves, and help in the house. Not like holy, bloody Win, always at that soddin' church.

Theresa turned into the ginnel dividing the old and new council houses, paused, had a quick look round, and with no one in sight rolled the top of her skirt over a couple of times. Adjusting the weight of her shoulder bag she strode out, as far as her short legs would allow, until she reached the bus stop in time to catch the seven o'clock bus.

This is it. I'm a student nurse. I hope there's a locker. This bag's bleedin' heavy to cart backwards and forwards every day.

Lolling against the wall outside the entrance to the School of Nursing, having a last drag on her cig, Theresa waved as she saw Maggie trudging toward her.

'Hiya, Maggie. You've worn your shoes to travel in.' Theresa wrinkled her nose as she considered Maggie's feet. 'I brought mine in my bag, there's no way I'm being seen outside in hiking boots.'

'Nobody's going to notice your shoes.' Maggie followed Theresa inside; through the entrance hall and into the cloak room. 'Not with your bum nearly on show. You can see your stocking tops.'

Theresa stood on her tip toes and peered over her shoulder into the mirror above the sinks.

'You cannot, and anyway we've all got to make the best of ourselves and show off our assets. You'll look fab when we get your weight down, Mags.'

Maggie shook her head, linked arms with Theresa and escorted her out of the cloakroom. Retracing their steps they made their way to the classroom they'd seen on the way into the building. A bevy of girls were already in the room wandering round examining the cream calico laundry bags distributed on the desks. A notice chalked on the blackboard instructed them that they should sit, in strict alphabetical order, at the desks designated by their named laundry bags.

'Why the bloody hell can't we sit where we want?' Theresa knitted her arms and shimmied her shoulders. 'Stop being so polite, push your way through,' she shouted to Jenny hovering in the doorway.

'What a scrum. Good morning, you two.' Jenny looked around. 'Where are we sitting?'

'You've worn your shoes as well. What? Oh, the places. We've no bloody choice. Find your laundry bag, they're in alphabetical order, and that's where you sit,' said Theresa dismissively waving her arms at the blackboard.

'Why can't we sit where we want to?' Jenny said.

'Please Jenny, don't get her going again. Theresa, think yourself lucky you've got Jenny and Sarah behind you. I'm stuck at the back with that fat, spotty cadet from the Infirmary and that miserable looking new girl,' said Maggie, nodding toward the back of the classroom.

'Nurse, not cadet, we're student nurses now,' said Theresa. 'Anyway, which new girl?' Theresa stood on tip toes. 'She looks a snooty cow, pretending to read her text book, who does she think she's kidding, and she's older than us.'

'Well, I'm stuck with her for the next eight weeks,' said Maggie. 'I wish I could sit with you lot.'

'I can't wait to get going. What say you, Nurse Booth and Nurse Smithfield?' Jenny said from the desk behind Theresa.

The new girl forgotten, Theresa smiled at Jenny and nodded.

How the bleedin' hell I've come to be pals with a posh bird like you Jenny, I do not know.

'Why are you sitting on the front row, Theresa? That's not like you,' said Sarah Green. She carefully removed her cardigan from around her shoulders, folded it neatly and looked for somewhere to put it as she joined the group gathered around Theresa's desk.

'You're behind me, Sal, next to Jenny. Mags is over yonder, at the back; with the misfits.'

'She might as well be in Siberia.'

'Don't worry Theresa, my bestest ever friend, you'll always be in my thoughts,' said Maggie.

Maggie was never really sure where her friendship with Theresa had come from. She remembered their first meeting at the cadet interview, all that time ago, in November 1963. It had been a cold, wet day. Theresa burst through the main door of the hospital and into the oak panelled corridor outside Matron's office, her hair plastered to her head and her ponytail hanging like a rat's tail down her back.

'It's a bloody long way from the bus stop,' she'd said, plonking herself down on the chair next to Maggie. 'Do you know where the lavvy is?'

'It's out of that door and down the main corridor.'

Maggie nodded toward an ornate panelled door inset with stained glass.

'Come on, come with me, we've got bags of time.'

'I think we'd better stay here.'

'Come on, don't be soft, we'll be back in a jiffy. I need to get myself sorted out.'

Maggie watched as Theresa soaked her handkerchief under a tap then wrung it out and rubbed at her mud-splattered legs. Her white socks were grey and damp.

'My poor dad spent bloody ages cleaning these shoes.'

Despite their wiping out on the roller towel, the shoes squelched as Theresa and Maggie walked back down the corridor.

'Don't you have a mac or umbrella?' said Maggie.

Theresa shook her head.

As they took their seats outside Matron's office, Maggie was taken aback to hear Theresa burst into song. 'Juliet,' she explained. 'It's my favourite song – The Four Pennies, they live round here somewhere.'

The door labelled MATRON opened. 'Theresa Booth? Come this way.'

Maggie heaved a sigh of relief.

On their first day as cadets Maggie had been surprised and a touch intimidated when Theresa had sought her out, stuck with her at meal times and then insisted on sitting next to her on their weekly day release from the hospital to Farnton Tech. Being with Theresa guaranteed attention. Where had Margaret gone and when did Maggie appear? She had unwittingly become a junior partner to the gobby fun-loving rebel. Maggie had refused the introduction to cigarettes, her dad's made her eyes water and her head ache, but she relished Theresa's tales of boys, necking sessions and the goings on in the Roman Catholic Church. Of one thing Maggie was sure; Theresa was the best friend she had ever had.

As the remainder of the twenty-four entrants for the May 1966 intake of student nurses assembled in the old classroom the noise level rose. Friends greeted each other and examined the contents of the laundry bags to find: three green dresses, twelve starched white aprons, three stiff white collars and three sets of starched cuffs. Shrieks of laughter pealed out as dresses were removed from the laundry bags, unfolded and shaken out. Theresa climbed onto her chair and held one of the dresses out in front of her. It was almost as wide as it was long.

'Bleedin' hell, I'm taking this back to the sewing room. The seamstress who measured me needs her eyes testing.'

'You'll need to return them today, we're expected to wear them from tomorrow,' said Jenny, holding her dress out for inspection. 'I might come with you. Mine looks a smidge on the long side.'

Desk lids banged shut, chairs scraped on the parquet floor.

The noise quietened as the heads of two tutors, a man and a woman, were seen passing the windows set high in the internal wall of what had previously been the dining room of the local work-house. The new recruits, who had not had the benefit of being cadets, were surprised when a short, plump woman unexpectedly appeared at the classroom door and followed her colleagues onto the raised platform by taking a sprightly leap. Turning to give a welcoming nod, she gave an agonised wince as she tugged at the skirt of her maroon sister tutor's uniform.

'Do be seated,' said the taller of the two women, peering at the group over the spectacles lodged on her hooked nose.

Theresa, already bored, toyed with the purse string neck of her laundry bag. She felt a sneeze gather in response to the sharp clean smell of the bag and its contents. *Well, Miss Bolton, you look a miserable old bugger.* She listened half-heartedly to Beaky Bolton as she introduced Miss Bennett and Mr Bradshaw and then went on to the correct way to wear the green dress and starched apron.

'... the hems of the two garments must be the same length and both must be fourteen inches from the ground at all times.' Theresa chortled, imagining what would happen if this rule were strictly imposed. *Me and Sal would end up with our keks on show when we made beds or changed some poor bugger. Look at Jen, fourteen inches from the ground would be just above her ankles. She would likely end up on her arse, lolloping off to fetch a vomit bowl. Mags would be OK, let's hope her apron stretches round her bum.*

Theresa turned her head, as far as she dared, to take a shufti at her classmates. She knew the majority of them, from day release at the tech. Maggie, herself and fifteen others had been cadets at the General. Four others, including Jen and Sal, were from the Infirmary and the others were new faces.

'It started as a dispensary in the town centre,' said Jenny in her *Top of the Form* voice. Theresa caught Sarah's upward glance as she dragged her attention back to the lectern. Mr Bradshaw had, apparently, asked a question on the origin of the Infirmary.

*Thank God Jen's always ready to stick her hand up.*

'Are you sure you don't want to live in with us, Mags?' Theresa said as she, Jenny, Sarah and Maggie walked back from the sewing room. Jenny and Maggie had each left two of their dresses to be altered. They had been left in no doubt by Miss Bolton that they were expected to turn up in their uniform dresses the following day, no matter how they fitted.

'No, my mum and dad, especially my dad, doesn't want me to and I'd miss our Elizabeth too much. Dad doesn't mind giving me a lift every day, so I'll leave you three to your cloistered lives.'

'Struth – cloistered, that's a big word for you,' said

Theresa, giving Maggie's arm a thump, 'and anyway you should know better than to torment me with visions of churches and anything else to do with nuns and priests.' *I hate the soddin' lot of em.*

'Does anybody fancy a night out on Saturday? That coffee bar near *The Farnton Evening News* offices is supposed to be good,' Theresa said to the small group of nurses relaxing in the shade provided by the wall of the old classroom. Sitting in the open glare of the sun was definitely out. The sludgy green dresses soaked up the heat from the early afternoon sun. Thick stockings, heavy brown lace-up shoes and rigid, starched collars that sliced into the sides of their necks had the girls fighting for the small patch of shade.

Theresa leapt into the centre of the group, stood erect, thrust out her ample chest, stuck her nose in the air, held her arms akimbo and continued in a nasal tone.

'Ladies, do let us celebrate the end of our first week as student nurses.'

She groaned as her gaze followed that of her sniggering audience. Miss Bolton glared at Theresa before she launched herself through the entrance to the reception area.

*Where the hell did she come from?* 'Are we on for it then?'

At the end of the first week of the Study Block, skills more or less mastered included: the making of beds, occupied and unoccupied, bed baths and care of the mouth. Miss Bennett's lecture on the correct procedure for giving bedpans and urinals emphasised the importance of keeping men from the ward, unless, of course, they were patients. Screens were to be placed across the ward doors to signal to the doctors and the men of the clergy that the ward was closed for the sanitary round. One of the new recruits was perplexed by the finer details of the procedures of the sanitary round.

'What do you do if a man, you know, can't, you know, put his thingy mi bob in the bottle himself?'

'Send for Tate and Lyle,' said Jenny.

Sarah came to the rescue. 'An auxiliary on 6C – men's surgical, who looks exactly like Olive Oyl, uses a large pair of forceps to lift the penis and place it delicately inside the bottle. She manages this without letting her eyes see or her hand touch the offending part.'

'Okay, but I still don't understand where Tate and Lyle comes in.'

'*Untouched by human hands*, the sugar advert?' Jenny said, raising her eyebrows.

'You get hold of it and shove it in the bottle for the poor bugger,' said Theresa.

The night out was on. Theresa was invited to have her tea and get ready at Maggie's house. Sarah accepted Jenny's invitation to 'come to my house to finish getting ready, there'll be no one at home, and we can walk into town together.' Sarah told her mother that Jenny had invited her to spend the evening with her family. The invitation to Chris Warrington had been firmly refused. Two others were undecided, with a 'probably not' from a girl hoping for a better offer from a boy she'd met at her ballroom dancing class.

'Do have a pleasant weekend,' said Miss Bolton, dismissing the group at the end of the first week.

As the group hurried down the hospital drive, toward the bus stop, Theresa shouted her instructions. 'Be in front of the gas showrooms at half past seven, and don't be late.'

# CHAPTER TWO

'Do have a pleasant weekend.' The phrase repeated and rattled round Sarah's consciousness as she stirred awake. It would be easier not to go; to stay at home and watch the television with her mum, to excuse herself at nine o'clock and go to bed and read. Yet, she knew she would go. She would fight the years of vows and promises she'd made as a Brownie, Guide and Ranger, the life of Sunday School, church bells, Walking Day and church choir, in order to deceive her mother. She was stifled by the constant scrutiny of her life; it was hard work being at the centre of someone else's world. That was the problem, she told herself as she lay on her back staring at her bedroom ceiling, running her hands absent-mindedly over the candlewick counterpane; her mother's life – limited to mithering about me, the church, and the Rev Evans; now wasn't that an embarrassment?

'Do have a pleasant weekend.' *I will Miss Bolton, I will, because if my mum finds out what I'm up to God only knows how she'll take it. What am I up to?* Sarah continued the discussion with herself. *I've told her I'm*

*going to Jenny's for my tea, which is true. What I've not
told her is that Jenny's family will be out and that we
are going to a coffee bar in Farnton. Perhaps, I could
tell her about the coffee bar; after all, what's wrong
with going out with my friends. We're only going to
listen to a pop group play music.*

'Hello dear. Are you awake?'

'Coming Mum, I'll be down in a minute.'

'I'll put the bread under the grill and boil the kettle.'

Mrs Green served Sarah her breakfast and then got on
with her baking.

'While you have your bath I'll nip over to the
vicarage and take the vicar a plate pie for his tea.'

'Is Mrs Evans away, or working?'

'No dear, or at least I don't think so. It's just that I
know he appreciates my cooking. I think his wife gives
him rather too much foreign food for his liking.'

'Foreign food?'

'Spaghetti.'

'We had it when Mrs Evans invited the Rangers
round; when she gave us a make-up demonstration and
then we had a meal for our Christmas party. I liked it.'

'Well that's as may be. I still think the vicar needs
proper food and for that matter I was never sure it was
the right thing; the vicar's wife encouraging young girls
to use make-up.'

Sarah took a slurp of tea to stopper her mouth.
Jousting with her mum about life at the vicarage was
fruitless. The suitability of a window-dresser at Kendal
Milne to be a vicar's wife was a constant agenda item
for the Mother's Union.

'That boy of theirs would probably still be at home if
he'd had a hotpot every now and again. I ask you Sarah,
would he have sacrificed the benefits of a university
education to flit to Germany to play in one of those
singing groups, swivelling their hips and screaming out

the music of the devil, if he'd have had …' Mrs Green blinked and glanced around as she emerged from her diatribe. 'Now what was I saying?'

'We're having plate pie for lunch then, Mum?' Sarah abandoned the idea of confessing her plans for the evening.

'Yes, dear. I must get on, Sarah. I need to get off to the vicarage.'

'Please may I leave the table, Mum? The plate pie was tasty.'

'Thank you, dear. Let's get the washing-up done and then you can get off to see Jenny and her family. Perhaps Jenny's father will bring you home in his car,' said Mrs Green.

'I doubt it, Mum.'

'Mind you leave her house in time to catch the last bus. I'll walk down to the bus stop and meet you.'

'Mother, I am eighteen years old and a student nurse, I can manage to walk two hundred yards on my own.'

'It will be dark by the time the bus gets to the Co-op. If your father had lived he would have come to collect you in his car.'

'I didn't know he could drive.'

'He couldn't, but I am sure he would have been able to by now, just like the vicar. Mr Hayes might know him.'

'Who?'

'Reverend Evans. The bishop thinks a lot about him, you know.'

'Must dash, the bus is due at any minute.' Sarah reached under the stairs for her coat and bag.

'Goodbye, my dear. Have a pleasant evening,' Mrs Green said to the front door as it clicked shut.

Sarah hadn't been sure about her dress before she left

home. The Simplicity pattern her mum favoured was fine for dos in the village but would it do for a coffee bar? She needn't have fretted: Maggie looked as though she'd stepped out of Marks and Spencer children's section and Jenny was in slacks and what looked like an old school blouse. Theresa blended in with the more trendy girls; in short skirts and white boots. The four girls made their way inside, adjusted their eyes to the dim lighting, found seats in a corner and ordered a Britvic pineapple each. Within minutes Theresa disappeared, and Jenny gave a shriek at the sight of the group and abandoned Sarah and Maggie.

'What do you think,' said Maggie, watching as Sarah craned her neck to take in the surroundings. 'Is it what you thought?'

'I'm not sure. What about you?'

'I've been once before; with our Elizabeth. My dad's funny about me being out at night on my own. Who's that with Jenny?'

'Everyone, everyone, this is Paul; we were at school together. Paul, this is Sarah and Maggie.' Jenny glanced around the coffee bar. 'Where's Theresa?'

'I think that's her,' Maggie waved her hand towards a distant corner, 'over there somewhere.'

'Sit down Paul,' Jenny indicated the seat next to Sarah.

'Hi, how do you know Jenny?' Paul said, inching closer to Sarah on the banquette.

'We've just started our SRN training – we're in the same group.'

'She's a smashing girl, always bright and cheerful. What's happened to her hair?' he said as he glimpsed Jenny and Maggie disappearing into the ladies lavatory. 'My name's Paul by the way.'

'Err, yes, I know, Jenny told us. Are you a musician?'

'No. I'm in the middle of A levels, but the parents have let me have a night off.'

Time zipped past as they talked about their schools and where they lived. Sarah felt Paul's hand touch her shoulder when he stretched out his arm and laid it across the back of the seating. She took a deep breath and felt her shoulders loosen and relax; she sighed, raised her head and smiled at Paul. She shuffled her bottom sidewards. She felt her thigh, warm, against his thigh. His hand crept onto her shoulder. The noise of the jukebox, the hiss and splutter of the coffee machine and the voices melted away. The world was still. Paul leant forward; Sarah sensed his movement and bent toward him. For the briefest time their lips met. Sarah felt her heart thump, she gulped, her throat was dry, she forced a swallow.

'Come on, Paul, it's time to get going,' called a distant voice.

Paul stood up slowly. He bent to kiss Sarah again. She stretched her back and reached her head forward until their lips met.

'Paul, come on, get a move on. She'll be there at the end.'

Sarah watched Paul walk towards the stage. He picked up his saxophone, lifted his head, looked at her and smiled. He closed his eyes. The haunting opening bars of *Stranger on the Shore* sealed the magic of her evening.

Maggie banged shut the passenger door of the van and waved good bye as her dad did a U turn in the entrance to the hospital drive. She turned at the sound of her name; a nurse, the ballroom dancer, was scurrying toward her.

'Maggie, Maggie, wait for me. Did I miss anything on Saturday?'

'Wait until you see Jenny, Sarah chopped her hair.'

'Those two didn't go out together when we were cadets?'

'Something to do with Sarah's mum being strict. She's only recently let Sarah go out on Saturday nights. Her mum thinks they stay in, with Jenny's mum and dad.'

'Did Theresa go with anybody?'

'Course she did. You should see her neck. She'll never pass that off as her collar rubbing.'

'Was the group any good?'

'Not bad. Jenny knew one of the boys. He went to her posh school.'

'Did you meet him?'

'Yes, course we did. You know Jenny; she dragged him over to meet us. He seemed to fancy Sarah but she had to go early. Oops.'

'Is something wrong?'

'I'm just wondering where I've put a piece of paper.'

'Is it important?'

'Could be.'

'Was he good looking?'

'Who? Oh, the lad who fancied Sarah you mean? Yes, sort of, not very tall, sandy coloured hair.'

Maggie stopped walking and rummaged in her pockets and bag.

'Did you meet your chap then?'

'Yes, yes, I did.'

# CHAPTER THREE

Week two of the introductory block was about to begin.

The remaining seven weeks were more or less uneventful. The pharmacist gave the same boring lecture twice. It would have gone unnoticed if Jenny hadn't piped up and informed him that he'd told them about poisons being kept in green fluted bottles the previous week. In week five a girl who had been experiencing a stomach upset from the first day of the study block didn't return. News reached the student nurses of a rapidly arranged wedding.

'Bloody hell, that's put an end to her high fallutin' plans for seeing the world in the Q.A.s,' said Theresa. 'Pass us the sugar, Mags. I'm having another cup of coffee. We've five minutes before we need to go.'

'Isn't that what Nurse Cherie Adams did? Or was it Sue Barton – joined the army?'

'Mags, what are you wittering on about? They aren't real, you know. They're characters in books for girls. We had them in the school library, I read them in the first year,' said Theresa.

'I know that, and well, it's wrong anyway.'

'What is?'

'Sex before marriage, you wouldn't catch me doing anything like that. It would really upset my mum and dad.'

'Heaven forbid, Mags. What have your mum and dad got to do with anything? Anyway chance ud be a fine thing.' *Nobody's going to look at you, luv. Until you lose some weight no bugger is going to want to grapple with you.* 'Come on we'd best get back to Beaky.'

On the Thursday of the final week of the study block, the first lecture of the morning had ended. Miss Bolton packed away her notes. The nurses stood, they knew better than to remain seated or to attempt to move from their places until she had left the room. At the classroom door she paused, turned and gave a rare smile at the expectant faces. Did she look straight at Theresa?

'You will find the ward and department change list on the notice board,' she said.

A small stampede ensued.

'Bloody hell, no,' said Theresa. Her head sagged and her shoulders drooped. 'Not Shitty Smith, she hates me.' *They've done it on purpose, Beaky and Shitty; I'll show 'em. The bloody nuns didn't grind me down and neither will them two – the bastards.*

Howls of protest were heard from another young woman as she envisaged the next ten weeks under the supervision of a sister whose evil bitch reputation preceded her. Chris Warrington had been allocated a women's medical ward. She turned her back on the boisterous crowd around the notice board to make a solitary journey back to the classroom.

Jenny stood outside the open door of her room in the nurses' home, taking it in.

'I'll leave you to get unpacked, Nurse Hayes.' The

home sister pushed past Jenny and dropped her suitcase on the bed. I'll be in my office if you need me. Your room key is in the door.'

'Thank you, Sister.'

Jenny watched the home sister bustle down the corridor. Stepping insider her home for the next ten weeks Jenny was aware of the mingled scent of flowers from lavender furniture polish and the strong sweet smell of the small bunch of freesias, in a cut glass vase, perched on the windowsill. She ran her hand over the flowered counterpane, touched the dressing table and the book rack on top of the small table that she presumed was meant to be used as a desk. She experimented with an alternative view of the room by sitting down in the moquette armchair. She sat up straight, her elbows resting on the wooden arms. *Here I am, on my own, home from home.* She hugged herself.

Unpacking was a joy. She had never had so many new things. With the money she'd squirrelled away over weeks she'd been on a shopping expedition to Marks and Spencer. Two new bras and five pairs of knickers, two pairs of pyjamas and a blue crimplene shift dress as well as a dark green cotton A line skirt and a pale green blouse. She would have liked a white cardigan but needed the money for a pair of shoes. The kitten heeled shoes with the pointed toes had been worth the sacrifice of the cardigan. She wasn't too sure if the pointed toes made her feet look even longer, but the shop assistant had told her they were all the rage. Jenny heard the squeak of shoes on the polished floor of the corridor, then voices.

'Thank you, Matron. Isn't this a lovely room, Sarah?' An older woman was speaking.

'I'm the home sister, Mrs Green, not Matron. I'll go now and leave you and your mother to unpack, Nurse Green.'

Jenny hoisted her suitcase on top of the wardrobe and went next door. Sarah was loading books into her book rack whilst her mother was making her way round the room, dabbing at the furniture with a yellow duster.

'Hello,' said Jenny.

'Jenny, come on in. Mum, this is my friend, Jenny.'

'How lovely to meet you, my dear. Is your mother with you?'

'No, she couldn't stay. She dropped me off earlier.'

'What a pity. I should so like to have met her, to thank her for inviting Sarah to your home so many times.'

'It was only a coupl...' said Jenny.

'If you've finished unpacking do you fancy making us all a cup of tea?' Sarah said ushering Jenny toward the corridor.

Jenny, changed and ready for bed, stood at her bedroom window and watched the distant hills disappear as the summer sky darkened over Farnton. It seemed ages since she had trudged over the moors with the school rambling club. One of her teachers had loved the view from the top of The Pike insisting that they sang *Jerusalem* in homage to the 'dark satanic mills.' She watched the mill chimneys lose the definition of their ornate brickwork collars as they became tall silhouettes, black against the fading sunset. *Let me be a good nurse. Let me show him*, she beseeched the last vestiges of light.

Jenny rootled about in her purse, searching for four pennies so that she could ring the General to see if Theresa had arrived and settled in. She had knocked at Sarah's bedroom door, on her way back from the bathroom, and was surprised not to get an answer.

# CHAPTER FOUR

Over the next days and weeks Theresa, Maggie, Jenny and Sarah settled into the routines of the wards. Their duties were much the same as those on their final ward allocation as cadets; making beds, cleaning lockers, helping serve meals and feed patients as well as emptying and cleaning bed pans and urinals. When time and staffing permitted they accompanied more senior student nurses and staff nurses to observe dressings being changed and medicines being dispensed: by mouth, as suppositories, as injections and through intravenous drips.

Sarah was in thrall to the notion of being Nurse Green; waking up in her room, seeing her green dress standing to attention on its hanger behind the door, her cape draped over the dress. The simple tasks of everyday life as a nurse were magical. She relished making her way to breakfast and listening to the gossip and chatter of senior students.

The ward sisters and staff nurse made a pet of Sarah. They had all been through the Infirmary, from cadets to students to state registration, and enjoyed seeing the infants of the profession pass through their ward. It was early July, the weather was warm, the windows were open, patients' visitors wore summer clothes and usually arrived smiling. Her mother's supervision did not reach to the wards or the nurses' home. But her shadow hovered over Sarah in the letters she received, on alternate days, about life in the village, particularly the life and times of the vicar, the Mothers' Union and the Sunday School.

In her letters home Sarah was vague about the workings of the off-duty rota. Staying in the nurses' home for her two days off without going home to her mother added to the frisson of being her new self.

She felt like royalty when the nurses' home maid courteously tapped on her bedroom door and then manoeuvred herself into the room bottom first carrying a large wooden tray. Sarah muttered 'good morning' and eased herself up the bed. The maid placed the tray across her lap.

'You enjoy that, Nurse Green – I made it miself.'

'Yes, yes I will – thank you.'

'It's a pleasure, luv. God only knows, you girls work 'ard on them wards. Eat it up and enjoy your day off. Leave the tray outside yer door when you're done wi it. Mind you, don't get used to this though, there's none of this up at the General. It's all fending for yerself up yonder.'

Sarah walked into town, to the hairdresser's she had heard older students mention. She pointed to a photograph of Stephanie Powers.

'I want it like that please, but shorter.'

The hairdresser combed out Sarah's hair. 'Are you sure you want to lose this, luv?' She looked at Sarah through the mirror.

'I am absolutely sure.'

'I must say you'll look fab with a short bob.'

Sarah felt liberated as the scissors sliced through her hair; the weight on her head lessened and cool air struck her neck. She closed her eyes and imagined the rest of her day; going shopping without her mother and best of all she was meeting Paul at the *Left Bank*. She had kept her meetings with Paul a secret from the others. From time to time she had been tempted to share the excitement of having a boyfriend but they would want all the details, especially Theresa.

Her mother had known every detail of her life. Sarah was resolute that she would be free of her mother's or anyone else's control – well – other than student nurses senior to her, staff nurses, sisters or the two matrons. Telling her friends about Paul would come soon enough.

'Sarah, Sarah, over here.'

Paul waved from the back of the café. Sarah shuffled sideways between the cramped, crowded tables. She couldn't believe that she, Sarah Green, was in the *Left Bank*. She glimpsed black and white photographs of the Eiffel Tower and steep streets and lamp-posts. Piano-accordion music underpinned laughter and chatter. She recognised three third year student nurses sitting on high stools at the counter.

'Gosh, Sarah, whatever have you done to your hair, it's beautiful.' Paul reached across the small table. 'Come here, let me kiss you.'

Sarah instinctively met him half way, to touch lips, before squeezing herself into the chair opposite him. He reached for her hands across the table. Sarah glanced at the nurses. One winked at her and smiled.

'Two coffees and two croque monsieur, please,' said Paul grinning at the waitress.

The girl looked nonplussed and glanced from Paul to Sarah.

'Cheese on toast,' said Paul.

'Why didn't you say so?'

Sarah heaved a sigh of relief as the waitress snatched the menu from Paul. She had never heard of crock whatever it was.

Sarah placed her knife and fork side by side on her empty plate. 'What time do we need to leave?' She glanced at her watch.

'We've bags of time. My shift doesn't start till three. It's the first time I've worked in the evening. I hope it's busy. What do hospital porters do in the evenings?' Paul said.

'Move meal trolleys, transport dead bodies, take patients from casualty to the wards, lots of stuff like that.'

'There isn't a casualty at The Beeches. Do people in private hospitals die? Anyway let's forget work and plan our day out tomorrow.'

# CHAPTER FIVE

For Chris Warrington the polite formality of office life, with the security of her desk and predictable office routines, was long gone to be replaced by unfamiliar ward routines run under the dictate of individual sisters.

'Before you go, luv, will you read that card for me?' Chris was finishing combing the hair of an elderly patient. 'I can't find my reading glasses.'

Chris reached behind a bottle of Robinson's Barley Water at the back of the patient's bedside locker. She took the card from its envelope.

'It's from Elsie and Jack.'

Chris felt a shove on her arm. The card was snatched from her hand and thrown on the bed.

'We've ward clerks for that sort of nonsense,' said the senior sister.

Chris wiped a glob of spit from her cheek.

'Yes, Sister.'

'If you have finally finished the beds you can collect the sputum mugs, then get yourself in the sluice and clean and sterilize them.'

'Yes, Sister.'

Chris had soon realised that she could deal with the emissions of the orifices below the patients' waists without revulsion. However, attending patients who were vomiting or honking up sputum had her retching alongside the patients she was meant to be nursing. There was nothing for it, she would have to face the task. She went from bed to bed collecting the stainless steel sputum pots; gingerly picking up the pots from the beside lockers, and trying not to turn up her nose, she carefully place the pots on the trolley. The thought of dropping a pot or spilling the contents and having to set about clearing up the gunk made her wretch. The collection completed, Chris trundled the trolley into the sluice. She felt bile rise in her throat when she lifted the hinged lids of the pots. She heaved until tears rolled down her face as she shook the green, yellow and sometimes black gelatinous mess from each mug until the contents plopped down into the sluice.

Chris's sense of loneliness and desolation lifted, albeit temporarily, when she realised the pitiless standards of the ward sister were not unique to her or indeed unique to nurses.

Toward the end of the tedious ward round of a demigod; wearing a hand-made suit and a bow tie, a bed ridden patient pleaded for a bedpan. A third year student answered the call, dragged resisting screens down the length of the ward and unfolded them round the bed. The nurse fetched a bedpan from the sluice, ensuring she was garbed appropriately. It was a serious crime to appear holding a bedpan without a long green gown securely covering the uniform dress and apron. Chris watched from the back of the ward round retinue as the nurse emerged from behind the screens pushed them back into place and turned to find a snorting bull facing her.

The ward was eerily quiet.

No one moved.

Chris held her breath.

'This is the ward round. What do you think you are you doing?'

The sister's jowls wobbled. Her eyes were wild and staring.

'Bedpan, Sister.' There was the sound of urine hitting stainless steel. 'The patient needed the bedpan.'

The nurse dropped her head.

'Get her off it. Now.'

The sister marched back to her supercilious idol and led him to her office for a cup of warm venom.

Chris inhaled deeply and joined the disgraced nurse at the back trolley.

Poorly patients whispered to both nurses as they tidied beds, ready for visiting time: 'sod the old bugger she needs a good seein' too,' and more gently, 'ignore her, you'll both make good nurses.'

At the end of the shift Chris dragged herself back to the nurses' home. Unlocking her door she stepped inside the room and slowly pulled her cloak from her shoulders. She reached up to hook it on the peg at the back of the door; the effort overwhelmed her. Weary and deflated she let the cloak drop to the floor. The room began to spin, what is this … what's happ… she was caught in a haze. She pushed herself away from the door and staggered toward the long mirror on the outside of the wardrobe.

'Who are you?' She peered at the image. 'I don't know you. I don't like you.'

Her image shifted as she yanked open the wardrobe. Chris stared at her clothes. Jagged thoughts scratched her consciousness. *I can't stay here, in this room, on my own night after night. I'm going mad. I'm leaving now, this minute, freedom, no more backsides, shit, pee. God, I stink of the stuff, it's seeped into my soul. How many paracetamol is a fatal dose? I can't cut myself. I want sleep to forever, if I can just get away ... but where can I go?*

Chris scooped her clothes into her arms; the wire hangers rattled and jangled against each other as she lugged the clothes toward her and threw them on the floor. She reached up to grasp the handle of her suitcase; she pulled and tugged, what was wrong with the bloody thing it was stuck on the shelf at the top of the wardrobe. Bracing her shoulders she gave an almighty heave ... Blackness surrounded her, occupied her, pins and needles prickled at her face. Chris opened her eyes, she felt drowsy, floating ... mingled thoughts, voices, singing, came and went ... Where? What? She was looking up at the underside of her washbasin, she tried to sit up; her head throbbed. Stroking the back of her head she felt a hard lump. Turning on her knees she crawled to the bed and slowly hoisted herself on top of the counterpane ... darkness again. *It's dark, I'm cold*; she shivered, she remembered – her clothes, the suitcase. *Dear God, help me. Somebody, anybody, help me.* Turning onto her back she startled at the pain from the lump. Easing up the bed and into a sitting position she swung her legs toward the floor. She felt queasy, took a deep breath and closed her eyes. *Didn't someone once tell me I was determined and resolute?* Perching on the side of the bed, Chris eased her arms out of her crumpled uniform. Stepping out of her dress she drew back the bed covers and folded herself into the sheets. *Whoever it was they should see me now. Mrs Metcalf, it was Mrs Metcalf, my fifth form teacher. She said I was a charming, intelligent girl who was determined and resolute and that I would achieve success in whatever I set my mind to. Look at me now Mrs Metcalf. What do you think I should do? Consider my options; is that what you would tell me to do? What have I got? Let's see; a roof over my head, reasonable food and a salary at the end of the month. That's a laugh; a pittance for being bullied and bossed about by miserable old bags. Yet, those girls love it, it's what they've always wanted to do – be a nurse, look after people. It's my fault I'm on my own Mrs Metcalf, not theirs. You'd like them, especially Jenny and Sarah. You'd probably think they were determined and resolute. Theresa, well you'd probably have her in detention for swearing and back chat, and Maggie – what would you think of her? You'd probably worry about her and keep your special close eye on her to make sure she wasn't led into mischief by her cocky friend. And me, Mrs Metcalf, what about me? Do you think the knock on the head has done me some good? Will it help clear my thoughts? What would you do Mrs Metcalf? Tell me to draw a decision tree, that's what we did isn't it, in our form room. Let's see. I need to get a grip and face the future. I have no alternative, with the way things are. I need a home and a job and that's what I get from being a student nurse. I need to find the person who can be determined and resolute. I'll tell you what Mrs Metcalf, I don't know if she exists any more but I need to look for her. But not now Mrs Metcalf, I'll do that in the morning after I've sorted this tip. Perhaps I won't wake up; that would solve everything, wouldn't it Mrs Metcalf?*

# CHAPTER SIX

'Telephone for Green or Hayes,' a voice called.

'I'll go,' said Jenny.

'Close the door behind you. We don't want Matron coming in here complaining about the noise,' said a body snoozing on the rug in front of the electric fire.

'Jenny, wait. I'm coming as well.'

The pair walked quickly, running was forbidden, to the phone booth at the opposite end of the corridor from the sitting room. Wedging the telephone between Sarah's left ear and her right ear, Jenny took charge.

'Hello.'

'It's me,' Theresa said. 'I've not got much money and the pips might go. I'm ringing to see if you want to come on holiday with Maggie and me. Maggie's aunty and uncle have a caravan at Knott End and we can have it for that one-week holiday at the end of August. Ring me back when you've thought about it. I'm on a late, so ring back after nine.'

The line went dead.

'I definitely do not want to go home for the holiday,'

said Jenny.

Sarah hesitated. 'Let's say we'll go then.'

'Virgin's retreat,' said a voice when they eventually got through to the home at the General.

'Theresa Booth, room 120, please.'

'Booth, someone tell Booth – phone.'

'It's us, we're coming.'

'Fab.'


'We could use the bottom cushions from the three-piece for them to sit on, Dad,' said Mrs Smithfield.

She stood in the drive, holding open the doors of her husband's A54 van and contemplating the floor space.

'Good idea, they can wedge their cases between 'em. That'll stop 'em sliddin about.'

'I can have the cake tins and the picnic in the front, between my feet,' said Mrs Smithfield.

'Margaret, take Theresa and the others and fetch a seat cushion each, off the three-piece,' said Mr Smithfield to the four girls gathered in his drive, surrounded by their luggage.

Loaded up, the red van set off through Chorley and Preston north on the A6 and then onto the coast road to the seaside at Knott End. Once the picnic lunch had been devoured Mr and Mrs Smithfield prepared to leave the crowded caravan.

'Be sure to lock the caravan when you go out,' John Smithfield said to Maggie. 'There's a telephone in the village if you need me for anything.'

'Dad, we'll be fine.'

'Don't leave the gas on and don't talk to strangers, especially men.'

'Mum, tell him we'll be all right.'

'It's time we headed for home, John.'

'Bye, bye – thank you.'

The holidaymakers waved as the van began its return

journey to Farnton, leaving them free to explore the caravan and the site.

'Crikey, Maggie, it's a long way to the lavvies. We'll need to plan in advance and besides that, what if it's raining?' Theresa said.

'Put your coat on and take the umbrella.'

'I've found the sink but where are the taps?' said Jenny from the cupboard of a kitchen.

'There are none. We need to carry the water from the tap by the lavatories. One of us fetches it in that blue container in the corner,' said Maggie. 'Oh, and we need to take the slops, from under the caravan, and pour them down the grid behind the lavatory block.'

'There's bugger all difference between here and the wards then,' said Theresa.

'What do you say, Sarah?' Jenny made herself comfortable on the built-in settee. 'Are we going to have a good time?'

'I'm sure it's going to be smashing, really smashing.'

Maggie was in charge of food for the week. Jenny took charge of fluid in and fluid out of the caravan.

'We should have brought a fluid balance chart,' said Theresa.

Sarah and Theresa were in charge of the metamorphosis of the furniture at each end of the day. On the first evening the two double beds were in place, the curtains closed and the calor gas lamps lit and giving off their quintessential smell.

'What on earth are you doing with your hair, Theresa?'

At Jenny's question Sarah looked up from her book and Maggie stepped out of the kitchen. They watched the intricate procedure. Theresa combed out a strand of her long hair, squirted setting lotion from a plastic bottle along the length of the shaft and then wound the hair around a large roller before bayonetting it in place.

'Do you do this every night?' Jenny said, patting her shorn head.

'Only when I'm going out and fellas might be involved.'

'My dad wouldn't want us to go with boys.' Maggie's voice rose an octave.

'Joke Mags, joke. Although, I did see you eyeing up that gypsy-looking lad on the dodgems.'

'I did not.'

'Should I make everyone some Horlicks?' Jenny said, climbing over Sarah and heading for the kitchen.

'Please Jen. Wait until tomorrow, you'll all be jealous when I look like Sandie Shaw.'

As the week went by Sarah, Jenny and Maggie had no choice but to become more familiar with Radio Luxembourg and Radio Caroline. Theresa fiddled with the transistor radio, balancing it in precarious positions in the caravan in her search for a signal. If The Kinks needed a girl singer for *Sunny Afternoon* Theresa was word perfect. She was working on *Paperback Writer*, muttering the words under her breath each time it was played on the radio.

Strolling along the path that skirted the muddy beach, sitting in the sun reading, day dreaming and chatting or walking together to and from the village to buy food, the young women talked.

Jenny shared her Cinderella-like existence and revealed her dad was really her stepfather and the father of her three half-brothers.

Sarah said, briefly, that her mother was strict and liked to know where she was and who she was with.

Theresa told of her affection for her parents, particularly her mum. The others were left in no doubt that she hated the parish priest's guts.

'There are six of us kids and our mum and dad; eight

to feed and wash and clean for. I ask you? We don't live in a big detached house, have a housekeeper to look after us and do nothing but pray all day. He's a stupid bugger who has no idea.'

Maggie, who already knew Theresa's story, had not realised how unhappy the other girls were. As she drifted off to sleep she was aware how fortunate she was. Her dad worried about her and Elizabeth, but that was because he had been in the war and seen bad things.

Four young women who had not long since left childhood behind were making changes on their journey to adulthood. Well, more or less.

'Have any of you ever used a Tampax?' Theresa said as she reached up to turn out the calor gas light over the bed.

'You are joking. My mother would have gone blue in the face if I'd dared suggested it,' said Sarah.

'Wouldn't it be uncomfortable?' said Jenny.

'What are you on about now?' said Maggie, abandoning sleep.

'Tampax. They're bound to be better than sanitary towels. I'm going to have a go with my next period. I'll get some when we go into the village tomorrow, then I'll be ready.'

'It might hurt, or get stuck, when you try and push it up. Then what will you do?'

'Jenny, just think, how are you going to get a fella's willie up your fanny if you can't manage a Tampax?' said Theresa.

'Correct anatomical terms please, nurses,' said Sarah nasally as she snuggled down.

'It's been the best day of my life,' said Jenny as the darkness deepened. 'The trip to Fleetwood, the dodgems, eating fish and chips from newspaper as we walked ...'

'Listening to Theresa sing,' said Maggie.

'What do you think, Sarah? Admit it; it's been the

best day ever.'

Jenny prodded her bed-mate with her foot.

'Yes, it was great, really great.' Sarah closed her eyes and pulled the blanket around her shoulders. 'Nearly as good as my haircut day and um, err …'

'It's time you came from under the covers and owned up, Sarah,' said Maggie.

'Why?' Sitting up in bed suddenly, Theresa lost two rollers. 'What's happened?'

'If you hadn't been off necking you'd have noticed,' said Maggie.

'Noticed what? Besides, I like necking.'

'We know that.'

'You're seeing Paul Thompson, aren't you?'

'Yes, Jenny, I am.'

'They say the quiet ones are the worst,' said Theresa. 'Details, give us the juicy details.'

Sarah took a deep breath and with a sigh realised she was ready to share her story about Paul.

The foundation of the friendships had shifted to firmer ground.

# CHAPTER SEVEN

'Can I come in?' Sarah said tapping on Jenny's bedroom door.

'It's open.'

'Have you been back long?'

'About two o'clock; there was nobody about at home so I collected some clothes and came back here. How was your mother?'

'Much the same as she always is. She wanted to know all about our holiday, what we'd done, where we'd been. She was put out that I didn't go home and spend the time with her.'

'Mr and Mrs Smithfield are great aren't they? It was good of them to take us and bring us back,' Jenny said.

'I enjoyed the singsong on the way back. I didn't know the entire family were into amateur operatics. Did you?' Sarah said.

'I don't think Maggie's over keen, but what the heck, they are a lovely family. By the way, that Warrington girl arrived this afternoon; she's on the other side of you.'

'What's she like?'

'I don't know how you'd describe her – a bit distant. I offered to make her a cup of tea while she settled in, she looked as though she was going to say yes, but then mumbled something and scooted off.'

'That's her loss. I'm sorry I'm dashing Jenny, but …'

'Are you meeting Paul?'

'Yes, I might see you later, if you're still up.'

Sarah all but skipped down the main hospital corridor that led from the nurses' home. On her way she passed Thorpe, the ward where she and Jenny would spend the next ten weeks. As she emerged from the revolving door Sarah saw Paul sitting on the garden wall waiting for her. They grinned at each other, instantly held hands and kissed briefly. It was chancy being seen 'carrying on' in the hospital grounds.

'I thought you might, err, like to meet the parents,' said Paul.

'That's a bit of a surprise.'

'Well I want you to meet them before I go to med school and that's only three weeks away. I've told them about you, and my mum, she trained as a nurse here, wants to know how things have changed.'

'Okay, if you are sure that's what you want.'

'It is – but I don't want to push you into anything.'

'Let's go then,' said Sarah.

'We can just call in, say hello and then go for a walk if you'd rather?'

Sarah shuddered at the thought of taking Paul home to meet her mother. The meeting with his parents had been bad enough. It was good that he had left her with little time to think about it. She liked his dad; he was really friendly, for a consultant. His mum though, she was different. Polite – but there was something Sarah couldn't quite put her finger on. She obviously adored

Paul, she watched his every move and her eyes lit up when she spoke to him. Sarah squirmed when she remembered how she'd blushed and stammered out answers to Mrs Thompson's endless questions, although she had seemed impressed when Sarah had talked about her exam results and the books she read. What was it about Mrs Thompson? *Does she think I'm not good enough? Well I'll just have to prove her wrong, won't I? Doing that will be a sight easier than facing my mum on my next days off, and telling her about Paul.*

The tea table was set; the tea poured, the bread buttered and the salad drooped on the plates. Sarah sitting across the table from her mum gasped as she realised with a jolt that she looked at Sarah in the same way that Paul's mum looked at him.

'Mum, I would like to bring a friend to meet you.'

'That would be nice, dear. Does she live in the nurses' home with you and Jenny?'

'It's a boy, my friend is a boy.'

'They let boys live in the same home as girls, dear me, dear, dear, me.'

'Mum, please let me tell you – he isn't a friend … well he is … I've met a boy. I've got a boyfriend; he's called Paul.'

'How long have you known him, this boy?' Mrs Green twisted her wedding ring round and round her finger. 'Was it him that persuaded you to have your hair cut?'

'No, I wanted it short.'

'So you've known him since then?'

'Since when?'

'The haircut and your clothes, what's wrong with the clothes … Sarah, my dear. I'm, oh dear, oh dear.' Mrs Green gazed at the photograph of the schoolgirl in pride of place on the mantelpiece. 'Where has my lovely girl gone?'

'He's a medical student in Manchester. His dad's the consultant radiologist and his mum's a health visitor. I've met them. His dad's lovely; very kind and thoughtful. His mum's a bit quiet but ...' Sarah paused to draw breath and sneak a quick look at her mother.

'The vicar has got a new surplice,' her mother said fiddling with the crucifix around her neck. 'I need to lie down.'

# CHAPTER EIGHT

Towards the middle of their second ward allocation Maggie, Sarah, Jenny and Theresa managed to meet in the *Left Bank* for a catch up – an achievement considering that they were at the mercy of the 'off duty'. Planning in advance was difficult given that it was not unusual for the rota to be pinned on the ward noticeboard on Friday for the week starting two days hence, on the Sunday.

Maggie greeted the others with the news that they were invited to her sister Elizabeth's twenty-first birthday party, arranged for a Wednesday evening midway through the next study block. The party would be in the upstairs room of her dad's local.

'It won't be posh,' Maggie said. 'My uncle playing the piano and pie and peas for supper.'

'Tell them about your new friend,' Theresa said when there was a gap in conversation.

'I wondered how long it would take you to bring that up.' Maggie nudged her friend. 'A very poorly old lady had to have an emergency tracheotomy on the ward –

under a local. The registrar, sister and staff nurse were doing all the important stuff at the top of the bed. I must have looked a bit sickly and green as they made the incision so the staff nurse, you know the one with the limp and the cripples shoe …'

'Get on with it Mags,' said Theresa.

'She said to me, "Nurse Smithfield make yourself useful and hold Mrs Almond's hand." I shuffled round the two housemen so I could be at the middle of the bed, slipped my hands under the theatre towels and stroked her hand. I must say having something to do helped me to feel better and I managed not to pass out.'

'How is the old lady now?' said Jenny.

'Poor old soul, she died next day.'

'She's not finished,' said Theresa, bouncing on her seat, 'let her finish.'

'Well, I was in the kitchen, making the sisters' tea, when Dr Gupta, the new houseman, came up behind me. He didn't half make me jump. Touched me on the shoulder and said he wanted to thank me for helping him through the procedure on Mrs Almond. I must have looked a bit surprised because he then said he was sure he would have fainted if I hadn't held his hand all the time!'

'He waves to her every time he sees her now,' said Theresa.

The time passed comparing notes and telling stories about sterilizers that had boiled over and flooded treatment rooms, being permanently short staffed, as well as how difficult it was trying to stick to the procedures that the three Bs had taught them, especially when the middle of the wards were overcrowded with extra beds. Theresa showed her chapped hands from her incarceration in 6C sluice cleaning bedpans with Chemico. Sarah admitted she was missing Paul now that he had followed in his dad's footsteps and gone off to medical school in Manchester. She told the others about meeting his parents and confessing to her mother about Paul.

'Struth, it must be serious then,' said Theresa. 'You won't catch me settling down with the first one that comes along, although Paul is going to be a doctor, which is something I suppose. Pity he hasn't got a sports car.'

'Theresa!' said Jenny and Maggie.

'On duty, Sister,' Chris Warrington reported at the ward office as she returned from the afternoon off, part of her split shift.

'Before we serve suppers I want you to go with staff nurse and carry out the last offices for the Ca liver on the right.' said the sister, glancing up from her paperwork. 'I've already rung for the porters so you'd better get a move on.'

'Yes, Sister.' Chris hesitated, gulped and took a deep breath.

'What are you waiting for nurse, stop gawping and get going.'

'Yes, Sister.' Determined and resolute Chris, she told herself, determined and resolute, you'd better go and find the staff nurse, always remember – determined and resolute.

'Have you laid a patient out before?'

'No, Staff, no, I haven't no, not yet,' said Chris bumping into a stainless steel trolley. 'Sorry, so sorry.'

'Calm down,' said the staff nurse. 'Come on let's gather everything together and I'll go through it with you.'

Chris watched the staff nurse set a trolley with a jug of warm water, soap, flannels, towels, dressings, luggage labels and a plastic shroud.

'We're going to wash the patient, comb her hair,

dress her operation site and then tie the luggage label around her ankle. You write the label with the name, time of death and the ward and then I'll check the details. Try and think of the patient as the person you enjoyed nursing and not as a dead body. Are you ready?'

Silence fell on the ward as all eyes followed the two nurses and their trolley. Skilled practitioner and novice, they walked the length of the ward to the screened bedside. At her first sight of the body Chris brushed away tears, fighting hard to stifle a sob. The quiet yet clear directions from the staff nurse helped Chris brace herself.

'Look at the patient, Nurse Warrington. She is the lady you've been nursing for the past few weeks. You weren't frightened to touch her body then were you? Come on love, you can do this; the first time is always the worst. The procedure is just the same as a bed bath; I'll sponge her, you can dry her. Grab the towel – come on.'

'Thank you, Staff.' Chris reached round the back of the bedside locker for a bath towel. 'I'll be fine.'

Chris braced herself to mirror the staff nurses actions until the bed bath was complete.

'Hold the feet together while I fasten this around the big toes,' the staff nurse said as she finished filling in the details on the luggage label, 'then we'll put her in a shroud and then you can draw the screens round the other beds and tidy away.'

'Shift your body, Nurse Warrington, get a move on and get the tables laid for supper.' The sister's jarring voice called down the length of the ward to Chris's retreating back as she wheeled the used stainless steel trolley back to the sluice. 'We'll never be ready for visiting time at this rate, and where on earth is that staff nurse? She surely doesn't expect me to serve supper?'

'Yes, Sister. I mean no, Sister.' Chris shoved the trolley through the sluice door and quick sticks turned back into the ward.

# CHAPTER NINE

'Morning' – knock. 'Morning' – knock. 'Morning' – knock, repeated along the corridor. Heads emerged from under sheets, blankets and counterpanes in response to the early morning call in the nurses' home at the General. Theresa dragged herself up the bed and leaned her head on the wooden bedhead; she groaned and slid back down the bed pulling the blankets over her head.

Why did I have that last pint of cider? The creep that bought it wasn't worth the walk to the bus stop. I can't stand clammy hands and, God forbid, he had terminal wandering palms disease; the cheeky bugger thought he'd got lucky. It's a good job that bus arrived when it did. He was a bloody big lad, I wouldn't have stood a chance.

With a mighty effort Theresa jerked herself bolt upright. Once the curtains facing her had stopped spinning she swung her legs over the side of the bed. Only slightly nauseated she lurched toward the washbasin and steadying herself on the sink she dared to raise her head. She squinted at herself in the mirror. *Not another bloody love bite? Perhaps I should play tennis like Jenny, or find a steady like Sarah or even sit at home like poor old Mags; perhaps not. Theresa will you pull yourself together, get in the bath and skedaddle home?*

Two buses and over an hour later she arrived home. Her mum was in the jungle of a back garden pegging out two worn grey sheets.

'Hiya, Mum,' said Theresa as she stood at the battered back door. The original glass was long gone – too many footballs had pelted it – replaced with a hotchpotch of hardboard and ill-fitting and mismatched glass.

'Hello, luv. It's good to see you. How long are you stayin'?'

''Till teatime. Why are you washing today?' Theresa said as her mother reached out to stroke her face.

'Little lads; they're a devil to get dry at night.'

'Let's have a brew and a natter before we set to with your jobs.' Theresa filled a battered pan with water and put it on the stove. 'Sit down Mum, have a bit of a rest while you can I've brought some Wagon Wheels for the little uns. Let's have one between us before the baby wakes up.'

Theresa thought her mum and dad were belting; the best. They worked themselves to a standstill to keep a roof over their children's heads and put food, however meagre, on the table. Yet, despite her deep devotion to her parents, Theresa was disillusioned with her family's need to scrimp to get through each day. She hankered for something different. She wasn't sure what, other than a vague notion that this couldn't be all there was for her mum and dad and little brothers and sisters. She had a long time to go to finish her training but it gave her hope that as an SRN she could get away from the overcrowded, chaotic life she'd been brought up in. All she had to do was stick at it; get decent ward reports, pass her exams, keep her gob shut and work hard.

'Come on Mum, lets shift that pile of washing that's dumped at the top of the stairs. It's a nice day, we'll get most of it pegged out and dry before the little uns get home from school.'

Theresa had emptied the dolly tub and was contemplating the process of shifting it back to its home in the corner of the kitchen when there was a tap, tap on the back door before it opened and a man stepped into the kitchen.

'Hello Bernadette, my dear ...'

'What do you want?' Theresa said to the local communities answer to Friar Tuck.

'And hello to you too, Theresa,' the priest said in his lilting brogue.

'Excuse me,' Theresa pushed the metal tub over his feet as she clumsily turned it over and rolled it into place. 'Mum, it's for you,' Theresa shouted.

'Will you be making us a nice cup of tea Theresa, and are they Wagon Wheels I can see?'

'No I won't and yes they are,' Theresa picked up the chocolate biscuits. 'But they're not for you.'

Theresa left the priest standing in the middle of the kitchen and went to find her mum who was making up beds.

'I'm off back to the hospital, Mum.'

'So soon? You've not seen your dad and the others.'

'Yon Holy Joe that our Win's so fond of is downstairs.'

'Did you make him a cuppa?' Bernadette left off the beds, glanced at her reflection in the mirror, patted her hair and bustled toward the stairs.

'Mum, I'm sorry I can't stay, not with him here.'

'Please, luv, stay for my sake.'

'No Mum, I can't.'

Sitting on the bus on the way back to the hospital Theresa was seething.

*One day I will kill that bloody priest. He didn't expect to see me. Bloody creep. Calling round at two o'clock when he thought she'd be on her own. He'll be going on at her about having more babies. Can't he bleedin' well see she's jiggered?*

# CHAPTER TEN

With ten weeks medicine and ten weeks surgery behind them, the young women were heading back to the School of Nursing for four weeks. Nine to four-thirty and three full weekends off as well as the firm, determined, yet, mostly, courteous approach of the three Bs – give or take Miss Bolton's moods and occasional nastiness. It felt as though there was a long holiday ahead. Finding their allocated places in the old classroom and being together as a group for the first time in twenty weeks, the laughter, loud voices and banging desk lids contributed to the din heard in the staff room.

'When are you getting married?' rang out from one group gazing at a sparkling chip on a left hand.

'Are we all ready to begin, nurses?' Mr Bradshaw raised his voice over the excited chatter as he arranged his notes. 'Nurse Booth, Nurse Smithfield will you please return to your seats.' Nurse Smithfield, I said … whatever is the matter, nurse?' Mr Bradshaw peered over the lectern at Maggie.

'My finger's swelling up Mr Bradshaw; it's the ring,

it won't come off.'

'You must be bloody joking,' said the potential bride, 'give it here, I said, give it here.' She lurched for Maggie's hand.

Maggie screeched.

The class were agog.

'Nurse Smithfield, will you calm down and sit down.'

Maggie was aware of Mr Bradshaw making his way down the classroom toward her.

'Rather a stupid thing to do Nurse Smithfield. Let me have a look.' Maggie gingerly held out her hand. 'There is only one thing for it. You will have to leave my lecture and go to medical emergency and have the thing sawn off.'

Maggie stumbled backwards as a hot sting suffused her face.

'You'll cop it Smithfield, when I get hold of you.' The girl lurched toward Maggie.

'Physical violence does not solve anything nurse, and you are as much to blame as Nurse Smithfield for being stupid enough to let her try it on. Now will you sit down or do I have to ring Matron's office? Nurse Smithfield what are you waiting for – medical emergency I said.'

Maggie looked forlornly at the door, fidgeting in her pocket for a handkerchief to blow her nose. She looked down the classroom to her friends. Jenny had her hands over her mouth, her eyes wide. Sarah looked to be wiping away a tear and Theresa was stood at the side of her desk her fists clenched and held in a fighting position. Chris Warrington reached out toward Maggie and then turned away as Maggie brushed past her.

During the trudge to medical emergency Maggie considered walking down the drive and catching the bus home. She trudged on; she had no option – her bag and coat were in the cloakroom. She licked and sucked her finger and twisted the ring. She wept, her nose ran. She felt stupid; fat and stupid. The ring had slid on and off everybody else's fingers.

She kept her head down as she walked up the main hospital corridor. At medical emergency she shuffled up to the desk.

'Ah, Nurse Smithfield? We've been expecting you. What have you been up to then?' said the staff nurse. 'Come with me, let's see what we can do.'

Maggie climbed clumsily onto the high examination couch with the staff nurse and the houseman watching her.

'Let's have a look then,' said the houseman.

Maggie saw him smirk.

'Nothing for it but the saw,' he said, holding Maggie's hand as though it were a piece of meat. 'It won't take a minute. Hold her hand still will you, staff nurse? I don't think local will do any good.'

Maggie tensed her hand as he approached her with a small saw that looked as though it came from her dad's tool kit.

'Relax your hand.'

Maggie held herself rigid as the houseman slowly slid the saw backwards and forwards and it ground into the ring. She felt sweat running down her back and between her legs. As the saw grated against her swollen skin she closed her eyes and bit her lips to stop herself crying out. The grating stopped. Maggie opened her eyes to find the ring resting in the trough of dress fabric between her legs.

'That'll teach you,' said the houseman as he tossed the saw into the sink.

'You arrogant bugger,' said the staff nurse to his retreating back. 'Come on luv, you'll live.' The staff nurse wrapped the mangled ring in a gauze square and handed it to Maggie. 'You'd better get back and face the music.'

'Staff, how much does a ring like that cost?'

'Twenty five – thirty pounds, I should think. But no doubt that one can be repaired. Best try and make it up with your friend.'

'I don't really know her, she isn't one of my friends.'


'The wanderer returns, just in time for coffee break,' Mr Bradshaw said as Maggie sidled into the classroom. 'Back in twenty minutes please, nurses.'

'Here's your ring.' Maggie couldn't bear to meet the girl's eye as she held out the gauze swab. 'I'm really sorry.' She curled her swollen finger into the palm of her hand. She could feel the eyes of the rest of the group.

'I bloody hate you. You fat bitch.' The girl pushed passed Maggie and marched toward the door. At the door she turned. 'You'll cop it good and proper when my Geoff gets his hands on you. He'll do you in.'

Maggie crumpled into the nearest seat, laid her head on the desk and cried.

'Come on Mags,' said Theresa, rubbing Maggie's back, 'let's get a cup of coffee.'

'You'll have to walk to the van with me this aft. Suppose he's waiting for me,' said Maggie as her friends escorted her from the classroom to the coffee queue.

'We won't leave you until you get in your dad's van.' Theresa glanced from Jenny to Sarah. 'Will we?'

Maggie sniffled into her hanky for the rest of the day. She couldn't understand how the ring had become stuck on her finger. Perhaps she shouldn't have given it that little push over her knuckles. She vowed she would never ever wear a ring. For the remainder of the study block she couldn't approach the car park without casting anxiously around. She was convinced that the demon Geoff would spring out at her and 'do her in'.

The future bride and her diamond chip did not return to the classroom. She was never seen again. Maggie, however, returned the next day and the next. Each morning Theresa waited for her at the hospital gates and walked with her to the School of Nursing. By the end of the week Maggie's finger had returned to its podgy normal size and the event lost its value as hot gossip.

Maggie stood up to admire her handiwork. The crepe bandage she had lashed to Jenny's leg was perfect; the layers of the bandage criss-crossed over each other in a line up the length of Jenny's lower leg.

'How does it feel?' said Maggie.

'Great, fab, very comfortable,' Jenny said. She levered herself up from her chair and hobbled towards Theresa and Sarah. She turned back when she saw Miss Bolton striding down the practical room, clipboard in hand.

'How will you get to the Eagle and Child tonight?' Maggie stood aside to let Miss Bolton scrutinize Jenny's leg.

'Well done, Nurse Smithfield. You can undo your bandage and change places with Nurse Hayes – and less gossiping.' Miss Bolton threw her shoulders back before she moved on to Theresa and Sarah.

'Loves young dream has offered me a lift,' said Jenny.

Theresa, who was spending the night of the party at Maggie's home, had seen the home sister at the General and been given permission to sign herself out of the nurses' home for the night of the party. Sarah, who wanted to save a late pass for the weekend, had suggested that she and Jenny sneak into the home at the Infirmary via the cellar.

Jenny stood in the gloomy passage entrance to the pub. The heady smell of beer, disinfectant and something familiar she couldn't quite place, in the cocktail of smells, tickled her nose. Which door? TAP ROOM or BAR? She could hear voices from behind the Tap Room door and distant laughter.

'Jenny, what are you doing there, come up?' Jenny, relieved to hear Maggie's voice, glanced around. 'Look behind you, I'm up the stairs. Where are Sarah and Paul?'

'Parking the car.' Jenny climbed the steep stairs towards Maggie.

'What are you smiling at?'

'Nothing, I'm glad to see you that's all. And to be here, in a pub. I've never been in one before.'

'Come on, I've bagged us a table.'

Jenny trooped after Maggie. Swivelling her head she saw tables and chairs set around a room with a space for dancing. There was a long table covered in a pristine white cloth with plates, cutlery and cups and saucers at one end with a birthday cake at the other. An upright piano was sitting off centre at the front of the room with the lid open and sheets of music piled on top. Jenny's slight feeling of unease as she settled herself to face the room was relieved with the simultaneous appearance of Sarah, Paul and Theresa.

'Phew, the bogs smell like the sluice on 6C,' said Theresa.

That was it, the other smell, Jenny thought – urine.

'I'll get us all dri…'

'No need lad, I'll see to that,' Mr Smithfield put his hand on Paul's shoulder. 'What'll you have, Theresa?'

'Cider for me, Mr Smithfield, thanks.'

'Jenny? Sarah?' Mr Smithfield looked from one to the other.

Jenny glanced at Sarah and raised her eyebrows.

'Sherry for me Mr Smithfield, thank you,' said Sarah.

'Me too, thank you Mr Smithfield,' said Jenny.

'And you too, lad. What will you have?'

'A pint of best please, Mr Smithfield.'

'Let's see then – cider, two sherries, pint of best and a Britvic Orange for our Margaret.'

'Why can't I have a sherry?' Maggie whined.

'One and one only, my girl.'

She doesn't know how lucky she is to have a dad who thinks she's special and cares about her, thought Jenny as Maggie grimaced at her dad as he made his way to the bar.

'Who are all these people, Maggie?' said Jenny, fascinated to watch people arrive, shout greetings to each other then set about shifting tables and chairs to make larger groups. Maggie gave a running commentary on who was who, waving and smiling as people looked around and caught her eye.

'Maggie, your dad is waving to you,' Jenny said.

'He wants us all to get up and dance,' Maggie tick-tacked back to her dad.

Jenny, Theresa, Sarah and Paul followed Maggie onto the dance floor for the progressive barn dance. Making introductions and catching up on family news was cut short mid-sentence as dancers completed a sequence and gracefully glided away from each other on to partners new, and fresh conversations or shy smiles. The Smithfield relatives and friends, a sociable and generous lot, soon had a line of full sherry glasses on the table in front of Jenny and Sarah. The beer and cider glasses were usually on their way to being empty.

'Don't you like sherry then?'

'This is my cousin, Dave,' said Maggie, turning towards Jenny.

'Hello. Not really, no,' Jenny blushed at the tall pleasant man smiling down on her, 'but I didn't know what else to ask for.' He doesn't suit brown, she thought – it makes him look spotty. 'Please, sit down.' Jenny drew out the chair next to her.

'I will, but first, should I get rid of some of these for you? The aunties and Grandma, who doesn't really drink, or so she says, are partial to a sherry.'

Dave set off to discreetly distribute the redundant glasses around the room, pointing out Jenny. The aunties and Grandma, not so discreetly, smiled, waved and held the glasses up to Jenny before swiftly downing the sherry.

'You're a friend of our Margaret's, aren't you?' Dave said, sitting down next to Jenny. 'Where are the others?'

He undid his jacket and casually brushed down his sharply creased trouser legs.

That suit looks new, thought Jenny, I bet he bought it especially for the party. I wonder who he's with.

'Maggie and Theresa have gone into the kitchen, Sarah is talking to that lady over there and Paul is getting ready to play his saxophone to give Maggie's uncle a break from the piano.' Jenny began to stand up. 'I'm sorry, but I said I'd help with the supper.'

'Stay here, with me, there's plenty of others in the kitchen. That's my dad on the piano by the way.'

Jenny reached out for a sherry glass, took a swig and coughed. It tasted vile.

'Would you like something else,' Dave said, smiling and nodding at the glass.

'No, thank you. I'm fine. I'll perhaps have a cup of tea later.'

Jenny danced with Dave for the rest of the evening. After the initial confusion over which of them should lead, being the tallest girl in her class had meant she'd learned to dance the male part, she enjoyed the St Bernard Waltz and the Veleta. The Gay Gordon's left them both hot and giddy with laughter.

'How are you getting home?' Dave said.

'With Sarah and Paul.' Jenny glanced at her watch. 'I

need to get a move on; we're due in the nurses' home by eleven o clock.'

'I could take you back, if you'd like.'

'I, I think I would like that, thank you. I'd like to thank Mr and Mrs Smithfield before I leave.'

'They're over there, with my mum. I'll see you downstairs.' Jenny watched as he walked toward the gents toilets.

Jenny said her thanks and goodbyes, and looked back at the table; there was no sign of Maggie, Theresa, Sarah and Paul. She rummaged in the back of the cloakroom for her coat. As she backed out of the enclosed space, Dave was waiting for her. He held out his arm for the coat.

'Let me help you.' He pulled her into his arms.

'Ooh.' She saw his lips closing in on hers. It's a bit wet, she thought as she closed her eyes. Jenny let go of her handbag and it clunked at their feet. *So this is it. I like it; I hope I'm doing it right.* She moved her lips in response to Dave's.

'Come on, we'd best go and find that bike.' He held out his hand as he turned to the stairs.

'Bike?' She took his hand.

At the bottom of the stairs he kissed her again.

Yes, I like it. I like it better than anything I've ever done before, she thought as the chill of the Farnton evening cooled her down.

Jenny and Sarah contemplated the revolving doors that led to the main corridor of the Infirmary.

'Perhaps we should have got late passes?' Jenny said.

'It's too late now and we're both on duty first thing so we wouldn't have been given them anyway.'

'You go first and when you're at the top of the cellar steps. I'll follow,' said Jenny.

'It's probably better if we're both in the door at once.

If it goes round twice someone might hear it. Come on, the corridor's empty.' said Sarah.

Sarah stood in the door and pushed.

Jenny entered the next segment.

They pushed the door slowly. It creaked its way round. Sarah darted out, turned sharp left and dived for the top of the cellar steps.

Jenny followed.

'I don't want to do that too often, it's too nerve racking,' mouthed Sarah as they tip-toed past Matron's rooms.

'It's all right for you titch, but I nearly knocked myself out on the overhead pipes.' The girls collapsed on the top step of the stairs, leading to their bedrooms, giggling. 'I could murder a cup of tea,' said Jenny.

'Too risky, we're bound to wake Matron. What was it like on the motorbike?' Sarah said.

'It was wonderful, great, smashing. I've never felt so, I don't know, free I suppose is a good word. I wasn't too sure about putting my arms around Dave but he told me to hang on tight or I'd fall off.'

'Did he feel nice and cuddly?'

'Honestly Sarah, you're getting as bad as Theresa.'

'I was going to suggest you came back in the car with us but then I went to get my coat and I saw the two of you having a kiss and cuddle. Well?'

'Do you think anyone else saw us? Theresa?'

'What does it matter? I think the Smithfields were out to fix one of us up with him and you were the obvious choice. I don't think he and Theresa would have been the perfect match. Do you?'

'His mother said something strange; when I went to say goodnight to Mr and Mrs Smithfield. "I'm glad you girls could come, especially you, love",' Jenny said fumbling to find her room key. 'Night, Sarah.'

'Night, Jenny. Sweet dreams.'

# CHAPTER ELEVEN

The student nurses straggled through the hospital grounds on their way to the mortuary. Dressed in their long, black, full-skirted out-door macs and black storm caps they resembled a flock of unruly ravens.

'I've been bloody dreading this,' said Theresa as the group waited for the mortuary doors to be opened. 'Thank God your Elizabeth's party gave us something else to think about.'

'Language, Nurse Booth. Get a move on nurses the pathologist is too busy to stand and wait until we deign to file in,' said Miss Bolton.

'I agree with you, Theresa,' said Sarah. 'I'd do anything not to be here. I'm standing behind Jenny then I can hide. I don't want to watch.'

In the mortuary ante room, Miss Bolton briskly gave the nurses a briefing. They were to watch closely, listen diligently to the consultant pathologist, and above all behave with dignity.

'Gather round, my lovely ladies,' said the pathologist, looking them up and down.

'He looks like he's sizing us up for the slab,' Theresa said out of the corner of her mouth.

'I think I'm going to faint,' Sarah muttered from behind Jenny.

'You, yes you. The little one with the face the colour of your dress hiding behind that bean pole. Step forward and as I indicate each cranial nerve you will name it.'

Twenty one others heaved a sigh of relief as the chosen one vacated her hiding place and took a step forward.

'You know the mnemonic, I presume, Nurse?' The pathologist grinned and pointed to the first cranial nerve with his long handled instrument 'Let's go then.'

'On, Old, Olympus, Towering, Tops, A, Fin…' Sarah muttered. She took a deep breath as the pointer indicated the first nerve, then the next and the next.

'Well done, Nurse. I thought you looked intelligent,' he said with a wink. 'I am sure in time someone will teach you the vulgar mnemonic, if they have not already done so.'

'Lecture theatre at eleven o clock,' said Miss Bolton, releasing the group to their break.

'Well done, Sal, you played a blinder,' said Theresa pouring coffee for herself and her friends.

'I thought I was going to vomit into the skull.'

'It's over with, let's forget it,' said Maggie. 'Did you all enjoy yourself last night?'

'It was a fab night out, Mags, and very successful with two fixed up now. It'll be your turn next, Mags,' said Theresa. 'You don't want to die wondering. Do you?'

'It's a little soon to talk of being fixed up,' said Jenny.

'You always go back to being hoity, bloody, toity when you're upset, or hiding something – like now,' said Theresa. 'I bet he kissed you. Come on, Jen, put us out of our misery. Are you seeing him again?'

'Tomorrow; for a meal, at the Red Cat.'

'My advice is don't bother to get a late pass, and then if he turns out to be a drip you can say you have to get back,' said Theresa.

Sarah sat back and relaxed, restored to normality by the banter of her friends.

Paul and Dave were standing together outside the Infirmary when Sarah and Jenny appeared through the revolving door. Sarah scurried towards the men. Jenny, walking behind her, gasped when Paul drew Sarah toward him and gave her a tender kiss.

'Hello, hello,' she said sidestepping toward Dave, flapping her hands.

'Hello to you too,' said Dave nodding.

'We could give you a lift into town,' said Paul.

'It's okay, thanks, we've bags of time and it's not far, so long as Jenny is good for the walk,' said Dave.

Jenny agreed. She had hardly slept and had thought of nothing else all day. The girls' teasing had been fun at first but then added to her anxiety. Who would ever have thought it – she, Jenny Hayes, had met a boy, kissed him three times and was going out on a date. She hadn't had to ask permission from her parents; would they care, probably not. What would she wear? She'd worn the blue shift for the party, it would have to be the green skirt and blouse. Thank goodness she'd bought the pointy-toed shoes. Now here he was in front of her.

She stumbled as she moved toward him.

'Steady now,' Dave said, reaching out and taking her hand.

It's sweaty, what will he be thinking, my hand is sweaty, she thought as she felt Dave move his hand around hers. With the minor adjustment their hands fitted together.

'Are you okay, would you rather have gone into town in the car, with your friends?'

'No, no I'm fine. Tell me more about your work, your job,' Jenny said hurriedly.

'What time do you have to be back?' said Dave, glancing at his watch.

'Eleven o'clock,' said Jenny without taking her eyes from Dave's face.

'It's ten to eleven.'

'Ye Gods.'

The bar of the Red Cat swam into focus as Jenny stood, grabbed her coat and together they made for the door.

'You are seven minutes late, Nurse Hayes. Sleep well,' a disembodied voice said from the depths of the night sisters' office.

'Bugger, I've drowned my baby,' said Sarah fishing a rigid doll out of the baby bath.

'Come here, I'll demonstrate for you. Move over and let me sit down,' said Jenny.

'Which way round does this vest go?' Maggie held out the tiny garment. 'Do the strings go at the back or the front?'

'Bloody hell, Mags, it's obvious,' said Theresa, grabbing Maggie's doll and feeding its arms through the sleeves and then tying the two sets of ribbons at the front. 'I thought you fancied doing your sick children's?'

'I can't help it if I've never dressed a baby before. Can I?'

*And what's this with the "bugger" Sarah Green? Not so much the miss goody-two-shoes these days. I wonder what else she's been up to, with lover boy.*

Paediatrics gave way to geriatrics as the study block progressed.

'When does old age begin?' Theresa challenged Miss Bennet at the end of the introductory lecture on the nursing care of the elderly. 'Surely any worthwhile life ends at thirty.'

'That's an interesting observation Nurse Booth, perhaps we can extend the upper age limit of old age so that I might be excluded from your definition.'

Theresa gasped when Jenny passed her a note: *Dave is 27*.

'Are you alright, Nurse Booth?'

'Yes, Miss Bennet. Nurse Hayes agrees with you, she's going out with an older man.'

'Theresa, will you ...' Jenny mouthed as the group giggled.

'Do you object to studying geriatric nursing, Nurse Booth?'

'No, I don't Miss Bennet, not studying it. But why do we have to spend time on the geriatric wards. It isn't acute nursing is it?'

'I absolutely agree and, given your intelligent and humorous observations and questions, I will explain my point of view. I am not in favour of the inclusion of geriatrics as part of the ward experience of student nurses. Studying the process of ageing and the associated disease processes, I agree with you Nurse Booth, is legitimate. Employing students to do nothing other than feed the confused elderly followed by the inevitable cleaning of faeces and urine, in some of the hospitals worst accommodation, is nothing but drudgery.' She paused for breath. 'The geriatric wards are chronically understaffed and do not provide a suitable training experience. To me the ward population of the general wards provides enough contact with elderly people. I know that I am seen as something of a radical and that my opinions and arguments will go unheeded as long as the NHS relies on student nurses as part of the ward workforce. Oh dear me I've gone on for far too long. I've said too much. I need to step down from my soap box.'

'Thank you Miss Bennet, I enjoyed that; it's the best lecture we've ever had,' said Theresa.

'Thank you, Nurse Booth.' Miss Bennet collected her notes and left the lecture theatre.

'Isn't she bloody great?' said Theresa to the room at large.

'See you in Marks and Spencer at four o'clock,' said Theresa over her shoulder as her group set off into town. The class had been split into small groups and were finishing their study of geriatrics with visits to homes for the elderly located around Farnton. Jenny, Sarah and Theresa and Maggie were planning to meet to investigate the phenomenon of tights. Lunchtime discussion had focused on the possibility of getting rid of stockings and suspender belts or panty girdles. The main stumbling block to tights was the question of knickers and if and where they should be worn. Suggestions included under the tights, over the tights, both under and over or no knickers at all. Theresa remained in favour of stockings and suspender belts.

'Tights, ugh, passion killers more like,' she said jumping from the bus in front of the others. 'I'll see you later.'

'At least tights would cover your bum,' Maggie called to Theresa, who wiggled her backside in response as she marched down the road.

# CHAPTER TWELVE

'I think it makes life more interesting, not knowing where one might be living or working.' Jenny looked down the corridor toward the staff room door and back to the vacant space on the notice board in the reception area of the School of Nursing. 'And it helps keep clothes and books tidy, constantly packing and unpacking.'

No one responded.

The coffee bar cum reception area was unnaturally quiet, with one or two nurses muttering between themselves. Others looked out of the windows, flicked through old copies of the *Nursing Times* or sat with their arms folded, gazing into space.

'At least I don't have to lump all my stuff across town every two months or so,' said Maggie. She reached into her bag. 'Does anybody want a bite of my Mars Bar?'

'No thanks.'

'Not for me.'

'No thanks.'

'Bloody hell Mags, you've only just had your dinner.

Well, we'll all soon be part of the SSU,' Theresa said, into the heavy mood.

She saw Chris Warrington look at her quizzically, and then look away when their eyes met.

'Shit Shovellers' Union,' Theresa said in explanation. 'Like I said to Miss Bennet, it's beyond me why we have to do geriatrics. It's only been on the syllabus since the introductory block before ours.' Theresa shrugged her shoulders, pursed her lips and gave the wall she was leaning against a backward kick. 'Who wants to look after confused, incontinent old biddies anyway? We won't learn anything, and anyway Bumble agrees with me. You all heard her say so.'

'What about nights?' Sarah said, pushing herself out of a low chair. 'Look out, here comes Bumble now ...'

The group moved into action, fastening collar studs and straightening skirts as they moved toward the notice board.

Tension mounted.

'Are you all looking forward to Christmas on the wards?' Miss Bennet said, reaching to pin the change list on the notice board. 'Final lecture in five minutes nurses, and it's then back to the wards next week.'

'How's it going?' said Jenny.

Sarah looked up from contemplating the pile of stuff on her bed to see Jenny poking her head round the door.

'Have you got everything packed?'

'Nearly there Jen, I've just my books and files to pack. Will you be able to give me a lift out to Paul's car with all this stuff?' Sarah stuffed books and study notes into a Richard Shops carrier bag.

'Yes, of course, give me a shout when you're ready to go. The handle on that bag looks a touch precarious. I hope it doesn't part company with the bag.' Jenny paused. 'Have you seen the Warrington girl?'

'Not since this afternoon, in the School. I would have offered her a lift to shift her stuff to the General. Paul wouldn't mind but, well, I haven't seen her.' Sarah shrugged. 'I can't help her if she's not here.'

'She's a funny old stick, won't join in, but she's always watching us,' Jenny said. 'Give me a call when you're ready to go. I'm putting my feet up for ten minutes.'

Sarah and Paul lugged the suitcase and assortment of bags from the car into the entrance hall of the home at the General.

'I'll see you in the car.' Sarah bent to heave up the suitcase. 'I'll be as quick as I can.' Sarah grabbed the suitcase and the Richard's Shop bag which immediately parted company with its handles. The books and files spilled out into the path of a small woman wrapped in a fur coat, her eyes peering out from under the brim of a matching fur hat.

'Miss Bennet?' Sarah peered at the figure stepping over her things. 'I'm so sorry.'

'No harm done, Nurse Green. Why don't you show your friend to the visitors' room and make him a cup of coffee while you sort out your paraphernalia? I'm sorry, I must dash. I'm off to the theatre.'

Miss Bennet peered toward the doors where a taxi had drawn up. She waved her hand toward a corridor leading from the hallway. She exited singing the words to *The Girl that I Marry Will Have to Be*.

Sarah and Paul looked at each other astounded.

'Wow Sarah, I'm allowed onto hallowed ground.'

'And you can have a cup of coffee. How free and easy is that?'

Upstairs, Sarah quickly unpacked her suitcase and then in a large cloth bag packed pyjamas, toilet bag, tights and a set of underclothes. She opened the wardrobe door and stood with her head on one side. She was staying overnight with Paul and his parents. Every time she thought about the evening at his house, sleeping the night and then spending the whole of the next day with him and his mum and dad, her mouth dried up and she felt her insides churn. She was well aware of the difference in her and Paul's backgrounds, something that didn't seem to register with Paul. Her thoughts skittered as her hands skimmed over the wire coat hangers. What should she wear tomorrow? She couldn't wear her best dress tomorrow as well as tonight. What would his mother think of her home-made clothes? Come on Sarah, she told herself, get a move on, it isn't as though you've got a lot to choose from. She dragged a skirt and jumper from their hangers and folded them into the bag. As she pulled on the camel coat her mother had given her the previous Christmas she felt perspiration trickle down her back. *Keep calm or you'll be a real sweaty mess by the time you arrive, and then what will his mother think.*

'All set then?' said Paul, springing up from the deep armchair and shrugging on his overcoat when Sarah called to collect him from the visitor's room. 'I'm really looking forward to this evening, aren't you, darling? Come here my lovely girl.' Sarah let herself be wrapped in Paul's arms. 'I love you,' he whispered as they returned their tongues to their own mouths.

'I love you too Paul, but I'm a bit bothered about ...'

He drew her to him again as they moved out into the corridor. Sarah glanced round anxiously as she pulled away from Paul. Thank goodness there was no one about, otherwise she would be in Matron's office before she knew it. How could he have the brass neck to kiss her in the nurses' home?

Relieved to be alone, in the 'green guest room', and free to think, Sarah was sure she would never get to sleep.

Her thoughts whirred round and round. Fancy being invited to a house where tea is called dinner; even the Reverend and Mrs Evans call the evening meal tea. *Did I dress up enough for Mrs Thompson? Oh bugger! Look what Theresa's done. I'll be swearing in front of my mother next. What will happen when I take Paul home to meet my mum? I am really, really dreading it. Plate meat pie; home-made and tasty, fair enough, with half a tomato and a piece of brown bread and butter served on the same small tea plate as the pie. All washed down with a pot of weak tea. I'll cook like Mrs Thompson when I have my own home. To start the meal: half a grapefruit spiced with nutmeg, butter, brown sugar and sherry, and grilled. Followed by cod in spicy tomato, onion and mushroom sauce served with fluffy rice. I hope I managed to look as though I'd eaten rice with a main meal before. I wonder if it's the same rice as pudding rice. I'll ask Jenny, she'll know. Why does his mother seem so stand offish? Is it because I'm not posh? Her accent isn't that different than mine. That sweet, come on Sarah – dessert – was fabulous. A pavlova; a meringue, crisp on the outside and like marshmallow on the inside, with thick whipped cream, not Carnation like at home, topped with mandarin oranges. Wine! I've only had sweet sherry before. It was as well I settled for iced water. Iced water, whatever happened to running the cold tap for a minute or two? Well let's face it, when Paul comes home with me he can have as much iced water as he wants at this time of year. That is if the water hasn't frozen in the pipes. His dad's lovely. The three of them are close. I liked his joke, and the way Paul and his mum groaned when he said his favourite Sinatra song had to be, because he is a radiologist,* I've Got You Under My Skin. *Come on Sarah, try and sleep you've all day tomorrow to get through. I wonder why his mother doesn't ...*

'Sarah, that camel coat is too good to wear to go rambling over the moors. Take it off.' Rose held out her right arm to take the coat. 'I'll lend you an anorak, and you'll find a spare pair of wellies in the back porch and I can find you a scarf.' She reached into the hall cupboard, deposited Sarah's coat and drew out a blue anorak.

All togged up, the four climbed into the Triumph Herald that Rose Thompson used in her job as a health visitor. They were ready to head for the moors, part of the foothills of the Pennines, surrounding Farnton.

'Paul, darling, throw those baby clothes on the parcel shelf.' Rose turned from the driver's seat and pointed to the back of the car. 'Then Rusty can sit between you and Sarah.'

'He can sit in front, between my legs.'

'Hugh, you know you are far too soft with him. He'll climb on your knee and block my view.'

Sarah took a deep breath and forced a smile.

# CHAPTER THIRTEEN

The warmth and comfort of being close to Dave's body when he held her encouraged Jenny to respond to his embraces. He nuzzled her neck, then sucked and gently bit her before his lips moved to meet hers. Practising kissing, at home in bed, by squeezing the tips of her first finger and thumb together and drawing her lips away with a loud smack had in no way prepared Jenny for the real thing. Her body tingled, particularly when he moved his hands to touch her breasts. She snuggled against him and sighed deeply. Her thoughts interrupted her bliss. *Ooh, ooh, should I push his hand away? Ooh. Between my legs feels damp. Have I wet myself?* Coming up for air she caught sight of Dave's wristwatch as it stroked her left breast.

'It can't be half past ten.' Jenny sat up suddenly, her voice rising.

'Do you have to be back by eleven every night?'

'Yes, unless I have a late pass or chance the cellar and I can only get a late pass if I'm not on duty at seven thirty the next morning.' She leapt up from the comfy settee in Dave's front room, tucked her blouse into her skirt and reached out for her boots, fumbling as she pulled them on ready for another hasty departure back to the Infirmary. 'I daren't risk going through the cellar, not since I was caught coming in late after we had dinner at the Red Cat.'

'Come on then, I can't have my girl getting in to trouble,' Dave sighed and pulled Jenny towards him, kissing her firmly on the lips. 'We'll have longer together tomorrow evening.'

His girl! Golly gum drops.

'Let's sit in the corner, by the fire.' Dave nodded towards a secluded table in the snug of the Dog and Partridge. Unwinding her School of Nursing scarf from around her neck, Jenny threw it over a Windsor chair, undid the toggles of her duffle coat, pulled out an upright chair and sat down. 'Relax, take your coat off.' Dave watched Jenny look around the room. 'What would you like to drink?'

'Cider, please.'

'Sweet or dry?'

'I've no idea. I've never had it before.' Jenny barked a laugh.

'You've given up on the sweet sherry then?'

'I don't know about drinks,' she blushed and turned away to give a faded picture of a hunting scene her attention, 'or pubs for that matter.'

'Go for the dry. It'll taste better with the chicken and chips and anyway the sweet stuff is just like drinking pop.'

'The chicken in the basket won't be long.' Dave settled himself in the chair facing Jenny and reached across the table. He took hold of her hand, lifted it to his lips, and kissed it. 'Do you still like your new ward?'

'Yes, I do. I'm glad I'm on male orthopaedics. I don't

mind old people but I'd rather be nursing young men who have been in motorbike accidents than old ladies who have fallen downstairs.'

Explaining helped Jenny relax.

'I swerved and fell off my motorbike last year.'

Dave let go of Jenny's hand and presented his for examination.

'It isn't very well sutured.'

Jenny let go of Dave's hand to make way for the baskets of food. Dave set to, dousing his chips with salt and vinegar. Jenny followed suit.

'I like a girl who enjoys her food.' Dave picked up a chip and shuffled it into his mouth. 'Especially one who likes her chips with loads of salt and vinegar.'

'We don't have chips at home, not allowed. They're very working class according to my dad – George.'

'You don't like him, do you?'

Jenny felt her cheeks burn. She carefully placed her knife and fork in the basket.

'Come on, eat your grub and then you can tell me about your dad. Have you seen our Margaret recently?'

Jenny cut up the food, carefully loaded her fork and pushed the food into her mouth. She chewed and swallowed, reported on seeing Maggie, sipped and swallowed until her basket and glass were empty. She saw Dave's concern and started her story.

'I've never told anyone before.' She hesitated. 'The others know some of it. I told them when we were at your parent's caravan.'

'Take your time.'

'George is not my father. Everyone thinks he is because we've all got the same surname – Hayes. He and Malcolm are cousins.'

'Who's Malcolm then? Are your mum and dad divorced?'

'Yes. No. I don't know.' Jenny's food had landed

heavily. 'Do you think I might have another drink?'

As Dave left the snug to go to the bar Jenny clenched her fists and banged on the table. The table felt sticky. Jenny saw the nicotine stained walls, the clumsily framed prints and the gaps in the curtains. *I am free, away from him. I will never go back.*

'Yes,' Jenny said as Dave appeared with the drinks.

'Yes? What does that mean? What a smile. Did I miss something?'

'It means I want to tell you – everything.' Jenny waited until Dave was settled in his chair. 'My mum married him, George, in Devon and then we moved here, to Farnton. I've never known my dad. He disappeared when I was a baby. No one ever mentioned him. Once, when I was growing up, I tried asking my granny where he was but all she would say was "I liked Malcolm, indeed I was fond of him, but the embarrassment he caused was unforgivable. He should never have married knowing he was like that." She told me that I should never ask any more questions or mention him again.'

Jenny told the tale of years spent listening; hanging over bannister rails, when she was supposed to be in bed, sitting quietly outside open doors when she was meant to be playing in the garden. Or best of all, hiding in the dark cave provided by the velvet cloth covering her Granny Ashford's dining table. Eventually she'd pieced together a story. Malcolm, her dad, and mother had met at a party given by George's parents to say farewell to Malcolm and George before they went off to the war. Malcolm had courted her mother, mostly by letter whilst he was away. He was away for a long time, in Army Intelligence. Their wedding was four weeks after his return home at the end of the war. George was the best man.

'I kept hearing the one word – annulled. When I was older I looked it up in the dictionary, but I couldn't understand. How could they not be married if they'd had me and did that mean I am,' Jenny glanced around the empty snug, 'a bastard? According to George I am, a bastard I mean. I looked that up in the dictionary as well.' Jenny hissed, under her breath. 'I hate them, I really hate them.'

Heaving sobs brought Dave to his feet. He pulled Jenny up from her chair, drew her into his arms until the sobs quietened.

'Her grandma died this morning,' said Dave to the landlord who had come to clear away the baskets and glasses.

'I'm sorry, so sorry what must you thin ...'

'I think you are lovely. Go and have a wash. I'll get us another drink.'

As Jenny moved to go to the Ladies he stroked her face with his thumb and kissed her on the cheek.

'Why are they so bloody awful to you?' Dave pushed Jenny's cider toward her.

'I suppose it's because I look like Malcolm. I'm the only one of the four of us with this frizzy mop, and then there's my height. George says I'm like an upturned mop that's been left outside to rot. He resents spending money on me. I failed the 11+. To his "utter embarrassment and shame." That's why I was sent to private school, for his sake not mine. It turned out I wasn't as thick as he made out. The effects of changing primary school four times had worn off by the time it came to O levels. He wanted me to go to secretarial college and then work in his office. I refused and, well you know the rest.'

Jenny flopped back and rested the back of her head on the rim of the chair. She sighed.

'But your mum's alright. Isn't she?'

'No, to be honest, she is just as bad as he is.'

'Do you get on with your little brothers? Are they

okay with you?'

'No, not really, but it isn't their fault. He encourages them to laugh at me. Although, he says it's teasing. I stay in my room, or did. I don't go home now, not if I can help it.'

'Jenny, what can I say?' Dave paused. 'I love the fact that at six foot two I've met a girl who can more or less look me in the eye. Your hair is glorious; you're lovely to look at, bright and cheerful and a joy to be with. Sod 'em, stand tall girl and be proud of yourself.'

'What? You can't mean it. Lend me your handkerchief, please.'

She reached forward to take it.

Dave reached for Jenny's elbow and drew her toward him.

Jenny pulled away and stared at Dave, her eyes wide, her mouth open. Then a slow smile became a grin followed by a laugh and then more tears.

Dave filled the space and told his story in a series of short sentences.

'I was engaged to Marion, a girl I went to school with. She broke it off a few weeks before the wedding. She did me a favour. We were in the habit of being together, nothing else. She said I was too quiet and boring. I've been out with other girls since but had nothing in common with them. You are the best thing that has ever happened to me.'

'Why?' Jenny handed back the soggy handkerchief. 'How can I be?'

'You are open and honest, innocent.'

'How can you say I'm innocent?' Lowering her voice and leaning closer toward him she said, 'I could be a bastard and I know what homosexuals do to each other. That's what my dad is you know – a homosexual. I've spent heaps of time in the library.'

Dave stroked her hair as more tears pooled. He felt in

his pocket, retrieved the soaked hanky and offered it back. Jenny shook her head and wiped her eyes with the back of her hands. To give her time to gather herself Dave told Jenny that his grandma was right. Marion was flighty; only interested in herself, her clothes, makeup, her hair, handbags and shoes and going dancing or to the pub. As he helped Jenny with her coat he leaned forward and whispered in her ear, 'I love you.'

Jenny sank into the nearest chair. Dave knelt down beside her, anxious that he had been too hasty.

'I'm fine. Don't worry, I'm fine. I love you too. I knew it more or less straight away but I'm scared. We've only known each other three weeks and two days.'

'I knew Marion for years but in the end it came to nothing. She was somebody I knocked about with, that's all. Come on, let's have a stroll before we get on the bike.'

Wrapped around each other they wandered down the lane at the side of the pub, Jenny felt her head begin to clear.

'Have you ever been out with other, you know … erm with other boys and that?'

'Tons,' Jenny said laughing. 'No. Not really. I met someone when I went to visit Granny Ashford in Devon last year but it fizzled out. I'm not the best letter writer in the world and he was even worse.'

'What are you smiling at now?'

'Something Theresa said. She told Sarah and me that we were like lambs to the slaughter, settling for the first boys that came along.'

'So you're settling for me, are you?'

'I might as well. Wait until I tell Theresa, she is going to love it.' Laughing as she ran away towards the bike, she shouted over her shoulder, 'She thinks you're virtually a geriatric.'

# CHAPTER FOURTEEN

'Permission to go off duty, please, Sister. I know it's five minutes early but the night staff are here and, well, can we go? It's Nurse Warrington. She nearly fainted. Heavy period, I think. I'm going to get her back to the home and in bed,' Theresa said, hovering in the doorway of the cubbyhole of the office on 1A.

'Yes, yes, go if all the evening jobs are completed. Where is Nurse Warrington?'

'In the staff lav, toilet, I mean. Good night Sister,' Theresa said as she hurried off.

Theresa reached for Chris Warrington's arm. 'Come on let's get you to the home.'

'Don't touch me, don't touch me,' Chris turned away from Theresa.

'Straighten your cap or you'll draw attention to yourself.' Theresa pointed to the lopsided head gear. *You look like something out of the bleedin' Adam's family if you ask me.*

Chris adjusted her cap and pulled her cape tight around her hunched shoulders. She followed Theresa out of the dreary geriatric ward.

'Let's go the long way round instead of cutting through the hospital. That way we're less likely to bump into anyone,' Theresa said, touching Chris on the shoulder as they stepped outside into the dark, wild night and crossed over the road that divided the annexe from the bright lights of the main hospital.

'Please, I've already asked you. Don't touch me. I'm filthy.' Chris flinched.

'What on earth's happened? What the bloody hell's the matter?'

'I'm filthy. Don't touch me. Don't come near me.'

'Well, I'm bloody stumped. I really am. One minute we're busy shit shovelling and the next minute you screamed and scarpered.' Theresa stopped mid stride. 'Hang on, that old codger touched you up when he was leaning against you. He did, didn't he? That's why you shot off and left me to sort him out. I'm right, aren't I?'

Chris mumbled a response.

'Come on. We're nearly there,' said Theresa. *Thank Christ.* She made sure she kept her distance.

As soon as she was in her bedroom Chris's knees gave way and she sank to the floor. Theresa, who had followed her into the room, was flummoxed. She was saved by a knock on the open door.

'What's happened?' said Sarah peering into the room. 'Is Chris ill?'

Sarah moved towards Chris, who was sitting on the floor slumped against the bed.

'For God's sake, don't touch her.' Theresa pulled Sarah backwards.

Chris was rocking and sobbing, muttering, 'I need a bath. I must have a bath.'

'Stay with her, Sal. See is you can find her nightie. I'll go and find a bathroom. Although, I have to say, finding one free at this time of night will be like pissing in the bloody wind.'

Chris carried on rocking and sobbing.

'Chris, your bath's ready when you are. I know I can't stop you locking the door but if you do I'm going to go on the sisters' corridor and bring the duty home sister to see you. Is that clear?' Theresa said.

Chris looked from Theresa to Sarah and in a barely audible voice said, 'Why should you two help me? I'm filthy.'

'Get in the bath. I'll lurk on the corridor. Sarah will make us all some tea and toast. Won't you, Sal?' Theresa raised her eyebrows at Sarah as she closed the bathroom door on Chris and positioned herself on the corridor.

'Ye Gods, what have you done to yourself?' said Theresa when Chris came out of the bathroom. 'Your face is red raw and so is the rest of you by the look of things. I knew you weren't fit to be left on your own.'

'I'm sorry, so sorry. Thank you for helping me, and all that stuff but I'm all right now, really I am. Please leave me alone.'

'You're a bloody liar, Chris Warrington. There is no way that you're all right, and no, I'm not leaving you. You need moisturising cream on that skin and some tea and toast. You're scared of joining in and getting to know the rest of us. That much I'm sure of.'

Theresa followed Chris into her bedroom and closed the door. Chris turned and faced Theresa.

'You don't know me. If you did you wouldn't keep trying to involve me … in stuff. I've told you I'm filthy, I can't get clean.'

'Hang on a tick. Something like this has happened to you before, hasn't it?' said Theresa quietly as she answered the kick on the door from Sarah who was carrying a tray holding tea, toast and fruitcake.

'What? What's happened to her before?' Sarah

lowered the tray to the floor.

'Chris, get into bed,' said Theresa. *I'm buggered if I know what to do next.*

'Would you rather I went?' said Sarah.

'No, Sarah. Stay if you want to. What difference will it make? There's nothing left for me to lose now. I'll see Matron tomorrow and leave as soon as I can.'

'Don't be so bloody daft. Why will you have to leave?' said Theresa.

Chris put her head in her hands and then dragging her hands down over her face looked at her captors. After a second or two of silence Chris started her story.

'Harry Jones, my stepfather, has made my life a living hell. He was always there, always lurking behind me, touching, feeling, and squeezing my breast and my bottom.' She paused, breathed deeply. Her head dropped. 'He crept up behind me when I was at the kitchen sink. He held me tight, around my shoulders, lifted my skirt with his other hand and put that bloody thing against me. I struggled and tried to stamp on his feet. I couldn't move. He bit my neck. When he had finished he whispered "Our little secret, eh Chris?" and walked away.'

'Bleedin' hell,' said Theresa.

'Did he leave you alone after that?' Sarah said.

Theresa cast a glance at Sarah. *Our little Sal is not so calm and cool as she makes out.*

'No. That's why I'm here. I had to get away. Coming here gave me a job and a home. I hate it. I'm not fit to be here and you lot won't leave me alone. I bet this will put an end to you and the others trying to be friends with me.'

'Go on, carry on, and tell us what happened next.' Theresa nodded encouragement, her mouth open, her eyes fixed on Chris.

'I tried to avoid him. I made sure I was only at home

when I knew he would be at work or when my mum would be there. One day I arrived home, I was sure it was safe. His car wasn't in the drive. I went up to my room.' Chris shuddered. 'The dirty old man, he had his back to the door. He was stood at my dressing table. I couldn't see what he was doing at first, but then he moved. He still hadn't seen me.'

'What was he doing?' said Sarah wide-eyed.

'He was masturbating. Rubbing his thing up and down with one hand and holding a pair of my panties in the other, massaging them with his thumb. I screamed at him to get out. He ignored me, smiled at me through the mirror and then turned round and the thing spurted. It spurted out. He wiped it, that disgusting thing. With my … I threw all my underclothes away.'

'Why didn't you knee him in the balls?' Theresa shifted her right knee.

'I tried, Theresa, believe me, I tried. But I missed and he caught me, pulled me toward him and said "That's my girl, come on give it to me again, hard, next time".'

'But why didn't you tell your mother, or a friend?' said Sarah.

'They all think he's wonderful. He and my mum have only been married a couple of years. It would be my word against his. Anyway, my mum is besotted with him and his money. You believe me. Don't you?'

'Of course we do. Don't we, Theresa?'

''Course we do.' Theresa said. 'What I don't understand, if it's been going on for a while, is what made you leave home when you did?'

'He announced that he was handing over the management of his engineering firm to his nephew so that he could spend more time at home. That was it. I had to get away. I considered packing a bag and catching a train to London, Birmingham, anywhere. To tell you the truth I was desperate and didn't know what to do.

Then I heard one of the women in the office talking about her friend's daughter leaving home to be a nurse. I rang the hospital and two weeks later I was here.'

'I've always wanted to be a nurse,' Sarah crossed her hands, held them against her chest and smiled.

'You don't like the shit shovelling and all the other grotty stuff do you?' Theresa said.

'I don't mind nursing women. I had begun to think I would be all right with men but look what's happened. I'll see Matron tomorrow.'

'Then he'll have got one over on you. Come on, stick it out. Show the bugger,' said Theresa. 'Let's face it. He's a bloody pervert who needs his balls cutting off.'

'Look at me, Chris, look at me,' said Sarah. 'I'm not religious, I've had too much of that at home with my mother, but I do believe that no-one is worthless. There must be a reason why he is like he is. He might be mentally ill. By the way, I hate anything to do with mental illness. This I do know, Chris, you are not going to leave. I will help you as much as I can; I'll stay with you tonight if you want me to. We could drag my mattress into your room.'

'No, don't worry, there's no need for that. I promise I'll be fine on my own. I've got a headache but I'll take two paracetamol.'

'Okay, if that's what you want. I'll give you a call at seven to make sure you get to breakfast. Theresa, it's your day off tomorrow. You can take Chris into town when she finishes her shift. She's got a half day.'

Sarah got up from the armchair and moved towards the door.

'Yes, okay, that's fine, boss. I want to see my sister, Win, tomorrow. She's coming for her cadet interview in the morning but I'm okay for the afternoon – Chris minding.'

'I don't need minding. I'm not going to do anything

stupid.'

'I wouldn't argue with Sarah when she's in this mood, if I were you,' said Theresa. 'I'm going to creep to the kitchen and make us all a mug of tea.'

Hauling herself from the floor Theresa realised she was tired as well as stiff from sitting too long in the same position.

'Sal, I've brought your tea,' whispered Theresa as she tapped on Sarah's door.

'Do you think she'll be alright?' Sarah said.

'God only knows.'

# CHAPTER FIFTEEN

'Why is the Warrington girl coming with us?' Jenny said as she and Maggie put their empty coffee cups on the serving hatch. 'Don't get me wrong. It's not that I mind. It seems a bit odd, that's all.'

'Something to do with being upset and they've got to know her better.'

'No doubt we'll hear all about it when we see them. If I don't see you before, I'll see you on Monday at the Red Cat.'

They parted company and made their way back to their respective wards.

Theresa, as usual, had organised the outing. On her afternoon in town, with Chris, they had called in the Red Cat. Theresa had beseeched, nay harangued, the manager to take pity on a group of hard working student nurses who would have very little time off duty over Christmas. She embroidered her pleas with a swirl of her hips and a slinky smile. The manager succumbed and agreed that they could have a table at nine o'clock.

Sarah told Theresa and Chris to make their way into

town without her. 'There's no point us all being on the last minute. I'll get changed on the ward; if I smell a bit of the SSU it will be too bad.'

Theresa spotted Jenny and Maggie. They were looking at the brightly lit Christmas window display in Drapers, Farnton's largest department store.

'Hiya, you two. Still planning your Christmas shopping?' Theresa said. 'Come on, let's get inside. It's cold enough to freeze the balls off a brass monkey.'

The fuss of getting settled at the table over, Theresa looked at Jenny and then looked again. 'Jenny, what in the name of God has happened to you? You look bloody gorgeous. She does, doesn't she, Chris?' Theresa gave Chris a nudge. 'Whoops, Sorry!'

'Theresa, forget it. I'll cope.'

'Cope with what? Thank you Theresa, I didn't realise anything was that obvious.' Jenny turned to Chris. 'What are you coping with Chris?'

Chris dithered.

'So come on. What's happened to you, Jen? You've got new clothes, a sticky out bust and you look even taller. Bugger me, its love. I knew it,' Theresa giggled. 'What did I say?'

'Yes, Theresa, you are correct, as always. Dave told me to be proud of myself and walk tall.' She drew herself up, sitting straight, peering down on her short friend. 'What do you think of my hair? I've had it cut and styled.'

'It suits you, the haircut and all that, but isn't it all a bit bloody soon, this love business?'

'I agree, it is sudden – four weeks and five days,' Jenny didn't pause for breath, 'What are you coping with Chris?'

Theresa groaned, reached out for the pile of menus at the end of the table and noisily distributed them. 'Come on, get choosing. I'm starving,' she said.

'I'm coping,' Chris fixed her eyes on the table mat, using her thumbnail she scraped at a dried tomato seed, 'I'm coping with being … with being … I think the word is … is, violated by my stepfather.'

Bleedin' hell, here we go again.

'Hello everybody, what's the matter?' Sarah headed for the vacant seat. 'You all look as though you've seen a ghost.'

'I don't want to talk about it any more, only to say that I am coping, but only just and that without these two,' Chris paused, wiped the tomato seed on her napkin, looked from Theresa to Sarah, 'I would be homeless and jobless. Will you tell me about your new boyfriend please Jenny, before I start to cry?'

'Man friend, you mean,' said Theresa turning her best incandescent smile on the waiter.

Chris was aware she had responded to Jenny but her voice was distant, not part of her. She surfaced to hear the girls laughing at something to do with sweet sherry.

'When are we all going to get together again? It's Christmas next week and then we start nights,' said Jenny.

'We're not likely to get together before the next change list goes up. Do you think there's a cat in hell's chance we could all be at the same hospital?' said Theresa.

Christmas plans were discussed. All the student nurses, at both hospitals, would be working for the whole of Christmas Day. The powers that be had decreed, in the spirit of fairness, that the shift would be from seven thirty a.m. until eight thirty p.m. On hearing that Chris and Theresa were not going home for Christmas evening – Theresa because the buses would have stopped running and Chris for obvious reasons – Maggie invited them to her home.

'My mum and dad won't mind a bit. It's our turn to

do Christmas and our Dave can give you a lift back, he lives near the General. Jenny's coming, with Dave. You are, aren't you, Jen? You can come as well Sarah, if you want to.'

'Thanks Maggie, but Paul's picking me up and taking me to his house and then, God forbid, we are going to see my mother on Boxing Day. I'm thinking of asking for a split so that we don't have to stay with her for too long.'

'Are you not going to see your family, Jenny?' said Chris.

'No, it's a long story, different than yours, perhaps not as bad but, let's just say I won't be missed.'

'Come on, look at the time,' said Maggie, pulling on her coat. 'I hope you inmates have got late passes.'

Christmas Day dragged on. For once there was an abundance of staff to carry out ward duties. Patients who were deemed fit enough to be discharged had been sent home, there were no routine admissions and with all the students on duty there was a fight to carry out the most mundane of jobs. Ward clocks move inexorably to eight thirty. Intermittent light relief was provided by visits from esteemed gentlemen; Father Christmas appeared and handed out gifts. He obviously had inside information that there was an imminent outbreak of the common cold. All his gifts were boxes of handkerchiefs. He, or his elves, had cleverly packed the women's presents in flat square boxes to distinguish them from the men's gifts. The senior consultant of each ward arrived prompt at midday to carve the turkey and mingle stiffly with the ward staff. Afternoon visiting was jolly; patients' friends and relatives were merry, fortified with Christmas spirits – holy and bottled. Presents for loved ones were often supplemented with gifts of Cadbury's Roses or Quality Street for the nurses. Finally, the night staff arrived and the student nurses were, at last, released to their own festivities.

Sarah arrived at Paul's house to find the extended Thompson family playing charades.

'At last, Sarah has arrived.' Hugh leapt from the settee and put his arm round Sarah to draw her into the sitting room. 'Let me introduce everyone.'

'Let the poor girl get her coat off.' Rose held out her hands for the coat. 'I'll get the supper while she says hello to you all. It was *The Night of the Iguana* by the way.'

Hugh's family; his parents, brother and sister-in-law and nephews said hello and politely asked about Sarah's day. In the general melee of rearranging furniture, visiting the lavatory and looking for missing handbags, Sarah, unsure of herself, but determined to get it over, gave her presents to Rose and Hugh.

'Sarah, these are lovely,' said Rose pulling on a pair of mittens in an Aran pattern. 'Have you knitted them? Aren't you clever?'

'Sarah, this is great.' Hugh wound a long scarf round his next. 'Thank you dear, very thoughtful.' He bent to kiss her cheek.

Rose knelt to reach under the large Christmas tree in the corner of the room. She handed three parcels up to Hugh before rising to her feet.

'For you, my dear.' He kissed Sarah again.

'Thank you, thank you very much.' Sarah looked from Paul's dad to his mum. His dad was beaming; the sharp look from his mother was quickly covered with a forced smile before she disappeared into the kitchen.

'Come on Sarah, open them.' Paul led Sarah to an armchair and sat at her feet while she carefully removed the sellotape of the first gift, drew back the folds of paper and lifted out the present.

'Get them ripped open, there's no need to save the

paper. Look, I'll show you.'

Sarah's treasure trove amounted to a pair of sturdy wellies in one parcel, a pair of thick socks in a second, and in the third a blue and white box decorated with a blue ribbon. The box held Blue Grass hand cream and a cylinder of talcum powder.

'Hugh, come and carry one of the trays into the sitting room,' said Rose, appearing from the kitchen with a pile of plates and linen napkins.

Paul pulled Sarah to her feet and kissed her. 'Merry Christmas, my darling.'

Grandma, who had appeared at the sitting room door, shot off into the hall calling for her husband. Sarah, who caught a glance of the old lady as she disappeared, blushed and attempted to pull away from Paul. Three presents, Hugh's attention, Rose's obvious irritation and Paul's blatant affection and endearments threatened to swamp her. In her world, presents were given in ones, wrapping paper was saved, and touching was for rare occasions of extreme distress. Paul pulled Sarah toward the tree to reach for his presents to her.

'Here they are.' Theresa turned from her vantage point by the first floor window, to Chris, who was sitting on the top stair. 'Come on, you'll feel better with a bit of fresh air.'

'I'm not sure I want to come. Maggie only asked me because she feels sorry for me.'

'Stop mithering and come on.' Theresa caught hold of Chris's arm and dragged her down the stairs.

'Merry Christmas you two,' Dave said as he opened the driver's door of his uncle's van and made toward the rear doors. 'My aunty put some old rugs in the back for you to sit on.'

'Merry Christmas.' Jenny squirmed round from the passenger seat.

'Merry Christmas,' chorused from the back of the van as the two new passengers wriggled their bottoms to get comfortable on the hard floor.

'What sort of day have you had with your old men?' Jenny said into the dark space.

'The usual; shuffle food in, wipe it up as it comes out the other end, with a break for visiting. What about you?'

'To be perfectly honest Theresa, it was disappointing. There were too many of us on duty and not enough work to do. We spent the majority of the time in the sluice eating chocolates. You have never seen such clean bed pans and the linen cupboard is immaculate.'

'I don't see why all of us have to work the whole day. I'm going to talk to Bumble next time we're in, oops, bugger, my bum, study block,' said Theresa.

'Sorry,' Dave said, 'it's time this cobbled road was tarmacked. Forget about work you lot, and try and enjoy what's left of Christmas.'

'You can't beat Christmas Day supper; turkey and stuffing butties,' John Smithfield looked fondly at the concoction in his hand, 'and pork pie and pickles.'

'Sandwiches, John,' said Dave's mum, flicking her head toward Jenny.

'Thank you ladies, for the supper. I think it's time I did my bit; who's for a singsong?' Brian Smithfield said, lifting the lid that sheltered the yellowing keyboard of his brother's upright piano.

'Let's start wi *Silent Night*,' said Grandma, who on her daughter-in-law's instruction reached behind her back to donate a soft cushions to Theresa who was sitting on the floor.

'Thank you,' Theresa said, returning the grimace.

'One, two, three,' Brian counted them in. The singing started and then quietened as a soft melodic voice was heard. Brian waved a free hand at Chris to encourage her to continue.

'Well luv,' Brian left the piano stool to give Chris, perched on the arm of the settee, a hug, 'you've made Grandma's Christmas.'

Theresa, Jenny and Maggie gasped whilst Grandma gave a gigantic snort into her hanky.

'What's up?' Brian looked at Maggie.

'Nothing, really nothing at all,' said Chris. She opened her eyes wide and stared pointedly at her friends. 'This is the best Christmas I've had for years – thank you for inviting me.'

'Come on, my favourite next – *White Christmas*,' said Brian.

During the break to replenish glasses Chris was asked about her singing. She explained that her mum was a good singer and had entertained the troops during the war. Her mother had been keen for Chris to sing and dance so she had been sent to weekly classes. She'd finally managed to escape with the excuse that she needed time to study for her O levels. She added that she carried on singing in the school choir, often as a soloist.

'Well Uncle Brian, what do you think of that?' said Maggie taking a sip of her drink. 'Mm, this pop is good Grandma. What sort is it?'

'I had one last week at the Over 60s, they know I don't drink but they said as I'd be all reet wi one of them. It's a called a Babycham and brandy. I don't mind a drop of brandy every now and then; when mi stomach's upset, but I'd never thought of mixing it with pop.'

Maggie gave a little belch. 'Watch yourself, Chris. You can't be involved with this family unless you sign your soul away to the Trinity Players. Dad, can I have another drink?'

Chris was puzzled. She didn't understand the

reference to the Trinity Players or Maggie's dismissive tone. She wasn't sure if Maggie was having a go at her, her uncle or the family in general.

'Ignore her; she's got one on her. Uncle Brian's the musical director of The Players and our Margaret was never that keen. Except when Tim Carter was there, she fancies him something rotten,' said Elizabeth from the other arm of the settee.

'I do not.' Maggie, sitting at her sister's feet, turned round and pulled out her tongue.

'She lost all interest in The Players when he went off to teacher training college. Didn't she, Mum?'

'Girls! Girls! It's Christmas Day,' said their mother.

'Well, for your information Margaret, he's back.' Elizabeth grinned knowingly at her sister.

'Dad, can I have some more of that pop?' said Maggie.

'I did not do it on purpose,' said Elizabeth when she and Maggie were helping to clear up after waving off their guests. 'If I had done it on purpose I would have told you there and then that he's not only back but he's engaged. So there!'

'Margaret, are you awake?' Elizabeth crept into her sister's bedroom carrying a tray.

'Mm, just about. What time is it?' Maggie pushed herself up in bed and half turned to look at her alarm clock. 'Ten o'clock. Ye Gods. My mouth feels dry and my heads all fuzzy.'

Elizabeth waited until Maggie had pushed herself up and was leaning back against the pillows she'd propped against the bedhead. She placed the tray across her sister's knee.

'I've made your favourite breakfast, boiled eggs and soldiers. I'm sorry about last night, honestly, I didn't mean to show you up in front of the family and your friends.'

'It's okay, don't mither yourself about it. When I had time to think about it I wasn't that bothered. He never fancied me anyway.'

The sisters set about the breakfast, taking it in turn to dip the soldiers into the soft yokes of the two eggs.

'Hutch up then and share your pillows.'

'So if you've given up on Tim Carter do you fancy anybody else?'

'No, I can't say I'm that bothered about boys. I'm jiggered when I get home, I can't be bothered to get dolled up and go into town. Theresa's the best friend I ever had. She looks after me and all that, but I can't be bothered to go out with her at night. I'm glad I don't live in with them; all they do is talk about clothes and sex; things I'm not interested in.'

'What's that Chris like?'

'I don't really know her; they've got to know her because she was in some bother and Theresa and Sarah sorted her out. She seems a bit snooty to me, pushing her way in.'

'I thought you invited her to come last night.'

'I did, but I'm not sure why.'

'Honestly Margaret, you don't know which way is up sometimes. It's a good job you've got Theresa to watch out for you.'

'Have you got rid of the hairs on your top lip?' Maggie peered at her sister's face. 'Theresa is always on at me about mine. She says I'll give any lads I snog beard burn.'

'Yes, I have. I used Dad's razor. I don't think he's noticed. I tried Veet, but my top lip went all red and sore. I didn't read the instructions until after I'd used it. It's for under-arms and legs.'

'I bet he'd soon notice if we both started using it.' Maggie took another squint. 'Let's buy a razor between us. Another thing we could do is get our hair cut. Jenny and Sarah look more grown up since they got theirs done.'

'Dad wouldn't like it,' said Elizabeth.

'Do you think we'll always be his little princesses?'

'Probably.'

Their mother disturbed their meandering musings by shouting up the stairs that there was enough hot water in the tank for Margaret to have a bath. She added, with a smile in her voice, that their dad was making turkey soup for dinner.

'Let's make an effort to join in a bit more with The Players and Dad might forgive us for having our hair shorn off,' said Elizabeth.

'Joining in and eating turkey soup?' Maggie swung her legs out of bed. 'Thank goodness he only tries to cook once a year. Ugh, turkey soup.'

# CHAPTER SIXTEEN

Theresa snuggled down in an attempt to catch another hour's sleep but the early morning clatter of nurses preparing for duty was no lullaby. Rubber-soled shoes squeaked on the polished floors of the corridors. Bedroom doors banged shut as the women pulled capes tight around their shoulders to shield against the cold weather. Without any thought for the sleepy heads still in bed they called out to friends to wait so that they could walk to breakfast together. Ten minutes of frenzied activity and all was quiet. Theresa turned her pillow over, gave it a thump and settled down. The noise of mop buckets clanging and the voices of the cleaning ladies persuaded Theresa that a hot bath was a better idea than sleep.

Bernadette leapt up from her chair by the fire at the sight of her eldest daughter making her way up the garden path. She dashed into the kitchen and was by the back door by the time Theresa had walked round the outside of the house. Mother and daughter hugged each other.

The ancient Christmas tree looked worse for wear, one of the branches had snapped off. Theresa remembered it had been hanging at a crazy angle when she and Win had packed it away at the end of last Christmas. One end of a home-made paper chain had escaped from its drawing pin and hung limp against the wall of the front room. Plastic toys, wax crayons and Christmas cards covered the threadbare rug.

'It wasn't the same over Christmas without you. Come and sit by the fire.'

Theresa leant forward in the chair and warmed herself by the coal fire banked half way up the chimney.

'Here's your tea, get your hands round that and you'll soon be warm.'

Bernadette shivered as she handed Theresa the mug of tea.

'Are you cold, Mum?'

'No more than usual love, it's this draughty house. There's gaps round some of them windows you can get your hand in. I bank up the fire one minute and it's burned through the next. I've a job keeping the house warm.'

'Let's hope it doesn't freeze like last year,' said Theresa.

'Jesus, Mary and Joseph our Theresa, I can't bring myself to think about it. Another burst would kill me, what with all that water to bail out and living upstairs crowded together like animals. Dear God, anything but burst pipes.'

A blast of cold air from the back door as it was thrust open to bang against the cooker, heralded the arrival of Win and the younger Booths.

'Our Theresa's here!' The baby whooped with joy and flung herself at her big sister. 'Did Father Christmas come to the hospital?'

Theresa and her bag of Christmas presents were the

centre of attention. Selection boxes were torn open and fought over by the three young children while Win dabbed Goya Black Rose behind her ears.

'You shouldn't have wasted your money on me as well,' said Bernadette wiping her eyes on the sleeve of her cardigan. 'It's lovely. It's a long time since I had a pretty nightie.'

'I'll leave these for Dad and our Tommy, for when they get in from work,' said Theresa putting two gifts on the sideboard.

As the afternoon darkened Theresa made her way back to the hospital. She had arranged to meet Chris when she came off duty. They were heading into town.


Chris inhaled deeply and then made an almighty effort to lift her sagging shoulders. Four and a half hours more and at the end of her two-five shift she could tick another day off her allocation to 1A and male geriatrics. She leaned against the ward door, paused and then pushing her weight against the door, she shoved it open. Two more steps and she was at the door of the sister's office. Despite the warmth of her new friendships and her vow to be determined and resolute she was verging on defeat.

'Nights for you next week, Warrington,' said the sister, raising her head from its cradle on the heel of her hand, her elbow balanced precariously on the edge of the desk. Easing up her specs, she rubbed her eyes.

'Thank you Sister, reporting back on duty.'

'Don't just stand there nurse, move your arse and go and get on with the back round. I'll never get the off duty finished at this rate.'

'Yes, Sister.'

The smell of stale urine, putrefied flesh and waste food mingled with Old Spice talcum powder revolted Chris. She gagged repeatedly as she and the ward auxiliary moved from bed to bed, cleaning up faeces, emptying catheter bags, dressing pressure sores and changing sheets. The vaulted ceilings of the ward and the shadows cast in the gloom of the inadequately lit room combined with the mutterings and cries of the elderly men, as they called for long dead wives or war comrades, intimidated her. She had survived the incident with Theresa, got through Christmas and now there was another hill to climb. Seven nights working twelve hour shifts in the dark doing nothing but shit shovelling, shit shovelling, nothing but shit fucking shovelling. Theresa was right – geriatrics was drudgery. She never imagined when she first sat in the School of Nursing in May that she would be doing this degrading work. Yet, this was preferable to being at the mercy of Harry Jones and his vile attempts to seduce her. She would grit her teeth, be resolute and determined and face it all: nights next week, five days off. Two more weeks back on days, and then a new allocation. Women or children please, she begged the guardian of the change list.

On Sunday morning Chris woke to the sound of the night nurse knocking on bedroom doors calling, 'time to get up, duty calls.' She turned over, pounded her pillows. She turned over again. She reached for her fob watch – quarter to seven. It had been half past four last time she looked. Chris curled up, pulled the bed covers over her face and sobbed. She had hardly slept. How was she expected to be ready to go on duty at nine o'clock tonight? How would she pass the time during today? How would she keep awake all night? Yet again she flirted with idea of packing her bags and disappearing. Where to? There was nowhere to go. There was no one who would care whether she lived or died; except perhaps Theresa and Sarah.

She'd done it, survived the ordeal; the first night was

over. It had been as bad as she'd expected, perhaps worse. Chris paused at the door of the annexe; the misty, damp drizzle matched her mood. She pulled her cloak tight around her body, hunched her shoulders and folded her chin into the deep collar. Head down she made a run toward the main hospital. Reflections of the long night buzzing around her head like a tormented wasp. The hour on her own, whilst the part-time staff nurse had gone to dinner was excruciating. She'd had to ignore the men's cries that 'I need a pee' or 'I'm going to shit'; there was no way she could cope with moving a bed ridden patient on her own. The men had been left to soil themselves, while each nurse, in turn, took her hour dinner break.

She'd been appalled when she was told that the night nurses at the General were responsible for making patients' breakfasts. She'd done as she was told and boiled twenty four eggs and then made egg butties and covered them in the wax paper from the sliced loaf. The concoctions were left to stand on the kitchen table until breakfast time at six o'clock. The majority of the old men weren't capable of feeding themselves. With Chris and her colleague trudging round the ward, tethered to the back trolley, there was very little time to spend with the men and coax them to eat. The majority of the egg sandwiches were thrown in the kitchen waste bin before the day staff came on duty.

Theresa and Sarah, in turn, followed Chris onto night duty on 1A. The only variation in their experience was Theresa's discovery of a transistor radio in the cupboard behind the sister's desk. Making the breakfast butties she happily bopped around the ward kitchen table when the signal was strong enough to pick up Radio Luxembourg. Her menu extended from the ubiquitous rubbery eggs to include such delicacies as jam or Marmite. Sarah managed to cast on the back of an Arran sweater, a gift for Paul's birthday, during the first night's dinner break. She was disappointed with her slow progress, she couldn't face her knitting for fear that the mingled smell of eggs, margarine and God knows what else might have been transferred to the wool.

# CHAPTER SEVENTEEN

Sister Cornthwaite appeared in the doorway of the sluice on Isherwood ward.

'Are you ready for your ward round, Nurse Hayes?'

'Yes, Sister.'

Jenny winced as she straightened up from stacking the stainless steel bowls, trays and kidney dishes she had unloaded from the steam sterilizer.

'Are you all right, Nurse?'

'Yes, Sister.'

Jenny took one or two mincing steps in an attempt to tighten her pelvic floor muscles. She couldn't believe that the Tampax she'd battled with before she reported for duty had won: the dratted thing felt as though it were hanging out of her vagina and her knickers were damp.

She'd read the instructions that came in the small blue box, looked at the diagram, imagined the cross section as part of her body, turned the picture upside down and round and round. Then she had unwrapped one of the packages and pulled it apart; two white tubes, one inside the other and an oblong of compressed cotton wool with a string attached. She lifted her left leg onto the toilet seat as directed by the instructions and poked and prodded the tampon she'd reconstituted against her resisting body. Memories of the length, breadth and rigidity of Dave's willie compared with the diameter of the short white tube made her persevere.

Sister Cornthwaite turned to her expectantly.

Jenny forced herself to stand tall. She wanted to impress the pretty woman who held herself like a fashion model and walked as though her sister's uniform was the latest gown to be shown on a catwalk. Sister Cornthwaite was engaged to a consultant geriatrician and had been the gold medal winner for her final year of nurse training. Although she had a reputation of being a 'stuck up know it all' she could be kind and supportive if the occasion warranted it. She was feared and revered by the nurses at the Infirmary.

'Sister, this is Frank Wylde, aged forty-three. He has a prolapsed lumbosacral disc caused by a work injury. Mr Wylde is being nursed on a board following a hemi-lateral laminectomy. He is four days post-operative. His nursing care is bed rest with four hourly pressure sore prevention and a daily bed bath.'

Jenny took a deep breath.

Sister Cornthwaite checked Mr Wylde's charts hooked on the bottom of the bed.

Mr Wylde snored.

'Sister, this patient is John Richards, aged thirty-three. He has had an open reduction and external fixation of a fractured fibular caused by a motorbike accident.'

Jenny and the Sister completed their safari around the dimly lit ward and made their way to the office.

'Please sit down.' Sister Cornthwiate graciously nodded to the chair adjacent to the desk.

Jenny lowered herself onto the chair.

'Is there anything wrong, Nurse? You leapt up as

though you'd sat on a drawing pin.'

'No, Sister. I was adjusting my apron.'

Jenny tentatively lowered herself back down onto the unyielding chair.

Sister Cornthwaite congratulated Jenny on her knowledge of the nursing needs of the men in her care. She encouraged Jenny to carry on with the knitting she had observed at the night nurses' station.

'It is a good way to keep awake, if the ward should ever be quiet,' she said.

Maggie was enjoying her first nights on Hilton, the female orthopaedic ward. She was teamed with a third year nurse whose state final examinations were imminent. As the pair moved from bed to bed the finalist guided Maggie through the night routines. She took the opportunity to practise for her finals by explaining the orthopaedic and medical conditions of the patients, alternating her tutorials with her insights into the life and times of the Infirmary ghost – The Grey Lady.

The first round of the night completed and the ward lights dimmed, the nurses set up two easy chairs in the middle of the ward. Individual patients muttered in their sleep; one called out, shouting instructions to a long dead husband.

The ward doors creaked on their hinges.

In the distance, the kitchen light flickered.

Maggie stood up and shifted her chair closer to her colleague's chair. The screech of the chair legs as they dragged across the floor pierced the spooky dimness of the long Nightingale ward.

'She appears mostly on Thorpe, but has been seen down in the nurses' laundry, checking the laundry bags. When you go to supper have a quick glance in Thorpe, you never know she might be out and about tonight.'

Maggie watched her senior glance warily around Hilton. She kept stock still, not daring to move a muscle.

'She's tall, obviously dressed in grey. She hovers, silently floating from bed to bed. Then she stops,' – Maggie caught her breath as the other nurse paused, for dramatic effect – 'stoops over her chosen patient and offers them a sip of water, or straightens their pillows. In the morning the patient is found – unexpectedly dead.'

Maggie shivered.

'By the way Maggie, before you go to dinner I need you to fetch a unit of blood from path lab. The patient's notes are on the desk in the office.'

The Blood Bank was on the second floor of the pathology laboratory. The long journey from Hilton included passing Thorpe and the laundry. As far as Maggie could see, as she hurried past and dared herself to look left into Thorpe, neither of the staff were levitating. Picking up her pace along the main corridor with its looming black marble pillars she turned left immediately after the imposing Board Room that doubled as the night sisters' office. Once off the main corridor Maggie was not likely to meet a living soul. Plaster theatre, on the left, was closed at night. Kershaw, the ear, nose and throat ward, in the distance at the top of the corridor, was notoriously quiet. Turning right immediately before the darkened operating theatres she glanced round, hoisted up her skirts and ran. The winding corridor was cold, heavy rain bounced against the windows. Maggie broke her step outside the laundry; she glanced into the gloom, the laundry bags, holding nursing staff clean uniforms, were laid out along the bank of shelves.

'Mum, Dad, help me,' she muttered.

When she reached the outer doors of the path lab she looked left toward the mortuary and heard the soft hum of the tiers of fridges, custodians of the recently dead. She shuddered, took a deep breath and bounded up the stairs into a small room. Maggie opened the door of the refrigerator with the legend 'Blood Bank' on the door. She shifted the contents until she found the unit of blood labelled with her patient's name.

Maggie's heart thudded and her hands shook as she lifted the unit of blood from the fridge. Conscious of the seriousness of comparing the information on the bottle of blood with the patient's notes and entering the correct data in the Blood Bank records, she muttered the set procedure twice. She wrapped the cold, slippery bottle in the dressing towel she'd brought with her and set off back to the ward. Tempted to run down the stairs and out of path lab she made herself walk slowly. She stuffed the patient's notes inside the bib of her apron, gripped the hand rail with one hand and clutched the bottle of blood to her body with the other. She watched her feet as they stepped gingerly down the stairs. She warned herself that she'd get well and truly done if she dropped the glass container.

'Everything alright in path lab?' said the finalist.

'No problems. I've put the notes back on the desk.'

The nurse took the blood from Maggie and walked toward the recipient's bed.


'It's a miracle.' Jenny was scanning the change list posted on the notice board of the nurses' dining room at the Infirmary. 'We'll all be at the same hospital.' She turned to face Maggie, hovering behind her.

Although the four young women had made passing relationships with other student nurses as they rotated around the wards, the only one that could be described as a new friendship was the one with Chris Warrington.

'Do you think your dad will lend Dave the van so that he can shift my stuff over to the General?' Jenny said as she and Maggie looked around for two adjacent places at the dining tables. 'I've done well to stay here for my first three wards.'

'I'm sure he will. After all, you'd have a job to move your stuff on Dave's bike.' Maggie slid into a place and looked daggers at a girl hovering with a full plate and about to sit next to her. 'He'll probably offer to move you himself. He likes to know what we're all up to. I'll ask him tonight.'

Jenny shuffled in next to her. 'That would be great; you are a pal, Maggie. So, it looks like you and me with Chris on 1F and Theresa and Sarah on 2F. It couldn't be better.'

Maggie curled her lips and shook her head as she prepared to load a fork full of mash and gravy into her mouth.

'I'm not sure about that. I'd rather it were just the four of us.' Maggie picked up and then scrutinised her lamb chop bone. 'That Chris Warrington, I'm not sure about her. She's taking up a lot of Theresa's time – going into town, sitting in her room at night and, well, loads of other stuff.' She stuck the bone in her mouth and gave it a good suck.

'Has Theresa said she's fed up with her?'

'No, she hasn't. It just that I wouldn't want to be spending so much time with her, that's all, and I don't see why Theresa should have to either.'

'Come on Maggie, she's friendly enough these days and, according to Theresa and Sarah, she's not afraid of hard work.'

'Do you want some apple crumble?' said Maggie.

# CHAPTER EIGHTEEN

'Chuck us a biscuit, Sal.' Theresa was wriggling about trying to get comfortable on the end of Chris's bed. 'This bed is as hard as nails.' She finally stilled with her back resting against the wall and her legs stuck out across the end of the bed. 'And will you pass my mug as well. Please? I'll never get comfortable if I move again.'

'See what we've had to put up with for six weeks, Jenny?' Chris said.

Sarah untangled herself from her place on the floor.

'Shit, shit and more bloody shit, that's what we've put up with, Jen,' said Theresa. 'I've said it before and you will certainly hear me say it again, geriatrics is a waste of time as far as our training goes. It should be for pupil nurses only. I'm serious about talking to Bumble about geriatrics.'

'Theresa, I don't think Chris and I disagree. Do we, Chris?' said Sarah.

Chris shook her head and mumbled, 'I agree,' through a mouthful of custard cream. She swallowed and added, 'I detested every single minute of it.'

'It's a waste of time ...'

'Theresa, will you bloody well shut up and do something about it?'

'Yes, I bloody well will Matron Green – have you any suggestions?'

'Write down what you want to say, all the stuff you keep going on about. Show it to us and we can see if we agree and then when Maggie and Jenny have done their stint they can comment as well and then you can give it to Bumble when we're next in study block.'

'Okay, consider it done, Matron.'

'What about paediatrics? You were on 2F as a cadet weren't you, Theresa?' said Sarah smiling at Jenny and Chris in anticipation of Theresa's informed insights into life on paediatrics. 'Isn't the senior sister supposed to be a bit of a sod to work for?'

'She's passionately in love with Doctor Little.' Theresa gave her friends a wise nod and a knowing wink. 'If she doesn't see him at least once a day she gets her knickers in a twist.'

'How very strange, being a paediatrician and being called Dr Little,' said Jenny.

'He's great, really old but very handsome, like an old-fashioned film star – like George Peppard.'

'You like him then, Theresa?' said Chris.

'Who doesn't? He's lovely with the children and their mums and dads. He always says hello to everybody, even the ward maids and cadets. I'm really looking forward to being back on 2F.'

'I'm glad you liked it. I'm not sure about it. I don't know if I'll cope with babies. I've no real experience of infants and I dread a child dying,' Sarah said, reaching out to relieve Theresa of her mug.

'Anything's better than male geriatrics. I admit I'm not sure about babies and children. At least you've helped with Brownies and Sunday School, Sarah,' Chris said.

'There's nothing to be bothered about, honestly. The sisters and staff nurses are great; they know their stuff and they're always knocking about on the wards. Not like some others we know, who hardly get their bums off their easy chairs in the sisters' office. They explain procedures and well … you'll soon see for yourselves.'

'I'll take your word for it Theresa, but I'm still dubious. I don't fancy being left on my own at night,' Chris said. 'What about you Sarah; are you not scared?'

'Chris, stop being such a bloody mither pot, you won't be put on nights until they are very sure you can at least handle a baby without dropping it.' Theresa shook her head.

'That's alright for you to say Theresa, but I'm not su…'

'Come on you lot, it's gone midnight and fretting about it won't make it any better.' Jenny levered herself up from the floor, stretched and yawned. 'We'd better make tracks for bed; see you at breakfast.'


'Are you on your way to lunch?' Chris said to Sarah as they simultaneously emerged from their wards that were directly facing each other across the main corridor.

'I am, and then I thought I might walk over to the School of Nursing. I want to read up on Battered Baby Syndrome while I'm off this afternoon.'

'What's that?' Chris screwed up her face 'I've never heard of it.'

'Well, apparently, some parents literally batter their children. I find it hard to believe, but it's true. We've got a little boy, I think he's about eighteen months old and he's got all sorts of marks – cuts, bruises and, worst of all, what look like faded cigarette burns on his body. Sister has told us that one of us has to make sure we're near his cot when his mum and dad are visiting.'

'What's it called again?' said Chris.

'Battered Baby Syndrome. It's only recently been described by a doctor called Kempe. I'm sure Sister said he was an American.'

'I'll walk over with you. If that's okay? It's time I started thinking about my case study. I'm thinking of writing up a pilonidal sinus from 2C. I really enjoyed it on there, the ladies were lovely.'

'I expect you'll soon get to the bottom of that,' said Sarah.

'Quick, I need the toilet.' Chris pushed open the doors to the dining room suite. 'I've laughed so much.' She scurried into the ladies lavatory followed by Sarah.

The menu board told them it was oxtail for lunch. 'That's a bit …' Sarah spluttered and burst out laughing 'of a bummer.' The pair dragged themselves along the queue tittering.

'I don't think I've ever laughed so much,' said Chris as she and Sarah walked side by side to find a place to sit.

'You look a lot better these days,' said Sarah, suddenly serious.

'I am Sarah. Theresa was right, as usual; the ward staff are great. I'm beginning to enjoy paediatrics.' They found a place to sit, undid their collar studs and folded their apron skirts across their knees. 'Now that we've calmed down tell me again about your case study.'

'I'm going to talk to Paul's mum before I decide, but I'm thinking of writing up the little boy with Battered Baby Syndrome. I'm on nights next week so, if we're quiet, I'll have time to go through his records.'

'What's happened to your hair?' Sarah looked up at Jenny. 'It's curlier than ever.'

'Steam tent.' Jenny plonked herself and her supper tray down and pushed back her damp, corkscrew curls. 'We've got a little girl with bronchitis in a tent. Every time I go in to top up the water I come out looking like a mop head.'

Jenny contemplated her sausage and mash.

'How's it going? You must be busy. I've been delegated to come over and help with the 2am feeds.'

Sarah breathed in and out and gave an exaggerated sigh.

'Okay, I suppose. Except, I'm not really sure about paediatrics or children, I don't think either is for me. I've decided I don't want children when I get married.'

'Why? What's happened?'

'We've got a baby, born a few days ago. It's got an enormous head and its spinal cord is exposed and its little legs are twisted. It's going to die soon. The poor little thing is in a cubicle with the curtains closed being specialled by the staff nurse who does regular nights. That's why we're short staffed; she's with him all the time.'

'Come on Sarah, just because one baby's been born handicapped doesn't mean …'

'I know what you're going to say Jenny, but suppose you went through nine months of a pregnancy and then had to cope with that? I don't think I could do it. I'm going to talk to Paul about not having any children, when I see him next week.'

'It's not like you to be so defeated.'

'I know. It's just that the parents look so lost when they visit. The mum's still on maternity, recovering from a caesarean. The dad brings her down, each evening, in a wheelchair.'

'Anyway, what's all this about talking to Paul next week? Is he coming home or are you going to Manchester to see him?'

'A bit of both. He's coming over for the day on Sunday. I hope I can stay awake all day; last time I came off nights I slept all day on the Sunday and ended up getting up as my mum was going to bed, she was in a right dither. Then I'm supposed to be going to see Paul in Manchester on Tuesday.'

'Err, will you be staying with Paul in Manchester or travelling backwards and forwards from home each day?'

'It's not like you to beat about the bush, Jen. What you mean is where will I be sleeping?'

'Weeell, I don't want to pry, but have you, well, err, have you,' Jenny gave Sarah a plaintive look, 'thought about birth control yet?'

Other nurses joined their table and talk turned to plans for the five nights off.

'We can talk later, after we've had a sleep, about you know what,' Sarah said as she turned into the entrance to 2F.

'See you in half an hour or so, when I come to help.'

# CHAPTER NINETEEN

Theresa used her days off to help her mum with the cleaning, cooking, washing and ironing. They'd been deep in conversation sat next to each other on the settee when Win bustled into the front room from the kitchen. She glared down at her sister.

'Theresa, keep your nose out of other folks business.' Win moved round the back of the settee and knelt at her mother's feet. She gently took hold of her mother's hand. 'It's private, between Mum and Dad and our Lord. Isn't it, Mum?'

'You are a sanctimonious nosey bloody parker, our Win, you really are. Listening at doors; whose business is it then that our mum is dead on her feet?'

'It's certainly not yours. I've told you it's up to Mum, Dad and our Lord.' Win crossed her hands over her chest. 'and besides that, don't swear at me. Tell her Mum?'

'Bugger off Win, and get real and while we're at it you could get off your backside and do a bit more round here.'

Theresa moved from the settee toward a chair piled high with ironing. Win eased herself up from the floor and shifted to sit next to their mother. She stroked Bernadette's arm.

'Ignore her, Mum, she's not like us. She doesn't understand, she's a heathen.'

Theresa gave her sister's head a heavy push with one hand as she walked past the back of the settee, balancing the pile of ironing on her other arm and hand.

Win jumped up, turned round and knocked the neat pile of ironing out of Theresa's arm and onto the floor. She stamped out of the front room, banged the door behind her and marched upstairs.

'Girls, please don't. I can't stand it,' said Bernadette.

'Mammy, why are you crying?' The baby appeared from the kitchen dragging a dishcloth fashioned from an old vest of her dad's. She pushed herself onto her mother's lap, wrapping her arms around Bernadette's neck. 'I've been doing washing.' The dishcloth dripped down Bernadette's back.

'I'm tired, luv, that's all. There's nothing to worry about. Theresa and Win are trying to help me.'

'Why are they shouting again?'

'I expect it's because they both think they know what's best for me.'

Bernadette eased the little girl off her knee, pushed the dish cloth to one side and bent to help Theresa pick up the scattered clothes.

'Don't go back to the hospital angry, luv. Make your peace with our Win before you go.'

'No, Mum, I will not speak to her. She's a pious twit, and you know it.' She stroked her mother's arm. 'I'm going to go and pack my stuff and go back. Promise me you'll try and rest.'

'I agree with Win, about it being none of your business.

Not the God bit though, I'm with you on that one,' said Sarah.

Theresa, Sarah and Jenny were in the laundry room at the General. Jenny was washing her knickers and bras. Theresa had hoisted herself onto the draining board to tell her story. Sarah was ironing a couple of blouses and her pyjamas.

'Well come on then, what do you suggest I do? My mum's worn out. She was younger than we are now when I was born. Her only life has been having babies, washing, ironing and cleaning. Lady Muck Win doesn't lift a bloody finger.'

'It's still none of your business though, Theresa. I agree as well, with Win and Sarah. All you can do is help when you go home,' said Jenny.

'Bugger, bugger, bugger. I don't want to have to admit you're right. I'm going to have to keep my gob shut, aren't I? But I'll tell you what. I'm sure as hell going to make sure I only have one or two children, if I have any at all.'

'Don't you start about not having children, Sarah has got it into her head she's going to have a baby with spina-bifida. She's talking to Paul next week about not having a family,' said Jenny.

'Which brings us to the question of,' Sarah paused and glanced at Theresa, 'birth control.'

'Why?' Theresa clapped her hands and rubbed them together. 'Are you two at it.'

'No, not really. Well we haven't done it.' Sarah's attention was riveted to watching her right hand as she pushed the iron between the buttons on her pyjama top. 'Paul and me, we haven't, well you know,' she paused and chewed her lips, 'gone all the way.'

'Us neither, I keep my knickers on and Dave tries to keep his, you know, his willie in his underpants.'

'Is it a big one then?' said Theresa.

'Theresa, honestly!' Jenny flicked a spray of water toward Theresa.

'So what are you love birds going to do? If you don't watch out you'll end up getting caught. Then you'll both be up the river without a paddle.'

'Dave said it's up to me, about us going to bed together. He's done it before ... with the girl he was engaged to.'

'Well I suppose at his age he was bound to have had it away.' Theresa pursed her lips in the attempt to suppress a smile. 'Is he good at it?'

'It isn't a joke Theresa, just suppose if we did begin to do it ... and I didn't do it right?'

'How can you do it wrong you daft bat, Jenny. It's just a case of legs open, willie in. Isn't it?' said Theresa.

'So you've never done it then, Theresa? Has necking ever gone that bit further?' Jenny said.

'Yes, come on, Theresa.' Sarah unplugged the iron. 'Tell the truth.'

'Nar. I've never met a chap I fancied all that much. The only willies I've really had a good gander at are little boys and old men. Anyway, I'm not prepared to risk getting pregnant. I don't want to end up like my mum. I'll wait until you two have taken the risk and reported back.'

Sarah told the others that she had heard of foam that the woman could use. She'd been sitting with a group of third years who were having a similar conversation at supper earlier in the week. Apparently, it was easy to use if you could use a tampon. The foam came in an aerosol container and was released when you pressed the tampon thing on the spout of the container. The girl pushed the tampon tube into her vagina and pushed the plunger. The foam killed the sperm stone dead. The sperm that survived the initial contact with the spermicide eventually died of exhaustion trying to swim through the thick white fog blocking their way in the vagina.

'Well that sounds a possibility. Do you know what the stuff's called? We can hardly go into Boots and ask for sperm killing foam,' said Jenny.

'I'm not sure. I think they mentioned two sorts.'

'Can't you wait until we're in study block? I know it's a while off but with half of the girls fixed up surely somebody will know something. That girl who does ballroom dancing is sure to be at it. All that bodily contact, rubbing up against each other on the dance floor will have put some rhythm into their lives. Ha! Get it. Cheer up the pair of you. You won't be virgins forever.'

Theresa left the reluctant virgins to get ready for their night duty. She intended to spend her remaining days off working on her case study.

'Let's go into town tomorrow morning and go to Boots before we go to bed,' said Sarah as she and Jenny walked over to the hospital to start their shift.

The change list had, as anticipated, indicated that Theresa, Sarah and Chris were bound for orthopaedics at the Infirmary, with Jenny and Maggie staying at the General for geriatrics.

The final ward of the first year of training passed without drama. Maggie and Jenny counted the days and nights on male geriatrics, mentally storing up comments to add to Theresa's script for Miss Bennet. Her experience of nursing old ladies with broken limbs on Hilton convinced Theresa that there was sufficient experience of working with elderly people on the specialist wards to justify her making a stand. She intended to use her case study of an elderly lady with a fractured neck of femur to support her argument.

Chris was surprised to find that she coped with, and at times even enjoyed, Isherwood. The ward was lively, the sisters and staff nurse held specialist qualifications in orthopaedics and were willing to teach and explain the impact of the men's injuries and bone conditions to the student nurses. The patients, and their visitors, were mostly pleasant and courteous.

Invitations to, 'Come and give us a good night kiss' and 'you can give my parts a rub any time' had sent Chris scurrying to the sluice during her first week's placement.

'Ignore the ignorant little buggers,' the terrier of an auxiliary nurse told her. 'They wouldn't know what to do with a pretty young woman like you. They're more interested in impressing each other. When they see you embarrassed it's a bonus. Nod and smile and get on with your jobs. They'll soon get fed up.'

Although Sarah thought the senior staff were great she was not over enthusiastic about the theory of orthopaedic nursing or caring for bed bound young men who were in hospital because they were dare devils or boy racers. It took so long for broken bones to knit together that the men, some of who were on the ward for months, were more aware of the ward routines than the junior nurses.

# SECOND YEAR

## CHAPTER TWENTY

Case studies were the key factor in deciding if a nurse progressed at the end of her first year of training. Each nurse was responsible for delivering her completed study to the admin assistant in the matron's office of her home hospital, by a given date. Appointments were then made for the students to present themselves to the relevant matron.

Those students who were intent on moving forward in their careers paid particular attention to their dress as well their nursing knowledge. Shoes reflected their passing acquaintance with polish, aprons were spotless, hair was off the face and above the collar, clean caps were held in place, on the top of the head, with white hairgrips, and dresses were the regulation fourteen inches from the floor; there was not a ladder in sight.

Both matrons held their audiences from thrones set adjacent to their imposing desks. At the Infirmary, nurses were invited to sit on a large, highly polished Edwardian dining chair housing a thin needlepoint cushion. It was imperative that a nurse sit decisively and firmly on the cushion, slipping into Matron's lap was not uncommon. At the General, nurses stood for their interview.

Each matron's interrogation included questions about the subject of the case study, why it had been chosen, followed by a determination of the main lessons learned as a result of the in-depth study.

At the Infirmary, ward and department reports were reviewed with Matron at the end of each placement. The practice at the larger General was to review reports at the end of the year. Further review only occurred if reports were not up to the expected standard.

'How will we find out if we've passed?' Jenny said to the group of young women pushing their way through the glass doors leading to the School of Nursing reception area. 'I don't know what I'll do if I fail.'

'Jenny, will you stop blathering on,' Theresa said. 'I'll tell you this for nothing, if Beaky has bloody well failed me, I'll do her in.'

'Both of you shush,' said Sarah, standing on her tip toes. 'Here Jenny, see if you can see.'

Jenny peered over the shoulders of the crowd in front of the notice board.

'No, there's nothing there. We can't have long to wait, our first lecture is in quarter of an hour.'

She joined the others leaning against the wall watching the staff room door.

'Who's taking us?' said Sarah, her eyes fixed on the door.

'All three of them, by the looks of it and here they come.' Jenny stood straight as the tutors passed them.

Miss Bolton looked straight ahead.

Mr Bradshaw muttered, 'Good morning, nurses.'

All eyes were fixed on Miss Bennet and the bundle of green epaulets she carried.

'Come on, nurses; the time has come,' she said.

'Well at least Miss Bennet is smiling,' Jenny muttered to Sarah as the two of them slid into the lecture theatre seats.

'How many pairs of epaulets are there?' Theresa turned to Chris and Maggie, sat each side of her. She leant over the desk to repeat the same question to Jenny and Sarah.

They each counted.

'I reckon it's eighteen,' said Theresa.

Jenny scribbled '17' on a piece of paper and pushed it along the bench top so that it could be seen from the tier above.

Miss Bolton welcomed the students to the study block and handed over to Miss Bennet who, with a smile, stepped forward. She shook her head at Miss Bolton who was pushing a sheet of paper toward her.

'Nurses, I know you are all anxious so I will put you out of your misery.' She paused. 'You will be pleased to know that all of you, here, in the lecture theatre, have successfully completed your first year of training.' She let the hullabaloo subside. 'Those nurses who have not been successful have chosen to leave rather than repeat the first year of training.' She went on to congratulate her audience and continued, 'Overall the case studies were judged to be good, the best for a long time. However, one or two were only just good enough to reach a pass mark.' Her eyes scanned the room, glancing fleetingly at two or three faces, and then her face lit up. She paused. 'And one was judged to be exceptional.'

The suspense mounted as Miss Bennet took time to explain that following discussion with her two tutor colleagues, both Matron and the chairman of the hospital management committee, it had been decided to put the said exceptional case study forward for publication in the nursing press. Miss Bennet raised her voice over the expectant muttering.

'I will write a paper to support the case study of – Nurse Booth.'

'Oh! Bloody hell,' said Theresa as her hand flew to her mouth.

'Very well done, Theresa,' Jenny said turning round as far as she could. As she twisted her head she saw Maggie looking daggers down the line of seats. She turned the other way, but couldn't see anything untoward. What could have upset Maggie – again? She smiled at Chris and Theresa who had their arms around each other.

'What on earth's upsetting Maggie?' Jenny said to Sarah.

'Nurse Hayes, Nurse Green when you are ready, we'll begin the presentation,' said Mr Bradshaw.

'Sorry, Mr Bradshaw, my fault,' said Jenny.

When Miss Bennet called out their name each nurse made their way to the front. Mr Bradshaw handed out the epaulets and shook hands. Miss Bolton nodded to each girl and said 'congratulations.' She appeared to be distracted by something outside the window as Roy Bradshaw shook hands with Theresa.

# CHAPTER TWENTY-ONE

Jenny couldn't believe her eyes when she saw Dave leaning against his car in the car park. He'd swapped his motorbike for a second hand Ford Anglia after Christmas. He'd told Jenny that he didn't like the idea of her hitching up her uniform to straddle the pillion, particularly in the cold and damp.

'Hello. What are you doing here?' Jenny said, beaming.

Dave reached out and pulled Jenny toward him. Their lips brushed briefly once and then again.

'Kissing you.'

They kissed again.

A wolf whistle disturbed them. Jenny waved to the whistler.

'We've all passed, by the way, well our little gang.'

'I knew you would, so I've come to take you into town to celebrate. I thought we might get your birthday present.'

'There's your Maggie. Should we offer her a lift?'

'I thought Uncle John picked her up.'

Maggie waved and looked toward the reception doors.

'I expect she'll want to wait for Theresa to see how she got on with Miss Bennet. She might have come over to say hello to you, but then, she is acting a touch odd these days.'

'Come on, let's get a move on, or the shops'll all be shut.' Dave opened the passenger door. 'Is Theresa in trouble?'

'No, the opposite.'

Dave parked his car outside Blackburn's, the swanky jewellers in Farnton. He leapt out of the car and hurried round to the passenger side. He opened the car door for Jenny, bowed and offered his arm as she stepped from the car.

'I could get used to this,' she said.

'Would madam like to step this way?' He tucked Jenny's arm through his and led her into the shop. As they stepped into the elegant enclave a man resembling a tailor's dummy came toward them.

'Good afternoon, sir,' he said. 'Can I be of assistance to you?'

Dave gulped, gripped Jenny's arm and said, 'We'd like to look at engagement rings. Please.'

Jenny squealed and stood still, rooted to the spot.

The man indicated that they should follow him. Dave grabbed Jenny's hand and hauled her after him. They were shown to a secluded booth furnished with a low table and three squashy leather armchairs.

'May I offer you a pot of tea?'

When he left to organise the refreshments Dave turned to the still stunned Jenny. He took her hand in his.

'You will marry me? Won't you?'

'Yes, yes.'

'That's good, otherwise I'd have looked daft on my own at the engagement party we're having on Saturday.'

'So your Maggie wasn't ignoring you. She knew why you were at the School?'

'Didn't she say anything?'

'Not a peep. Mmm, but then she has a thing about engagement rings.'

They eventually chose a small round sapphire surrounded by a circle of tiny diamonds set on a white gold band. Jenny was oblivious to her surroundings as they left the jewellers. She couldn't take her eyes off the ring.

'Jenny, did you hear me, love? I said we're going straight round to see your parents.'

'No, Dave, please? No.'

Dave held up his hands.

'Look love, we've made three or four attempts to see them and they've always fobbed us off. We're going to go and surprise them. I intend to do this properly and ask their permission.'

'They'll spoil everything.'

Jenny pulled the passenger door closed. She looked at her ring, glanced at Dave and could see no way out.

'Dave, please don't stop, drive out of the other gate, please,' Jenny said as the car crunched on the gravel in front of the house.

'It's got to be done love, and I've made up my mind. Come on let's get it over with and then I can tell you my bit of news.'

'What news? Dave? What news?' Jenny shook Dave's arm.

'Later.'

Jenny watched Dave turn away, slide his legs out of the car and hoist himself up. She hesitated. How could this be happening? How could happiness disappear in a flash to be replaced by fear, loathing and dread? She reached into her handbag for her front door key before thinking better of letting herself into the house. Her mother answered the door-bell.

'Jennifer! This is a surprise, why didn't you let us know you intended to visit?' She looked at Dave. 'You'd better come in – with? Who is this …?'

'What's going on, darling? Oh, who have we here, the – the bad penny, well well. What do you want?' George turned his sneer on Dave, 'and who is this?' He hesitated his sneer gathered depth and feeling.

Dave held out his hand. George shook his head at the proffered hand and stepped toward Jenny.

'I said what do you want? Are you now deaf as well as thick as shit?'

Jenny took a step backwards, her head down.

Dave moved toward Jenny.

'She's up the duff; she's come here in that uniform to cover up the damage. You've got her up the fucking duff, that's it isn't it?' George started pacing; walking five steps, turning and walking back again. 'Always expected that she'd go for the ladies, be a dyke – a chip off the old block in every other way, don't you know.'

Dave took a stride, anticipating George's step. Jenny gasped. Dave's face was corpse white, his breathing was rapid and his eyes wide and staring.

'Mr Hayes,' he shouted and turned to Jenny's mum. 'Mrs Hayes,' he said more gently. 'I have come here to ask for Jenny's hand in marriage.'

George stopped pacing. He pushed Dave in the shoulder. Dave stood still, looked down on him and shook his head.

'Come on Jen …' Dave reached out to grab Jenny's hand.

George stepped between them. 'She's as thick as two short planks, so it's as well she's good in bed.' Spittle foamed at the side of his mouth. 'Might have known she'd spread her legs for a bit of rough. What is it you do? Manual work – road sweeper, on the bin round or the dole? What the bloody hell do I care. You can take her off. Yes, that's it, take her off out of my sight and do not return, either of you – ever.' He opened the front door and with a sweep of his hand pointed to the drive.

Jenny raised her hand and dropped her keys on the table in the middle of the hall.

The front door slammed shut.

'Dave, I know you are really angry but let's get in the car and out of the drive. Please, start the car and drive round the corner,' said Jenny.

Dave turned the key in the ignition. It stalled. He thumped the wheel with his balled fists.

'The fucking bastard, I could kill him for what he's done to you.'

He sat back in his seat and reached out to turn the ignition. Gravel spat from under the wheels as the car circled the drive, and turned through the gateway onto the road to stop a hundred yards or so from the house.

'Bloody hell Jenny, love, I never imagined he was as bad as that'. Dave bent his head. 'How the hell you've stuck it, I don't know.'

Jenny reached out and stroked his cheek. He lifted his head and turned to her. She saw tears in his eyes.

'Come on; be positive,' she forced a smile. 'I'm free and I'm relieved. It's over. I've always known I was on my own, apart from Granny Ashford, but now I've got you and your family, as well as the girls.'

Dave pulled Jenny toward him and kissed her tenderly at first and then with growing passion.

'Err Dave, I think we'd better make a move.' At the edge of her vision Jenny glimpsed a neighbour peering at them through the car windows as she walked her dog. 'Come on, we've time to go and see your mum and dad before we meet the others at the pub. I want to show them the ring.'

'Egg and chips aren't what you would call a celebratory tea,' said Mavis Smithfield as she set about the King Edwards. 'We didn't expect to see you until the party on Saturday.'

'Egg and chips are great. Thank you for making our supper. I think it helped calm Dave down, telling you about me.'

'Aye luv, there's nowt to tell. It's your mam and dad need talking about, not you.'

The senior Smithfields had been finishing their tea when Dave and Jenny arrived. Jenny watched the concern cross Mrs Smithfield's face when she looked at her son.

'What's up luv?' She'd got up from the dining table and moved toward them as they took their coats off, 'you've been crying.'

'It's my fault, all my fault.' Jenny buried her head in Dave's shoulder.

Dave told his mum and dad his and Jenny's story, from meeting Jenny at the School of Nursing to arriving at their house.

'How'd you feel now luv?' Mavis relieved Jenny of the brandy glass she was holding.

'I'm relieved for lots of reasons; that I don't have to pretend any more, that you know the truth, and,' she paused, 'as I keep telling Dave, I'm free.'

'You're welcome in this family, that's for sure. Let's celebrate. Dad, why don't you get us all a nice glass of sherry? There's some left over from Christmas. It's in the sideboard, next to the brandy bottle.'

'Is it a double celebration then?' Mavis nodded to Jenny's shoulder.

'No, triple,' said Dave.

'You're news, Dave. I'd forgotten you had some news …'

As they'd sipped the sherry Dave told his astounded

parents and fiancée his news. He'd had a letter from his HNC tutor asking him if he'd be available to cover the classes of a colleague who had suffered a heart attack.

'Can you do that when you've only just qualified, yerself?' Mr Smithfield said.

'I've been qualified a long time, Dad. The HNC was something to do to try and get promotion.' He squeezed Jenny's hand. 'I'm going to do it. I wasn't sure at first but after that nasty bugger ...'

'Dave?' said Mrs Smithfield.

'Sorry Mum, after Jenny's dad looked down his nose at me I made up my mind – I'm going to do it.'

'Well Mother, what do you think to that, our lad's going to move up in the world and be a teacher, and we're going to have a lovely nurse for a daughter-in-law?'

'Life couldn't be better Dad, that's what I say.' Mavis glanced at the sideboard. 'Shall we have another drop of sherry?'

'What a day,' said Dave as they made their way into the Eagle and Child for the pre-arranged meeting in the pub.

'Are you going to tell them, about what's happened – with your mum and dad, sorry, George?' Dave said quietly as he took Jenny's coat.

'No, not until we get back to the home.' She faced him and straightened his tie. 'You offer to run Maggie and Elizabeth home and tell them as much as you want them to know. I think you should tell the girls about your new job though.'

'It's very part-time,' he said.

'It's something to celebrate; we've got so much to celebrate, Dave. Haven't we? Come on, let's go and tell the others and your Elizabeth.'

'Well I don't know how I'm going to compete with you set of clever clogs,' said Elizabeth. 'All of you passing your exams. Our Dave's going to be a lecturer, no less, and a new cousin in the family, whatever next?'

'Do you think people would believe all that's happened today if it were in a novel?' Sarah said. 'An engagement, us lot passing our exams and Dave's job.'

Jenny and Dave exchanged looks and ruefully smiled at each other.

As they hoofed it back to the home Jenny suggested a nightcap in her room.

Theresa took a sip of her Horlicks.

'Let's get it out of the way. I'm sure we're all really pleased with the engagement, but Jen, you're not,' she nodded sagely in the direction of Jenny's abdomen, 'you know what, are you?'

'Oh Theresa!' chorused Sarah and Chris.

'Theresa, if and when I am pregnant, I promise you that you will be one of the first to know. But, I do have something to tell you all, about earlier tonight, when we went to see my parents.'

'Oh bloody hell, I knew it was all too good to be true – go on Jen, what's happened?'

'When we were at Knott End I didn't tell you everything about my family.'

Jenny described the events of the early evening from leaving the jewellers to arriving at her parent's home.

'Bleedin' hell it's like something from the telly,' said Theresa. 'Jenny, can I just ask? Is it a big hall then, to have a table in it?' Theresa said as Jenny finished her story.

'Yes, Theresa. I might have scratched it. Such a pity. It's two hundred years old.'

'You posh lot don't half have a bloody funny way of carrying on. What with Chris's lot and now this. Although Paul's lot are okay, aren't they Sal? I don't suppose there's any funny sex and other goings on there.

Is there?'

'They are fine, Theresa. The three of them are very close. His dad is smashing with me, always has been. His mum was a bit standoffish at first, but she's fine now. She seems to have got used to me being around.'

'Us poor folk are so busy making ends meet, washing and ironing and trying to keep the place tidy there's not much time for falling out. Well, apart from the odd religious set to between me and Win and the little uns squabbling,' said Theresa. 'You know Lennon and McCartney were spot on when they told us to get on with our short lives and not waste time falling out with each other.'

'That's exceptionally philosophical,' said Chris laughing.

'From two other exceptional people – Mr Lennon and Mr McCartney.' She rose, majestically, bowed and waved goodnight in the manner of H.M. The Queen.

'Goodnight Theresa,' said Jenny.

Sarah and Chris followed Theresa to their beds.

Jenny undressed slowly – what a day! She checked her watch. 12.30. Dave would be asleep. She yearned to speak to him. Perhaps she could persuade him to have a telephone installed.

The following day Jenny was the centre of attention as news of her engagement spread. She was repeatedly asked, what was the ring like, had they set a date, were her parents pleased? She responded with: sapphire and diamonds, no not yet and I'm sure they're glad to see me settled.

The lecture programme for the remainder of the two weeks was of mixed interest to the students. Ear nose and throat, ophthalmic and theatre work were all usually considered fiddly and fussy. The reputation of the senior theatre sister at the Infirmary and the senior sister on

Jones, the ophthalmic ward, as out and out tyrants added to the brave but stoical endurance that these allocations fomented in the majority of the nurses. The more fickle of the girls persisted with their chronic whimpering; pleading for mercy at the altar of the change list. Of personal interest to all the young women was gynaecology: the anatomy and physiology were relatively easy to understand, they had all survived the menarche, the mechanics of sexual intercourse was a top favourite, closely followed by methods of birth control. The majority of the class of May 1966 had, until they started nurse training, scant formal sex education, from parents or school. They relied on each other's knowledge and information, or misinformation, to guide them on the uncertain path of intimate relationships with men.

# CHAPTER TWENTY-TWO

'How you can find ophthalmics interesting, I do not know,' said Maggie to Sarah as the group walked over to the dining room for their lunch.

'Did you see the look Beaky gave me when I yawned? She's a miserable bugger,' said Theresa squeezing between Maggie and Sarah and linking arms with each of them. 'I bet even she was bored out of her skull.'

'I was on Jones for seven of the twenty months we were cadets. The nursing care on there is the best ever. The three sisters are sticklers for attention to the smallest detail. There are never any bed sores even though patients spend ages flat on their backs. They are the greatest nurses ever.'

'I thought that was Florence Nightingale.'

'Be serious, Maggie.'

'I'll take your word for it but let's forget about it and talk about our holiday. If we don't get a move on we'll be too late to book anywhere and we'll end up back at Knott End,' she lowered her voice and turned her head toward Sarah, 'and I am telling you for nothing, I am not sleeping with Chris Warrington.'

'What are you whispering about, Mags,' said Theresa.

'Nothing, it doesn't matter.'

'Hang on you two, let's wait for Jenny and Chris to catch up.' Theresa stopped and looked back up the path. 'Where are they?'

'You two wait and I'll go and bags places for us,' said Maggie.

'We can't keep you away from your food can we, Mags?' Theresa said, her attention on the progress of her friends. 'Ye Gods they're on their way – with Beaky? The creeps.'

'Suit yourself, I was trying to be helpful,' said Maggie setting off on her own.

'We need four places, Mags.'

Maggie flicked her eyes over the table for eight; four places were taken, she shrugged her shoulders.

'Why didn't you sit at one of the empty tables?' Theresa said, her head questioningly on one side.

'What does it matter where we sit?' Maggie's face and neck flushed.

'It's you that wants to talk about the holiday. You'll have to bloody well move if we're going to do that.'

'You can have our places now,' said a voice from the other end of the table.

Amid the shuffling out and in of the diners Theresa sat down next to Maggie and hissed at her, 'What the hell is up with you Maggie, one minute you're as right as rain and the next as miserable as sin?'

Maggie looked away from Theresa.

'Mags, come on, join in. You're my best mate and I don't like to see you upset.' Theresa pushed her shoulder against Maggie. 'Come on, cheer up. I'm sure you'll survive if the change list puts you on ophthalmics; that's what this is all about. Isn't it?'

Maggie gave a weak smile.

'That's better. I don't know if anybody ever told you but you are a really ugly crier, Mags.'

'What are you two whispering about at that end of the table,' Chris leant forward. 'You'll have to speak up Maggie so that I can hear.'

Maggie developed a sudden interest in the cruet set.

'So come on, what about this holiday? I want to get away so that I don't have to live at home for the whole of the two weeks. Come on Maggie, what do you fancy doing?' said Sarah. 'I don't mind if it's got to be Knott End again.'

'London, I think we should go to London,' Maggie said decisively.

'Bloody hell! Where's that come from?' Theresa said, throwing her arm round Maggie's shoulders. 'See, I know you, Mags. Once you owned up about not wanting to do ophthalmics you cheered up.'

'You'll all have to forgive me, I would love to come but Dave and I are working on the house, clearing out his junk and decorating.'

'London!' I don't think so.'

'But, Dad …' Maggie tried to speak.

'Don't "but Dad" me, you are not going and that's an end to it.'

'Tell him, Mum; it's not fair – I'm nineteen.'

Maggie gave her dad a withering look.

'You can take that look of you face, mi lady.'

'John, would you let her go if I went with them?' said Mrs Smithfield. She stood up to clear the pots from the table. 'I could leave your books for a week, couldn't I?'

'Mum, thanks and all that, but, well I don't know what the others would say.'

'Why, what are you intending getting up to, that you

don't want your mother to know about?'

Maggie pushed her chair back from the table. The chair toppled over.

'Let go Dad, you can't treat me like a little kid for ever.'

Maggie stamped out of the dining room and marched up stairs. She slammed her bedroom door shut. Flinging herself on her bed, she reached out for Pussy.

A knock on her door woke her from an uneasy sleep. Her mother sat on the end of Maggie's bed.

'Go and rinse your face and then come down and say sorry to your dad.'

'But, Mum …'

'You might find it's worth your while. Go on, into the bathroom. I'll see you downstairs.'

Once downstairs, Maggie sidled up to her dad's chair. 'Sorry Dad,' she muttered, head down.

Her dad tilted his head. Maggie grazed his cheek with a kiss.

'I've talked it over with your Uncle Brian and the vicar.'

'What's it got to do with them? Mum, I thought you sai…'

'Margaret, sit down and listen to what your dad has to say, before you go sulking again,' said her mother patting the settee. 'Come here and sit next to me.'

'Take it or leave it but if you want to go our Elizabeth has to go as well. I've asked her and she said she'll go with you. I agree with Brian; that young woman Chris has something about her. Sarah is a quiet, sensible girl and well, if Theresa is a bit flighty, she's still a good friend to you and will make sure you come to no harm.'

'What do you say to that Margaret?' her mother said, smiling at her.

'It's okay, I suppose.'

'It better be or you are not going.'

'Tell her the rest, Dad.'

Maggie was not thrilled with her dad's tale of contacting the vicar and his advice on a suitable guest house.

'He stays there when he has to go to London. He says it's close to Euston station so you won't have far to cart your bags and they give you a hearty breakfast.'

'He'll be glad of that, the hearty breakfast. It'll be a change from having to fend for himself,' said Mrs Smithfield.

'Don't you be wasting your sympathy on him, our Mum. He's a decent chap, I grant you that, but since his wife died certain ladies of this parish have waited on him hand and foot and he has a woman what does, as well.'

'Why do they do that, wait on him?' said Maggie.

'The less said about that, the better. The sooner he marries again the sooner certain ladies will come to their senses. Them two lads of his need a mother. As senior churchwarden it's my job to keep him out of trouble.'

'What sort of trouble?' said Maggie.

'Hadn't you better telephone your friends and see if they fancy this guest house? If they do I'll ring and see if they can fit you in. I can have a chat with 'em all about keeping their eye on you at the engagement party.'

'Dad?'

'You do want to go don't you, Margaret?'

'You know I do,' Maggie said through gritted teeth.

'Well less of your lip then, lady.'

# CHAPTER TWENTY-THREE

Brian Smithfield tapped the side of his glass with a fork.

'It's a real pleasure to see you all here at our Dave's. Now will you please raise your glasses to toast the engagement of our son David and our lovely, future daughter-in-law, Jennifer?'

'David and Jennifer,' rang out in a formal chorus as glasses were raised toward the happy couple.

'I don't know about the rest of you but it's well past my teatime. Let's have our supper, prepared by the Smithfield ladies – thank you to them, one and all. Then we'll get down to the serious business of the night, a singsong.'

Dave thanked his dad for the toast and announced that the wedding would be on the 23rd of September at Holy Trinity Church and would be conducted by the Rev Fred Cummings. Despite having taken a swig of beer Rev Fred managed to nod and smile at his future wedding congregation.

The plates were cleared and Brian stood ready to conduct the a capella singing, starting with *I'm Getting*

*Married in the Morning.* Chris followed with *Moon River.*

'Ee that were grand,' said Grandma Smithfield wiping her eyes. 'What are you singing next, luv?' She tucked her hanky back up her cardigan sleeve.

'Have you thought any more about joining us at The Players, Chris?' Brian said, handing Chris her drink.

'I have, and I'm interested but I wouldn't be all that reliable about attending rehearsals every week because of my shifts.'

'Come when you can, you've too good a voice for the chorus but you'll really lend it some extra oomph. Won't she, vicar?'

'Certainly, certainly, and I am sure Jennifer will be persuaded to help out in some way or other. The Smithfield family are the stalwarts of The Players.'

'It's Jenny, we call her Jenny,' Chris said.

'Yes, quite so. How is it you are with the other girls? Are they not junior to you?'

Chris blushed.

'Have I said something amiss?'

'No,' Chris reached out and touched Rev Fred's arm, 'we're all about to start our second year. Let's just say they've adopted me.'

'Yes, I see. Like the Smithfield's have adopted Jennifer? Sorry Jenny.' He reached out to take Chris's empty glass. 'Can I get you a refill?'

Maggie stood apart from Theresa, Jenny and Sarah, watching them as they ogled Chris and the Rev Fred. They were being silly, nudging each other and pulling faces. She saw Chris catch sight of them and blush. What was the joke? She didn't understand, but then there was so much she didn't understand these days, so much she felt left out off since Chris Warrington had appeared and taken over. Why couldn't things be like they used to be when she and Theresa were cadets? She wanted

Theresa to herself; to be tempted with smoking and lads and make up. She hated Chris Warrington.

The next day, Maggie, relaxed and happy, watched Theresa stare intently into the mirror as she layered a third coat of mascara onto the lashes of her right eye.

'Don't go without me,' said Maggie before locking herself in a lavatory cubicle.

'I've been thinking, over the weekend,' Theresa said to the lavatory door reflected behind her. 'Being a student nurse means that's all you can do. You can't arrange to go out, unless you ask for a specific off duty and get a late pass. They've got us by the bloody short and curlies.'

'What's brought this on,' said Maggie, emerging from the lavatory.

'If anybody asked what you did, what would you say? You'd say you were training to be a nurse and expect them to understand what that meant. But they don't – do they? Do you want some lippy by the way?'

'Theresa, what are you on about? No, what do I want with lipstick?'

'That priest, sorry, vicar, at the party. He made me think. He said "it sounds like jolly good fun." I tried to explain about how often we changed wards and hospitals and that we weren't all together, having "jolly good fun" all the time. It was then it dawned on me how disjointed our lives are.'

'I don't know what you're on about. Come on or we'll be on the front row.'

Theresa blinked at herself in the mirror. *Bloody stunning.* She smacked her lips at the reflection. 'Come on Mags, this should be interesting, for once, Mr B holding forth on that new Act of Parliament.

'I must be naïve or I've led a sheltered life in the

village,' said Sarah. 'I knew back-street abortions existed, from the novels I've read, but the number is staggering.'

The group were assembled in the lecture theatre waiting for Miss Bennet to arrive. Mr Bradshaw had left them reflecting on his lecture on the anticipated Act to legalise abortion.

'Why would anybody want one?' Maggie looked from one to the other of her friends. 'None of us would have one. Would we?'

'The Catholic Church has done too good a job on me, so no, I don't think I would,' Theresa said trying to remove a blob of mascara from the line of vision in her right eye. 'Although, I suppose it would depend on the circumstances.'

'It might be the answer if you'd been raped. What are you doing Theresa?' said Chris.

'I'd never thought about it before today,' said Sarah. 'Here Theresa, turn round and I'll have a go with my hanky.'

'Me neither. You look as though you've been crying black tears from your right eye,' said Jenny.

'Bloody hell,' said Theresa. 'Here's Bumble. Maggie, you'll have to lend me your notes to copy up later. I can't see a bloody thing.'

# CHAPTER TWENTY-FOUR

'Dad, there's no need for you to come into the station with us,' Maggie said as the girls piled out of the back of the van and heaved their suitcases onto the pavement outside Piccadilly station. 'We can manage from here. Can't we Elizabeth?'

'It's no bother. I'll see you safe inside; make sure you find the right platform.'

At the ticket barrier Sarah turned.

'Thank you for the lift, Mr Smithfield.'

'Yes, thank you very much,' said Chris.

'Thanks a lot,' said Theresa.

Sarah, Theresa and Chris set off toward the train.

Maggie and Elizabeth surrendered themselves to their dad's embraces and inevitable watery eyes.

Settling into their reserved seats the girls found that their catching up would have to wait until they reached the guesthouse. It hadn't been possible for Maggie's dad to book five seats next to each other. Theresa gazed out of the window then leafed through her *Beatles Monthly* magazine, glancing up as the Cheshire and Staffordshire countryside whizzed by.

*This is me, Theresa Bernadette Booth, travelling to Swinging London. Bloody hell! Who would have thought it?*

Maggie popped up, over the back of Theresa's seat, to hand out parcels of sandwiches and cake provided by her mother.

'Thanks Mags. Oops, sorry,' Theresa said to the man next to her as she dropped her greaseproof paper parcels in his lap. 'Oh look! The Ovaltine factory.' Theresa wiggled her head and shoulders in time to her humming of the Ovaltinies theme tune.

The man laughed as he handed over her parcels.

'My daughter is a great fan of Radio Luxembourg, as am I. She's been an Ovaltinie since she was a little girl.' He nodded to her magazine. 'Do you like popular music?'

As they continued their conversation about music and the proposed new BBC radio station Theresa was aware of Maggie's ear pressed in the gap between the seats behind her and her travelling companion. When the train pulled into the gloom of Euston station Theresa felt a sharp tap on her head.

'Theresa, come on, we're here,' Maggie said, leaning over the back of Theresa's seat.

'It's been a pleasure to travel with you. I hope you and your friends enjoy your holiday.'

'Thank you.'

The man smiled at Maggie, who immediately flopped down into her seat.

'Honestly Theresa, you'll talk to anybody. Haven't your mum and dad warned you about talking to strangers?' Maggie shuffled up the aisle of the railway carriage after Theresa.

'Mags, grow up. You're never going to meet a chap if you think of everybody outside your family and the hospitals as strangers. Come on, lead the way – you've got the directions.'

The five travellers lugged their suitcases towards the barrier, and found their way out of Euston Station across Melton Street and into Euston Street to the bed and breakfast. They were shown to the two bedrooms they would be sharing. Once shut of the landlady they settled in the larger room to get their breath back, review their day and consider plans for the evening.

'I know it was good of the Reverend Fred to write and introduce us, but I wish my dad would let us grow up and do something on our own, for once,' said Maggie.

'He seems like a lovely dad, Maggie; I don't think he interferes, not in comparison with my mum. To be honest, without your dad I wouldn't be here; my mum hit the roof when I told her we were coming to London. She only calmed down when I said your vicar recommended the guesthouse and that your dad was making all the arrangements,' said Sarah.

'Well, you'll see. One day I'll show him I'm not a little girl.'

'What the bloody hell's this?' Theresa held up a lump of balding grey fur from the top of Maggie's open suitcase.

'It's Pussy; my pyjama case.'

Maggie snatched her treasure from Theresa and held it to her chest.

'She can't sleep without it,' said Elizabeth.

'I can. Why don't you push off and go next door and unpack, Elizabeth?'

'Come on Chris, let's go next door and leave softy baby Margaret loving her cat.'

'I don't know why we invited our Elizabeth and Chris Warrington to come with us. They're both stuck up,' Maggie said as the bedroom door closed.

'What have you got against Chris? Anyway, never mind them, Mags. I suggest you, me and the cat in the double bed and Sal in the single. No offence Sal, but I'd rather share with Mags and her dead cat than have you thinking I'm Paul and putting your arms round me,' Theresa smacked her lips together a couple of times, 'and kissing me during the night.'

'It isn't dead,' said Maggie tucking the pyjama case in the double bed, its head resting against a pillow.

As the five girls clumped downstairs the lady owner of the guest house appeared out of a door marked 'Private'.

'Have you unpacked and settled in? Do you have everything you need?'

'Yes, thank you,' said Sarah looking round at the others who, other than Theresa, nodded and smiled.

*Nosey bugger. She looks as though she could be Beaky's sister.*

She looked each girl up and down, sniffing as she looked at Theresa's skirt, and then held out a key to Chris.

'The Reverend Cummings has asked that I keep my eye on you, and make sure you come to no harm. I know that you are all used to being in your rooms by eleven o'clock – my niece is training to be a nurse in Sheffield. By the way, I bolt the front door at eleven o'clock prompt.'

*Christ Almighty, this is supposed to be a holiday.*

'Could you suggest somewhere for us to eat, please?' said Chris.

'You'd best make your way toward the university ...'

'Wahey – students?' Theresa rubbed her hands together. 'Boys galore.'

'As I was saying,' the landlady sneered at Theresa, 'there's plenty of café's that would suit you round there.'

They found a café that didn't look too posh, ordered

their evening meal and settled down for the catch up. Theresa had cautioned them that she had a 'bloody unbelievable tale' to tell as they battled to cross the late rush hour traffic on Euston Road.

'Go on Theresa; tell us what's been happening,' Chris said.

Theresa swallowed her mouthful, took a deep breath. She glanced at each girl in turn and started her tale.

'We were having a bloody fab week. My mum and dad had switched the beds round, the baby ...'

'How old is she now, the baby?' said Sarah.

'Nearly three, anyway where was I? Yes, well the baby was back in with them and I was in with the other girls. Win and me were the best we've been for ages. My mum was laughing and joking, she looked miles better, less tired and worn out. I'd been helping with the little uns and doing jobs all week. So, I thought to myself wouldn't it be good if we could get Mum and Dad to go out, you know, as a thank you for all they do for the lot of us.'

'You really are the most thoughtful person I know Theresa,' said Chris, looking around the table 'Isn't she?'

'She's not bad, not bad at all,' said Sarah, smiling.

'Maggie, what do you think; about Theresa.' Chris looked pointedly at Maggie.

'Sorry, I didn't hear what you said. I thought Theresa was telling us about her family.'

'Ignore her Chris, now where was I again? Tommy, that's it – well I got him to have a word with our Dad and suggest he take Mum out, down to the Catholic Club – I told Tommy to say me and Win would see to everything – tea for the little uns, bedtime and all that. Our Dad didn't need much persuading; he likes his beer.' Theresa took a slurp of her coffee and a mouthful of egg and chips. 'The tea was bloody fab, if I say so myself – bacon hot pot, made by yours truly. We set the table and all squashed round – well, except our Tommy. He was late.'

'Why?' Maggie said.

'Let her carry on,' Chris grizzled. 'Go on Theresa.'

'I'm going to the toilet,' said Maggie shuffling out of her chair.

'Well me and Win did the pots, got the baby in bed and persuaded the other two little uns to sit in bed and read while I helped Mum get ready. It had been a real bugger of a job persuading her to get dolled up but when Win, believe it or not, backed me up, she gave in and let me choose her clothes and make her up. She's the same size dress as me, although she's taller than me, and these days her boobs are a bit dangly. She looked bloody fab, in one of my skirts, knee length boots, and a blouse I'd never worn. She said the top button was too low, but we tightened her bra straps to hoist up her boobs and she looked fine. Dad had nipped to the offy to buy me and Win a bottle of cider; we were set for the night, listening to Radio Luxembourg while I tested Win on her history GCE.' Theresa paused. 'You'll never guess what happened next – it was bloody awful.'

'Poor Theresa, what happened?' said Chris.

'What's up Mags?' said Theresa, watching Maggie squeeze back into place at the table.

'Nothing, why should there be something up? When are we going back to the guest house?'

'Put your face straight and let Theresa finish,' said Elizabeth, giving Maggie a savage nudge with her elbow.

'Take no notice of her, go on, Theresa,' Elizabeth said.

'Our Mum was in the hall, trying to find her coat when there was an almighty banging on the front door. Frightened out of her skin she stepped back, stood on a dinky toy, skidded and ended up showing next week's washing as she fell back on the stairs. The banging got louder; my little brother was leaning out of his bedroom window shouting "go round t'back". You should have heard the din, it was enough to wake the devil; anyway, it woke the baby. I opened the door, as far as it would go, and a snotty little bald man tried to force his way in. He got stuck half way.'

'Why?' said Sarah.

'He couldn't get through; we don't use the front door. Well, we can't really, there's too much stuff cluttering up the bottom of the stairs. Anyway, he pushed and shoved and heaved his way in. "Where is your father?" he said to me. He barged into the front room followed by a fat woman and a young girl, who was crying. Just then my dad appeared, with the bottle of cider. He'd been in the lavvy while all this was going on. Mum appeared carrying the baby; somehow her blouse had come unbuttoned and one of her boobs was nearly hanging out. The other kids came down and then our Tommy appeared through the middle door. When the fat git saw our Tommy he started balling and shouting, stuff from the Bible ... It's a real bloody mess.'

'Theresa, are you okay? What was the mat...' said Sarah.

'Didn't I say? Our Tommy, the bloody idiot, has to get married. He's got the girl, Esther she's called, in trouble.'

'My dad wouldn't like it if one of us got in trouble,' said Maggie, 'would he Elizabeth?'

'Will they definitely have to get married?' said Elizabeth, ignoring her sister.

'They will that, and in some soddin' church we've never heard of. Esther's dad went on and on about Catholicism, the pope and loads of other stuff. The upshot is; the shotgun will be in a couple of weeks, immediate family only, with no do afterwards and our Tommy will move in with them. The fat git says she, Esther, still has to sit her O levels. And then what? I've no idea.'

'How have your mum and dad taken it?' said Sarah.

'My mum's taken it badly. It didn't help that the bleedin' cow of a woman stood there sniffing, her nose in the air. She gawped round the room and looked my mum up and down as though my mum had stood in dog shit. Then, to make matters worse, whenever the mother mentioned something or other religious our Win crossed herself. The mother looked as though she'd have a myocardial. I have to say, looking back, that bit was funny.'

'Dear me, Theresa. What a mess. Is there anything we can do to help?' said Chris.

Theresa glimpsed Maggie mee-mawing Chris's words and actions.

What the bloody hell is she doing?

'Not really, thanks for listening. You see, it's a kick in the teeth for our mum and dad. They want us to have a better life than they've had. They've given up stuff, nights out and that so that me and Win could stay on at school. Our Tommy refused to stay for O levels. He stayed on for an extra term to do the exams he needed for his apprenticeship. He's a lovely brother,' she sniffed and reached for the paper serviette, 'he's my best pal – well other than you lot. He'd never do anybody any harm and now he's in deep, deep shit – poor sod.'

'Does he have to get married? Is there no other choice?' Chris said.

'No, not where we live. He's going to end up married to a girl he hardly knows. He said they haven't done IT, well not properly, they were just messing about. He'll be stuck with her mum and dad – miserable buggers. No telly, no doing anything on a Sunday other than going to church, chapel or whatever they call it, three times. Her dad's going to get them a council house, or so he says; he's something important at the town hall.' Theresa shuddered. 'Look at your faces. Come on I'm spoiling our night out. What are we doing for the rest of the week? Lead me to the lads.' Theresa saw Maggie's panic stricken face. 'Joke, Mags. Joke.'

The days were passing quickly. Unable to break the habit of rising early the young women were up, dressed and eating breakfast by eight o'clock each morning. They enjoyed jostling with the commuters as well as people watching on the underground. Tottenham Court Road, Goodge Street, Warren Street; they felt like girls-about-town as they anticipated the underground stops to and from the guesthouse.

'I must say I'm not over impressed with Carnaby Street,' said Theresa, catching hold of the seat in front of hers as the underground train swung to the right. 'Mostly tat and stuff for tourists.'

'I agree. Where's all the trendy stuff?' said Chris.

'Well, we all bought a tote bag – they'll look fab in Farnton,' Sarah said.

'Did we all manage a different colour?' said Elizabeth.

'I didn't buy one,' Maggie said.

Bleeding hell Maggie, straighten your face.

'Sarah's and the one we bought Jen are both luminous orange,' said Theresa.

'I paid my share to that.'

*Hoo bloody rah for you, Mags.*

167

# CHAPTER TWENTY-FIVE

In Farnton, Jenny was settled into the box room at Mavis and Brian Smithfield's home. Dave had moved back into the bedroom he had shared with his brother for the fortnight of Jenny's holiday. The couple travelled back and forth to Dave's terraced cottage, their future home, to get on with the jobs they'd set themselves.

Jenny had been relieved when Dave told her he thought they should wait before they 'went all the way'. Her stepfather's jibes had stayed with her and made her absolutely determined she would not give him the satisfaction of her being pregnant before her wedding day. The tender acceptance of Dave's mum and dad and their willingness to share their home with her was astonishing. The only time she'd felt anything akin to being so treasured was when she was with Granny Ashford. Anxious not to be a burden to Mr and Mrs Smithfield, Jenny took it upon herself to help set about chores while Mrs Smithfield was at work.

'Jenny, luv?' Mrs Smithfield said, opening the back door.

'Hello, Mrs Smithfield.' Jenny heaped mashed potato onto the minced meat and onions she'd already cooked and put into a Pyrex dish. 'I hope you don't mind me getting on with supper?'

'Do I 'eck as like.'

I wonder why she did that bobbing motion?

Jenny watched Mrs Smithfield duck her head as she went under the clothes rack suspended from the kitchen ceiling. She's walking okay now, Jenny thought, as Mrs Smithfield shrugged off her coat and went through the door into the lounge to hang her coat up behind the front door. She's done it again.

'Where are the ...' Mrs Smithfield looked startled, took a step back and pointed to the empty rail.

Jenny smiled as realisation dawned.

'I'm hope you don't mind. I did the ironing and then helped myself to the stuff for the meal. Dave said it would be all right for me to ...'

'Don't fret yourself Jenny, luv. I feel like a lady coming home and all my jobs done. Haven't you been over to the house today?'

Jenny explained that they'd spent the morning clearing out cupboards but had left at lunch time to allow Dave to prepare for his evening classes.

'I hope you don't think I've been prying; looking for the iron and ironing board, but Dave said you wouldn't mind ... I'm really sorry ...'

'Don't get upset, luv.'

Jenny turned her head away, breathing deeply, willing herself not to cry.

'You must treat this house as home from home. Sorry luv, sorry, I didn't mean anything about your mam and dad's.'

'Don't worry, Mrs Smithfield, don't worry about them. I'm fine,' Jenny smiled. 'Honestly, I'm fine.'

'Let's have a nice cup of tea and a sit down; my legs

are killing me, market day is murder in that post office.'

'I'll do it, you sit down.' Jenny reached for the kettle. 'By the time this boils I'll have finished washing the pans.'

'You do the pans and I'll make the tea and butter us a Chorley cake each.' Mavis rummaged in her shopping bag and extricated her treat. 'Then there's something I want to talk to you about.'

Jenny froze.

'Don't look so worried, luv, it's something and nothing. Come on sit down and I'll explain.'

Jenny watched as Mrs Smithfield eased the tea cosy over the teapot then reached out to take Jenny's hand in hers.

'I've been thinking about us, you and me.'

'Why? Is ...'

'Don't worry luv, there's nothing wrong. Let me explain.'

Mavis told Jenny that although she'd always got on with Grandma Smithfield she had never been sure what to call her. 'Mother' had never felt comfortable and 'Mrs Smithfield' seemed odd once she and Brian were married.

'I avoided calling her anything until Dave was born and then I latched on to calling her "grandma".'

Jenny sighed and said. 'I know what you mean. I've been thinking about that myself. I wasn't sure ...'

'Well, what about "Miffy"?'

Mavis explained that when Dave and young Brian were little their friends had worked their way from 'Mrs Smithfield' – 'a mouthful for anybody' – to 'Mrs Smithy' and then 'Miffy'.

'Elizabeth and Margaret call me Aunty Miffy now.'

'That would be super – Miffy,' said Jenny through trembling lips.

'Let's open this letter. Don't cry Jenny, luv, you'll

get me going.' Mavis reached across to the draining board for the vegetable knife. 'With luck, it's our Brian writing to say he can make it home for the wedding.' She slit open the flimsy blue airmail letter.

Jenny, perched on the draining board of the large stone sink in the laundry room, was keeping Theresa company while she caught up with her ironing. The draining board shifted in time to the swinging backwards and forwards of her gangly legs.

'If you're not careful that thing'll come away from the wall.' Theresa shook her head. 'Jenny, are you with me?'

'Sorry, did you say something?'

'I knew you weren't listening. I was saying our Tommy's wedding won't be a wedding like yours is going to be.'

'Well ours won't be a big affair, we can't afford anything fancy. I've got enough savings to pay for mine and Sarah's dresses. Although Sarah has offered to pay for the material for hers but I'd rather stretch myself and pay for it, that's what the bride's family usually do, isn't it – pay for the bridesmaids' dresses? By the way, did you know her mother has offered to make our dresses?'

'Well dresses or no dresses, at least you're happy to be getting married, to the love of your life and all that. Our Tommy, well, it's just a soddin' mess.'

Jenny's thoughts wandered to her own wedding. She was embarrassed that the Smithfield's were insisting on paying half of the reception as well as flowers and most of the other paraphernalia that went into making a family wedding. Dave had some money put away as well as his extra pay from teaching evening classes. He would pay for the taxis and photographs and the other half of the reception. Maggie's mum had offered to make the wedding cake as a present to them.

'Jen, are you with me; you're not listening, again. What's the matter?'

Jenny's whirling brain clunked back into the laundry room and joined the rest of her body perched on the draining board.

'Sorry, I'm really sorry, Theresa.'

'You've lost the blushing bride look. I thought you were happy.'

'I am happy but, it's just that I don't like being beholden to other people. You know, after George and all that.' She hopped off the draining board. 'Dave's family are paying more than their fair share, and well, just think about the church and the service. Who's going to give me away? Where will I be married from – the nurses' home? Besides all that, what do I do about Granny Ashford? I sent her a postcard to tell her I was engaged. She sent a letter back asking heaps of questions. When I wrote back I didn't answer them. I sent her a picture postcard of the town hall and told her I was here, at the General. She must think me awfully rude.'

They were interrupted by a staff nurse agitating to use the ironing board.

'Come on, let's get some fresh air before we go for our supper. We can walk to the park, they might have set out the pitch and put. I bet you sixpence I win,' said Theresa.

'Righto, see you at the front door in five minutes.'

'Jenny, you need to sort yourself out. Come on, steady the buffs,' she told herself. She shrugged off her green uniform dress in favour of slacks and a polo neck jumper. *Be jolly thankful you're wanted as part of his family and that his parents are looking forward to the wedding. George and my mother can go and fuck themselves.* She bobbed down to check her appearance in the dressing table mirror. *Fuck, fuck, fuck. I feel fucking marvellous saying fuck to myself.*

By the time Jenny and Theresa had walked to the park, played a round of pitch and put and walked back to the hospital, Jenny felt as though she'd been on the holiday to London thanks to Theresa's running commentary.

'I thought you knew it was David Niven and not Sean Connery in *Casino Royale*,' said Jenny.

'Not only was it the wrong bloody actor, the plot was useless as well. *The Graduate*, now that's another story. We had to explain the plot to Mags – she's a case. I'm in lurve with Dustin Hoffman.'

'Even more than Dave Berry?'

'Umm, I don't know. I'll have to think about that one,' said Theresa, smiling and then muttering tunelessly something about *Mama* as she waved her arms about and contorted her body.

# CHAPTER TWENTY-SIX

'How are you enjoying gynaecology, Nurse Booth?' said Miss Bennet.

Theresa was nervous, unsure of how to behave with this figure of authority that seemed intent on treating her as though she were normal, accepted and acceptable; it was a strange feeling. When Theresa had knocked on the staff room door in The School of Nursing she'd been invited into the inner sanctum and offered a cup of tea. She'd quickly refused, particularly when Miss Bolton had looked daggers at Miss Bennet and exclaimed, 'Beatrice! Whatever next!' Theresa and Miss Bennet were now closeted in an alcove in the library to discuss the way ahead with their article.

'I love it, Miss Bennet.'

'I was a sister on gynae; I loved it as well,' Miss Bennet sighed, 'but that's some time ago and we need to look to the future, so we'd better get on or you will have wasted your afternoon off.'

'I don't mind Miss Bennet.' *No, I really don't mind. I'm enjoying this; I think.* 'Honestly.'

'Well, I've made progress, that is to say I have arranged for us to attend the next Hospital Management Committee meeting to present our paper to the members before we proceed toward publication.'

'Err, Bumble, sorry,' Theresa covered her mouth, 'I mean Miss Bennet, I won't have to say anything, will I?'

Miss Bennet laughed.

'Nurse Booth, you are a bright girl. I am confident that you are more than capable of answering a few questions.'

'Well I suppose I will have to practise speaking properly,' Theresa said in her version of a posh voice, as she sat bolt upright in her chair, her nose in the air.

'You are fine as you are. Why don't you tell me about your experiences on geriatrics?'

Sharing her thoughts and observations on nursing old men, most of whom were not acutely sick but pleasantly disorientated yet able to knock about the ward, and in some cases make a bid for freedom out of the ward, helped Theresa relax. They compared the patients with the residents of the care home Theresa had visited and concluded there was very little difference between a significant number of the residents in the homes and the patients on the wards. They discussed staffing levels, the ward routines and the quality of care and nursing. Theresa explained her theory that the work on the geriatric wards wasn't nursing but more like fighting a battle that could never be won.

'Why should men, and women, who've never done anybody any wrong end up like that; behind cot sides? Most of them don't get visitors, they just lie there looking sad. Something needs to be done about the men but also about our training.' *Bleedin' hell look at the time.*

'Before you go, Nurse Booth,' Miss Bennet took a deep breath, 'there is something from years ago that I would like to share with you – in confidence.'

Shit, what's up now?

Miss Bennet looked wistful.

Please God, help me.

'I enjoyed my nurse tutor training. It was intellectually stimulating to be with nurses who were bright and loved the profession. I trained here at the General and, well, best not go into that.' Miss Bennet raised her eyebrows at Theresa. 'I'm sure you know what I mean? The student tutors came from all over the country, from prestigious hospitals – they had all been ward sisters. The lectures were lively. We were encouraged to question and challenge accepted ideas about nurses and nurse training.'

Where the bloody hell is this going?

'Well,' Miss Bennet hesitated, 'one day, after a particularly lively seminar, that I'd chaired, one of my fellow students, who spoke just like Princess Margaret, said to me "you know Bea, considering the way you speak, you really are quite bright".'

'The cheeky bugg…, blighter. What did you say to that, Miss Bennet?'

'I thanked her for the compliment. The moral of the tale Nurse Booth is never be afraid to be yourself, always remember your roots and take strength from them but don't hesitate to have the courage to move on.'

'Thank you Miss Bennet, thank you – for telling me.'

Theresa left Miss Bennet to tidy the desk. She closed the door of the library behind her.

She's bloody marvellous. I'm going to be like her. One day I'll be a sister tutor. Bleedin' hell Theresa, you a sister tutor – dream on.'

Work on the two gynaecological wards was interesting and busy. It was occasionally funny and often emotionally taxing. The intimacy of the diseases and the nursing procedures required to support the patients' recovery, coupled with the fact that the women were, for a short time, free of the responsibilities of marriage, motherhood and other family concerns led to the patients unabashed sharing of life experiences, particularly in relation to the mechanics of sexual intercourse.

Ladies undergoing hysterectomy frequently asked, 'Will I lose my feelings?' and 'Will everything be all right down there – for my husband?' Faced with these questions, Mr Stone, the consultant gynaecologist, would respond, 'Don't you worry my dear, you'll find I've taken the nursery but left the playpen.' The young unmarried nurses were left to more fully explain his comments, often with the use of clumsily drawn diagrams.

Tears and tantrums from the women were not unusual. The patients were placed randomly in the long Nightingale wards. A woman coming to terms with the loss of an unborn child could be in the next bed to someone who had been butchered by a back-street abortionist. Women undergoing investigations for infertility could be in the next bed to a patient with a large family who had opted to be sterilized.

Flowers were a constant bind. There were vases and vases of the blithering things all needing to be taken out of the main part of the ward at night and brought back to the correct bed in the morning, having had the water changed and dead blooms removed.

Jenny and Theresa were both allocated to nights for the third week of their gynae allocation. Theresa had requested night duty so that her days off would be Friday and Saturday – the day of Tommy and Esther's wedding. She cobbled together a wedding outfit: a skirt from Sarah, who had persuaded her that she needed a tad longer length than she usually wore. The skirt wasn't one that Theresa would have chosen. It was muted yellow, brown and orange in a swirly paisley pattern. She'd bought a long sleeve blouse pleated across the chest. It was one she could get some wear out of later on. Having been persuaded into flesh coloured tights her modesty was ensured. Chris supplied her with a black handbag to match the kitten heeled shoes, slightly too big, that she borrowed from Maggie.

# CHAPTER TWENTY-SEVEN

Chris walked around the side of the Accrington brick church hall looking for a way in. The door, when she found it, refused to budge when she turned the large wooden door knob.

'It sticks; you need to give it a bit of a wiggle to get it to shift. Let me have a go.' The vicar that Chris had met at the engagement party wiggled the door handle and pushed at the same time. The door grated over the parquet floor beneath it.

'It's Chris, isn't it? Good to see you. Come on in, I know Brian will be pleased to see you.'

'Thank you …' Chris hesitated, not sure how to address a vicar.

'Chris, Vicar, come on in, find seats where you can and then we'll get started,' said Brian Smithfield.

Chris was relieved to see Elizabeth had saved her a seat on the back row.

Brain Smithfield clapped his hands. The assembled Players quietened as their leader welcomed the company back to the church hall for another round of rehearsals.

'We've got four months to get the show up and running. As you are no doubt aware we've settled on *Oliver*. However, due to difficulties with copyright, the show will have to be re-titled *What the Dickens*. Another difficulty that I have discussed with one or two of you, is that we will need to change our usual date from the end of September to the beginning of the month because our Dave is marrying a lovely nurse, Jenny, who has no say over her holidays.'

The assembled company broke into spontaneous applause.

'Thank you for that, especially since we would like to invite you all to the evening do – providing, that is, you all agree to sing while Jenny and our Dave are signing the register. Let's get going; we'll go through everything as a group so that we all get to know the words and music before we rehearse as principals and chorus.'

Chris, hesitant at first, cast her eyes around the room at her fellow singers. They were a mixed bunch, mostly middle-aged with one or two younger; Elizabeth, herself, Dave and three or four others. The room reminded of her of her primary school hall, high ceilings with patches of damp in the corners, tall windows with pull down sections to let in air on the bottom panes. The piano sounded tinny but the singing couldn't be faulted. Chris stood tall, breathed from deep down in her chest and joined in. It felt liberating to be singing in a group again.

'Hello, it's good to see you here; we didn't get time to talk at the beginning did we?' The vicar hovered behind Chris and Elizabeth in the tea queue. 'Will you be able to manage to get to rehearsals then, Chris?'

'Hello. Yes, I hope so. I'll have to miss the odd Tuesday, when I'm on nights or a late shift, like Maggie and Jenny are tonight – well Jenny is on nights I'm not really sure about Maggie, but I should be able to make it most weeks. You see, on most wards the sisters don't mind if you ask for particular lates or earlies. Although it doesn't mean we always get them.' Stop rambling on, she told herself.

'Do you work late often?'

'Twice, sometimes three times a week.'

'Goodness gracious me! How many hours a week do you work? I'm sorry, I don't mean to pry.'

'You're not prying. Really, you're not.' Chris blushed. 'We work eighty-eight hours a fortnight. When we're on nights we do most of that in one week.' *Christine, pull yourself together. Why are you enjoying this? He's too old – handsome though and his brown eyes are ...* 'No sugar thanks,' Chris reached out for the cup of tea that Maggie's mum was holding out to her.

'Have a clean saucer, love. You've slopped tea over your custard cream.'

'Thank you, Mrs Smithfield.'

'Watch out,' Elizabeth whispered to Chris as they shuffled along the row to reach their seats for the second half of the rehearsal. 'He's on the lookout for a wife.'

'Honestly Elizabeth, what a thing to say.' Chris picked up her folder of sheet music.


Chris escorted her patient into the treatment room; she linked her arm through his to give him support on his first day up and about following removal of his bandages after cataract surgery. She left him sitting in the treatment chair in readiness for the sister to observe his eyes and administer his drops and then set off down the corridor to fetch another patient. As she passed the telephone table, the phone rang.

'Jones, ward Nurse Warrington speaking.'

'Hiya Chris. It's me; I've rung for my off duty.'

'Just a tick Theresa, I'll nip into the treatment room and get it for you.'

Chris read out the following week's shifts for

Theresa.

'What's it like on there? Is it as good as Sal says, or as bad as everybody else says?'

'Thank you, Nurse Booth. Goodbye,' Chris said in her best telephone voice as the sister strode past, pointed down and instructed, 'Next patient if you please, nurse; in your own time of course. This isn't a holiday camp.'

'Sorry about earlier – the sister was on the prowl,' said Chris into the telephone.

She settled herself on the wobbly chair in the flimsy telephone cubicle. As nurses came off duty the queue for the phone grew. Those waiting in the queue lounged on the nearby staircase laughing, joking and nattering to each other. They were variously dressed for the evening ahead; pyjamas and dressing gowns with newly washed hair in rollers, summer dresses for a couple of hours out and about, with one brazen hussy who regularly used the phone wrapped only in a large white towel.

Nurses heard speaking softly into the phone were usually whispering sweet nothings or indulging in juicy gossip. If snippets of the one-sided conversations were overheard by the gang on the stairs, whoops, kissing noises and less than helpful comments punctuated the phone calls.

'What's it like at The Main Road?' Theresa said.

'It's fine. Old fashioned and a bit like a rabbit warren, but comfortable with lovely breakfasts in bed on your days off, and wait for it because you'll never believe this – you are given a key to let yourself in when you get a late pass.'

'Bloody hell.'

'Don't get too excited – the front door gets bolted and locked from the inside at midnight.'

As second years the nurses at the Infirmary moved to the home at the front of the hospital. Late passes meant the treasured key to the front door. No more reporting to the night sisters, running along the cellar or bumping into Matron. The ruse at The Main Road was that one nurse asked for a late pass and then arranged to meet the other at eleven fifty five. Climbing in through a ground floor window had disappeared as an option after one of the older resident sisters disturbed a man climbing through the window late at night. It was reported that he fled in fright, scared to death at the sight of the Old Mother Riley apparition. All the sash windows were now firmly screwed down.

# CHAPTER TWENTY-EIGHT

Sarah was in the treatment room clearing away the equipment she'd been using when the staff nurse poked her head around the door.

'There you are, Nurse Green. We've got a young girl on her way from medical emergency – threatened abortion. You can admit her while I get on with the pharmacy order.'

'Yes, Staff. Any particular bed?'

'Second on the left.'

As Sarah stepped out of the treatment room the porters were wheeling a trolley, holding a recumbent figure, out of the lift. She led the porters to the designated bed.

'Hello, I'm Nurse Green. Can you manage to wriggle off the trolley and onto the bed?' No wonder she's scared, the poor thing is only a child, thought Sarah as she arranged pillows under the girl's head and straightened the bedding. 'Are you married?' Sarah looked askance at the girl's left hand.

'Yes, only just – we've been married for three weeks

and two days.'

The girl rubbed snot and tears on the arm of her cardigan sleeve.

'I've lost my handkerchief.'

'It doesn't matter. I'm going to get you into a clean gown and wash your hands and face – I'm sorry, what's your name?'

'Esther, Esther Booth.'

Sarah looked more closely at the girl.

'Is Tommy your husband and Theresa your sister-in-law?'

'Yes. How do you know?' Esther began to cry. 'Please can I see Tom? Are you a friend of his sister's?'

'Yes, I am. Come on let's get you sorted out. Is Tommy with you?'

'He's outside with my mother and father. I don't want to see them, not if I don't have to.'

Sarah helped Esther out of her cardigan and blood stained nightdress and into a white theatre gown. All the time she was helping Esther she talked to her, encouraging her to try and relax and explain what happened. In a halting whisper Esther told Sarah that she and Tommy had 'you know, been together, last night.' Then she'd got up to go to the toilet and found one or two spots of blood on the toilet paper when she wiped herself. She hadn't thought it was anything to be bothered about: there had been one or two spots of blood in her knickers once or twice before. When she woke up in the morning, she found more blood, lots of it, on the sheets. Tom had insisted that they would have to ask her mother if they could use the phone to call the doctor. The doctor had sent for the ambulance.

'Is the baby still there?'

'We'll know more when the doctor has seen you – look, here he is now,' said Sarah pulling the screens closed as the doctor stepped up to the bed.

Tommy and Esther stared at Sarah dumbfounded as she stood at the bedside and explained the process of the incomplete abortion that Esther had experienced and the need for her to go to the operating theatre later in the afternoon.

'Thank you, nurse,' said Tommy, his head down as he scratched at the counterpane. 'Esther says you're a friend of our Theresa's. Will you be able to let her know what's happened? I think she's just been moved to the eye ward at the Infirmary.'

'I'll ask the staff nurse if I can give Theresa a ring. I'm sure she'll say yes.'

The boy lifted his head and gave Sarah a half-hearted smile.

Esther was sitting up in bed absent-mindedly sipping a cup of tea, a slice of cold toast solidified in front of her on the bed table, when Theresa arrived on the ward.

'Hello Theresa, you made me jump.'

'You were miles away. Do you still feel groggy?'

'A bit, I wish Tom were here.'

'He'll be back tomorrow, at visiting time.'

Theresa prattled on about anything she could think of. Esther nodded her head occasionally and made half-hearted replies to Theresa's questions. After half an hour of watching the ward clock drag around Theresa pushed her chair back from the side of the bed.

'I'd better go now, Esther. I was only allowed in to see you because the staff on here know me; it was my last ward. Why don't you close your eyes and try and have a rest.'

I'm whacked, I might nip and see if Sal's about. I can cadge a cup of tea before I go back to the Infirmary.

'Sal, are you in?' Theresa said as she knocked on Sarah's door.

Theresa was turning to go when she heard signs of

life and the bedroom door opened.

'You look knackered. Were you fast asleep?'

'Come in.' Sarah stretched and yawned. 'I was having forty winks before Paul comes to pick me up. Have you been to see Esther?'

Theresa didn't need any persuading to join Sarah and Paul on their night out. They abandoned the idea of the pub and decided to chance a call at Dave's house to see if Jenny and Dave were in.

Paul and Dave's dispatch to the offy left Jenny, Sarah and Theresa free to catch up on news. Jenny concentrated on slicing bread while Sarah grated cheese as she and Theresa patched together their understanding of what had happened to Tommy and Esther. Jenny, intent on listening to the story, yelped.

'Whoops, bugger.' Jenny dropped the bread knife and stuck her thumb in her mouth. 'I've cut myself.'

'Did you say bugger, Nurse Hayes?' said Theresa, shifting the bread to her side of the table and holding out her hand for the knife.

'I'm swearing a lot lately and it bloody well helps,' said Jenny. 'Come on Sarah, what happened next? Don't say anything to Dave – about the swearing.'

It turned out that Esther's father wouldn't take no for an answer when he was told that his daughter refused to see her parents. He'd stormed onto the ward in the middle of afternoon visiting, followed by his wife. They'd stood at the bottom of the bed while he shouted at Esther to 'repent of her sins'. He quoted passages from the Bible, while the other patients and their visitors watched mesmerised. Esther had clung to Tommy, both of them were crying. At the sight of the porters, called by staff nurse, Esther's dad had stormed off the ward, with her mum in tow, turning to yell at Tommy and Esther that 'the day of reckoning is at hand'.

'That miserable wedding was all for nothing.'

'Was it very bad?' said Jenny.

'Bad? You must be kidding, bad doesn't go anywhere near it.' Theresa gave a snort. 'It was more like a bloody pantomime, never mind a wedding. In between wailing, the mother kept shouting out questions to "Dear Jesus" and God knows who else. The father, miserable bugger, didn't even link Esther's arm, you know like brides and their dads usually … Oh, bleedin hell, sorry, Jen.'

'It doesn't matter,' Jenny flapped her arms at Theresa, 'go on.'

'Well, he stormed up the aisle and Esther trooped after him. You should have seen her outfit, mine was odds and sods, but hers – well!'

'That's my best skirt, Theresa,' Sarah said, feigning being piqued.

'Sorry Sal, well anyway – she wore her navy school skirt with an old-fashioned pale blue twin set. When they were taking their vows I leant forward and peeped over the pew to see if she was wearing white socks. She wasn't, but she did have school shoes on. Not a flower in sight, well not in that miserable place or on any of them. We made up for it though – all decked out in buttonholes our mum had made for us, even the little uns. Although, the baby picked at hers and ended up with just the safety pin in her cardie.'

'What do you think will happen now?' said Sarah.

'Difficult to say. Esther managed to sit her O levels, but I don't know what's going to happen, other than they are two kids who hardly know each other who are forced to live with the God Squad from Hell – poor sods. Stick that cheese on the toast Jenny, I'm starving.'

'Have you three had time to catch up?' Paul said, settling himself in one of the well-worn armchairs.

'No, you've come back too soon,' said Theresa grinning, as she came through from the kitchen carrying a plate piled with cheese on toast, 'go away again. We were about to start on Jenny and Dave's wedding. We've done our Tommy's.'

'Well, there's some better news about that. We were talking about it when you arrived, weren't we, Dave?' Jenny patted Dave's head before folding herself down to sit at his feet. He had settled himself in the chair on the opposite side of the fireplace to Paul.

'We were, love.'

'It looks as though it's going to be all right, about me being given away and all that other stuff I've been getting in a tizzy about.' Jenny swallowed her mouthful. 'I've had another letter from Granny Ashford. She's coming to visit – she usually does once a year but the big thing is, this year, she's staying at the Crown and Mitre not with my mum and dad – George, I mean. I refuse to call him Dad, ever again.

'Does she know about that obnoxious bugger and what he said about you?' said Theresa.

'She must have guessed something was amiss. She wrote to tell me George had written to her to tell her about my and Dave's visit to announce our engagement, and she asked for my version. I wrote back and said it was to be a quiet wedding and that they – Mum and George – were busy on the date we'd planned. I also told her that Mrs Green was making my and Sarah's dresses. She wanted to know what arrangements George had made to cover the cost of the wedding. I had to tell her that Dave and his mum and dad were well … you know the rest.' She waved her hand dismissively. 'So Sarah, do you think you and your mum would be free to come to tea at The Crown and Mitre next Tuesday? I know it's short notice but I only found out today. I was going to ring you tonight.'

'Is this Granny of yours dead posh?' said Theresa.

'Well she's a touch grand, like the Queen Mother, but she's really kind and gentle.'

'How grand,' Dave hesitated, 'is grand?'

Well, her father was something important in India. I think he was an honourable something or other, but surely that doesn't matter. She's my granny and she wants to meet Dave and his family and my friends. Theresa, you and Chris and Maggie, of course, are invited as well.'

'Thanks Jen, but you've enough on without us three tagging along.' *Bleedin' hell what next, from hell fire and damnation to toffs all in one easy step? I'd best start practising my curtsey.* 'We're a motley crew – poor and posh, aren't we?'

'All the better for it,' said Paul 'being different I mean.'

*If only you knew how the other half lived, Paul, you might change your mind. I bet my mum would swap places with your mum any day.*

# CHAPTER TWENTY-NINE

Jenny and Miffy emerged from the shade of the Crown and Mitre lobby into the sunshine of Makin Square. The statue of Alderman Makin stood before them in the centre of the quiet leafy enclave. The old dispensary, the forerunner of the Infirmary, now converted to prestigious offices, was on their right.

'This'll be a grand spot for wedding photos,' said Miffy, looking around. 'Dad and me would have been happy to help with the reception you know.' She smiled up at Jenny.

'I know and I will always appreciate ...' Jenny concentrated very hard on the head of Alderman Makin '... you and Dad have been so good to me.'

'Why would we not be good to you? Jenny luv, there's something I need to ask you?'

'Miffy, what is it?'

'I didn't make a fool of myself, did I, Jenny, luv?'

'Why would you think that?'

Jenny struggled to see anything privileged or beneficial in her upbringing, other than her Granny

Ashford. She wanted what Dave, Maggie, Theresa, and if this afternoon was anything to go by, Sarah had – a loving family who supported each other, no matter what. When Miffy linked her arm as they made their way to the bus stop Jenny felt warm and wanted.

'We're not posh though. Are we?'

'You are the kindest people in the world. Granny really took to you. Did you enjoy it – the afternoon out?'

'I did, luv, it were grand. I had a bit of a struggle getting changed in the back shop, but it were worth it to meet your grandma and Mrs Green; she's a nice woman. That afternoon tea will do me for today. When I get off the bus I'll nip in the butchers and get Dad a nice piece of undercut.'

'It was kind of you to invite Granny for supper tomorrow.'

'I don't know how that happened. Are you sure she'll want potato pie and rice pudding for her tea?'

'Of course, I'm sure she'll be delighted. I'll walk to the Crown and collect her and then we'll get a taxi and be with you for half-past five. Dave can run her back when he takes me back to the hospital for my night shift. Here comes your bus.'

'Do you feel better, love, now that things are getting sorted?' Dave said as he manoeuvred the car through the side entrance of the hospital and up to the front door of the Infirmary.

'I do, and are you more comfortable being with Granny now that you've met her and spent some more time with her?'

'I'm a daft bugger. I should have known she'd be smashing. After all she is your granny. What do you think she thought of her tea?'

'She said it was delicious and I know she meant it.'

'Thank God, my mum must be worn out. Dad said

not only was she beside herself having her tea at the Crown and Mitre but then she was up at the crack of dawn cleaning and polishing.' Dave shook his head and smiled. 'I've never had spud pie off the best china before.'

'The tea was brilliant. Your mum's been giving me lessons on the perfect potato pie and rice pudding.'

'Did you see the dirty look my dad got when he went to stir his jam into his rice pud?'

'Yes, I'm busy watching your mum for hints and tips on husband management.'

'Come here you, I'll show you about wife management.'

Dave reached across the gear stick and hand break and pulled Jenny toward him. Emerging from the kiss, Dave said, 'Are you sure your granny is all right about the reception – it's a lot of money for one old lady to stump up. My dad was a bit concerned, when we were washing up.'

'I don't think you, or he, should worry about money. George was always telling my mum that "it will be fur coats and champagne all the way when the old girl shuffles of this mortal coil".'

'The bastard, sorry love – saying bastard!'

'Dave, forget it.'

They kissed again.

'Were they mentioned – when you were on your own with your granny?'

Jenny recounted the events of the early afternoon. She'd arrived at the hotel to be told by the receptionist that Mrs Ashford had requested that Jenny make her way to room 148. A tray of tea and biscuits was delivered and, once Jenny was settled with her cup and saucer, Granny had asked what happened when Jenny and Dave announced their engagement. Jenny had begun with an edited version, when she was told to start again at the beginning and to tell the whole story. Granny Ashford had not been surprised that Jenny knew about her natural father – Malcolm. The taxi had arrived and they carried on their conversation in the car. Apparently, George was not a patch on Malcolm, who was unfailingly kind and considerate. He always put others first and tried to do his duty to his family, which was probably why he tied himself in knots and ended up trying to live a lie. The upshot of the conversation was that Granny Ashford had visited her daughter and son-in-law the previous evening. It was a short visit. Jenny's mother would attend the wedding but not George or his sons. George was no longer welcome in Devon but his sons could visit, with their mother, if they chose to do so, and that was it.

'We arrived at your mum and dad's and nothing more was said, and if I know my granny nothing will ever be said again; well not to me anyway.'

Changed and ready for their night duty, Sarah walked with Chris toward the hospital.

'How did it go at the Crown and Mitre yesterday?'

'Really well, my mother was in her element. The vicar and Mrs Evans will never hear the last of it.'

'Did she get on with Dave's mum – the granny I mean?'

'Yes, she's lovely, posh in the way she speaks. You can tell she's a kind person. She invited Dave's mum to sit next to her and kept asking for her opinion and advice.'

'Is she coming to the wedding?'

'Not only is she coming, she's giving Jenny away. She's remarkable, it must come from being upper class – my mum hardly said a word. Well, other than inviting Jenny to be married from our house, the dress will be there after all, and offering to make a supper for us all the night before the wedding. I can't believe it.'

'That was kind.'

'I thought she would faint with delight when Jenny's granny patted her knee and said "I do hope you will be my guest at the wedding and reception".'

'What did she say?'

'She was flabbergasted. I thought she might curtsey on the way out, but I managed to get her away before any damage was done. See you at first supper.'

# CHAPTER THIRTY

For the first time since she was a child, Chris was at peace with herself and her life. She'd accepted that she would have a tenuous relationship with her mother as long as she remained Mrs Harry Jones, which she was likely to do. His affluence afforded her mother an extensive wardrobe, holidays, a social life through his masonic lodge and a comfortable home. She surmised that what he got in return was sex as and when he wanted it – the dirty old man. The thought of him touching her mother made Chris's flesh creep. She mused on her nana's relationship with the swine. Nana was nobody's fool. Surely she knew that he was a creep?

The friendships of Sarah, Jenny and particularly Theresa underpinned the reawakening of her self-esteem. She valued her growing friendship with Elizabeth. Maggie she couldn't fathom. In some ways she was a child, and a spoilt child at that. Yet, she had a reputation as a capable, caring nurse. The attention from Fred, well – it was wonderful, unexpected, glorious. As the weeks of rehearsals passed they had moved from speaking in the refreshment queue to sitting next to each other after the break, listening while the principal singers rehearsed. The first time she'd felt his leg warm against the side of her leg her whole body was suffused with a glow she'd never imagined; that and the hand brushing as one or other gathered the other's crockery in order to return the used cups and saucers to the tea ladies. Was the leg touching an accident, Chris asked herself, fearing the answer. She needn't have doubted, with a bit of shuffling and cautious shifting of seats the leg touching became a regular occurrence. One stormy night, when Jenny was working and Dave teaching an extra class, Fred wouldn't hear of Chris catching the bus back to the nurses' home.

'I absolutely insist, you will be drenched to the bone if the rain comes on again and it isn't really out of my way.'

'Thank you,' Chris said, her head down to hide her blushes, 'that would be kind, especially since you only live next door.'

'Like I said,' Fred gave Chris a sideways look and smiled, 'it's not really out of my way.'

Chris shrugged herself into her coat and made her way into the back hall to wait. Fred appeared seconds later.

'This way, my dear.' He led the way down the side of the hall and through a gate into the vicarage garden. 'Here,' he held out his hand, 'take my hand. The path is dark and a touch overgrown. It wasn't always like this; but, well, never mind that now.'

Chris felt the wet plants and grass brush against her legs and the bottom of her coat, her stockings were soaked and her shoes squelching by the time they reached the car. Fred unlocked the passenger door and saw Chris into the seat. 'We'll soon have you back at the nurses' home warm and dry; we couldn't have you getting wet. Could we?'

Rounding the corner, in front of the church hall, Fred beeped his horn and waved at the group standing on the pavement waiting for John Smithfield to lock up. The group waved back, with one or two of the women bending down to peer at the passenger side of the car.

'They're a good group, very kind and solicitous, I've always thought,' Fred said.

'Yes, I'm sure they are.'

Chris stared into the dark streets, the glow of the sodium lights twinkling in the damp night. *I've imagined it all. He's a kind man who's taken pity on me. I've talked myself into a dream. I hope I don't catch a cold, my feet are freezing.*

'Chris, is it possible, that you would …? What I am making a hash of saying Chris, is would you like to go for a drive with me on your next day off? If we can arrange it, that is?'

Chris nodded to the head and shoulders of the man intent on staring straight ahead as he steered the car through the damp streets.

'Yes, thank you, I would, I really would. My days off next week are Tuesday and Wednesday.'

'Tuesday would be good. Would ten thirty be suitable, then we can make a full day of it and be back in time for rehearsals. Although, that is quite a long time to wait. Would you like to go for a walk later this week?'

'What about tomorrow evening?'

'I'll call at the home and pick you up at around seven. We could perhaps find somewhere to eat.'

Chris wished away the hours between one meeting with Fred and another. She didn't think of their meetings as dates – they were special times, private times that didn't have a name. It was one of the periods when she didn't see much of Theresa, Sarah or Jenny. Days off and shifts didn't coincide or if they did one or other of them was busy with concerns of their own. Chris attended rehearsals and enjoyed the singing. Fred was right, the ladies were kind. They seemed to want to include her and they were always asking her questions; was she well, was she busy at the hospital, which ward was she on, how old was she, did she have a boyfriend, did she come from Farnton?

The meetings with Fred, their drives out and meals in country pubs and tea rooms, as well as attendance at Tuesday evening rehearsals had sharpened Chris's interest in the weekly off duty rota. Before Fred the shift patterns had been something to endure, something else to survive, something to defeat and subdue her in the life she had fled to. Now, since Fred, the weekly posting of the rota meant freedom, liberation and excitement. She begrudged the intrusion of the unsocial shifts into her precious time with the charismatic man she wanted to be with more than anything else in the world. Hectic days, sore feet, bad tempered sisters, obnoxious tasks faded into insignificance when she thought of Fred.

'Please, please,' she silently begged anybody or anything that might be listening as each rota was posted, 'not a late on a Tuesday.'

The pleading didn't always work. One Tuesday after a particularly draining split shift the sister refused to let the day staff off duty until she had taken her time giving the night staff the report. Chris cussed and mumbled as she ran down the hospital drive to the bus stop. Fred would wonder where she was. Perhaps he'd think she wasn't interested in him. John would be cross, she'd let him down. He wouldn't say so but ... well she knew. They'd know she was useless all of them. They seemed like nice people but ... She didn't like people to make allowances for her, it made her conspicuous, obvious, attention seeking.

Chris leapt from the bus and scuttled toward the church hall. Overly conscious that she was late Chris discreetly made her way into the church hall. Brian smiled at her as she dumped her coat and sidled toward the piano to join the rest of the chorus.

'I'm sorry I'm late,' she mouthed.

'Good to see you, luv. When you've got your breath back will you start us off with *As Long As He Needs Me?* Joyce can't make it tonight.'

Chris found the music and nodded to Brian that she was ready. The rehearsal went well. The break was spent considering the draft programme for the show. Fred was busy; a parishioner had nipped into the church hall to catch him about a christening. Chris and Fred had surreptitiously caught each other's eye but hadn't managed to speak.

'Thanks for stepping in Chris, you're a goodun,' Brian called across the hall as the choir pulled on their coats and made for home. 'It was a good rehearsal, thanks to you.'

Brian tidied away his music and shut the lid on the piano. John supervised the stacking of the chairs in the corner of the hall.

'Thank you, Brian and John, for a good night's work,' Fred said as he shrugged on his coat.

'I think our Elizabeth was looking for you,' said John as Chris carried the remaining chairs toward him. He nodded toward the ladies lavatory.

'What can that frown be about?' said Fred bending himself into the driving seat of his old Morris Minor.

'Something Elizabeth said. She's asked me to ring her tonight, even if it's late. I hope everything's all right. Maggie can be a bit off at times, I hope there's nothing wrong.'

'Oh dear, oh dear! I don't think anything is amiss at

the Smithfield residence. I think we've been rumbled. John came over, in a bit of a lather. He's asked to see me tomorrow lunchtime.'

'Rumbled. Oh, you mean …?'

Fred pulled into the side of the road, turned off the ignition, took hold of Chris's right hand, raised it to his lips and kissed it.

'I was planning something a little more romantic my darling, darling girl but, the thing is … Do you think you could possibly …? I know this is all very sudden. Chris, will you marry me?'

'Yes Fred, I will. I will, I will.'

They looked at each other, flabbergasted.

'Fred, we'd better get a move on, it's eleven o'clock now.'

The car kangarooed off from the side of the road. It was ten past eleven when they reached the home.

'I love you, my dearest Chris, but I don't want to push you into anything with this sudden declaration. But in my position, you know, the parish, the boys and everything …'

'Fred, I understand. I love … Ye Gods is that the night sister on her way back to the hospital?'

Chris leapt out of the car and ran after the cloaked figure.

'Sister, I'm really sorry but my boy er man … well he's just proposed.'

'At this time of night?'

Fred had followed Chris.

'This is my fault, Sister.'

'Yes, well, we'll let it go this time.' She turned back to the nurses' home, jangling the keys.

'Chris bent her head to say goodnight to Fred through the car window.

'Chris, put Elizabeth off. Whatever she says to you don't tell her about tonight. I need to see the Bishop before it gets out in the parish. I love you.'

'I love you too, good night.' Chris waved as Fred drove away.

'Very nice, very nice indeed Nurse, I must say. I'd confess my sins to him any day,' the sister said, pulling the door toward her and locking it.

Through a combination of swapped shifts, days off and missing supper to finish early, Theresa, Sarah, Jenny and Maggie with Elizabeth managed to meet for a meal at The Red Cat.

'I'm glad we're having a get together, and all that but where's the fire? It seems bloody strange to me, Chris ringing round, leaving messages and saying it's urgent. Do you think she's gone and jacked in her training?' Theresa said.

'She's here now,' said Sarah, peering toward the door. 'That's odd, it looks as though she's come with your vicar, Maggie.'

The girls twisted round and craned their necks as Chris and Fred made their way through the crowded pub and restaurant.

'Hello, can we make room for Fred as well?'

The girls shuffled round the large booth, casting questioning glances at each other.

What the bleedin' hell's going on?

'I don't know what to say now I'm here. I've been practising but well …' Chris and Fred glanced at each other. 'Fred has asked me to marry him.'

'Bloody hell fire, oops, sorry Father, I mean Vicar, sorry,' Theresa said.

As they laughed, the tension relaxed. After he had ordered a round of drinks, Fred made to leave. He wished them all a joyful and talkative evening. Theresa watched him bend to kiss Chris on the lips.

*She'll be another one traipsing off to Boots for the*

*sperm killing foam.* Theresa glanced round. *Put your face straight Maggie, you'd think you'd just emptied a pongy bed pan. Although, I bet he's older than our Dad. She's supposed to be freaked out by older men – well she's obviously got over that pretty quickly.*

'I'm sorry if I was pushy about us getting together but Fred's announcing our engagement to the parish tomorrow and I wanted you to know before the rest of the world gets hold of it.'

'My dad won't like it,' Maggie muttered.

'Shut up,' Elizabeth muttered back. 'Show us your ring again, Chris.'

# CHAPTER THIRTY-ONE

At the sound of her mum's footsteps on the stairs, Maggie thrust the envelope she'd been examining against the vase in the middle of the sideboard, and throwing herself onto the settee picked up the *Woman's Realm* and feigned interest.

'I could murder a cup of tea, trying to decipher your dad's handwriting doesn't get any easier,' she said as she stepped into the living room. 'I keep telling him he'll be forever in my debt. A bookkeeper would charge him a fortune.'

'Sit down Mum, I'll make the tea,' Maggie said, ignoring her mum's familiar complaint. She and her sister were well aware that their mother was the brains behind the decorating business. Her mum managed the house, the business and her dad with quiet efficiency. She was the rock that they all relied on.

'Is that a letter? Pass it across, Margaret.'

'It's for our Elizabeth.' Maggie handed the letter to her mother.

'It's franked Farnton Royal Infirmary.'

'Is it? I hadn't really noticed.'

Maggie watched as her mother peered inside the window of the envelope. She shook it and tipped it up and down then held it up to the light, in much the same way that Maggie had done earlier.

'I can see the date, it was written two days ago.'

'Was it really?' said Maggie.

'I hope she isn't poorly.'

'How can she be? You'd know about it. You always come to the doctor's with us.'

'Here Margaret, put it back on the sideboard, our Elizabeth's coming up the path.'

The tea forgotten, Maggie hovered behind her mother as she opened the front door.

'There's a letter for you, from the Infirmary. Is there anything wrong Elizabeth, anything I should know about?'

Maggie watched as Elizabeth took her time opening the letter. She read it, smiled and then handed it across to her mother.

'What is it, Mum? What's up?' said Maggie.

'I'll tell you what's up, our Margaret. From September there are going to be three nurse Smithfields but only one of them will have a moped.'

'I don't know what your dad's going to say,' said Mrs Smithfield. 'All I know is I need that cup of tea and a piece of cake. Do you two want a piece?'

'No, not for me, Mum. I told you, I'm on a diet.'

'You must be joking,' said Elizabeth.

'No, I'm not. I've started to lose weight anyway with being on my feet all the time, so I've decided I'm going to help it along and then get some new clothes.'

'I'll believe it when I see it.'

'You will see it, Elizabeth. I'll show the lot of you I'm not the daft kid you all think I am. Why you've applied to the Infirmary is beyond me.'

Maggie never felt comfortable at the Infirmary. She had a vague feeling of being a visitor, of not quite fitting in. Her discomfort was aggravated when permanent ward staff commented, 'Ah, you're from the General,' as though being from the other hospital explained a multitude of undisclosed sins. She counted the days to being back on the other side of town.

According to Maggie, you knew where you were at the General with the wards branching off the long, undulating main corridor. She felt hemmed in at the Infirmary. Apart from the two new male surgical wards opened in 1964, the remainder of the hospital was more or less a hundred years old with odd bits added here and there in a higgledy-piggledy fashion. Space for extending the hospital was limited on a site that was closely bounded by the large County Borough Park and two busy main roads. She thought Kershaw, the ear, nose and throat ward, was just about okay. It was saved from being classed as boring because of the work with children. Maggie was happy to spend time distracting the little boys and girls who were crying and distressed after being left in an alien environment with strangers who constantly reassured them that they were going to be all right. On the edges of Maggie's memory were pictures of herself sitting lost in a huge white bed crying for her mummy. She remembered enjoying the bowls of ice-cream fed to her to ease her sore throat.

Maggie watched her Dad savour a mouthful of crispy potato from the top of his Lancashire hotpot.

'If I ever need anything doing with my nose, believe me Dad, I won't be doing anything about it.' Maggie munched; the mingled flavours of the onion, potatoes, carrots and lamb soothing her and momentarily distracting her from the trials of her day. Fork and mouth empty, she continued. 'I was sent to watch a sub-mucous resection, they call it a SMR. It's when the surgeon chips away up the patient's nose with a chisel and toffee hammer and believe it or not – the patient is awake. Chip, chip, chip ooh it ...'

'Margaret, for pity's sake, do you think you could leave all the gory details until you girls are in the kitchen and doing the pots?'

'But Dad, you like us talking about work; he always says he does,' Maggie turned to her mother and sister. 'Doesn't he, Mum?'

'Yes John, you're always telling the girls you want to hear about what goes on at the nursery and the hospital.'

'What are you smiling at, Mum?' Elizabeth said.

'Nothing Elizabeth, nothing.'

'Elizabeth, Margaret, I am interested, you know I am. It's just that well ...'

'He's squeamish, your dad is squeamish. Aren't you, Dad?'

Maggie looked from her mum to her dad. Her mum was trying not to smile and her dad was looking at Mum with his eyes narrowed.

'So that when you, Margaret, talk about pressure sores or leg ulcers or different sorts of vomit and when you, Elizabeth, delight us with the content of babies nappies, it turns his stomach. Doesn't it, Dad? For my part I find it all very interesting. Did the poor man having his nose fixed complain of pain, Margaret?'

'Let's give up on bodily functions. The thought of having the two of you going on and on is enough to make me eat in the kitchen. I bet your friend Chris doesn't go on to the vicar like you do.'

'She isn't my friend. I keep telling you all; she isn't my friend.'

Theresa and Maggie were back at the General, allocated to six weeks in theatre. Theresa was not happy. She found the lack of natural light and the quietness of the theatres oppressive. Finding theatre clothes to fit her short curvy body was well-nigh impossible. The green theatre dresses that fitted around her bust dragged on the floor. She attempted to hoist up a dress using two old crepe bandages tied together and wrapped around her waist with a fetching bow at the front. The senior sister, an eccentric and excitable woman from somewhere that sound exotic and had a lot of vowels in its name, was not amused. Despite many of her instructions being difficult to follow due to her accented speech, further distorted by a thick cotton mask, Theresa was left in no doubt that her bastardisation of the dress was not acceptable. Cussing and swearing she climbed into the smallest pair of surgeons' green trousers she could find, rolled up the legs and tied her makeshift crepe belt around the waist, as tight as she could. She pulled a baggy green top over her head. A pair of white theatre wellies and a green cap completed her ensemble.

'I look a right bloody sight,' she said to Win when she bumped into her sister one lunchtime. 'It takes me forever to get in and out of that get up every time we're let loose to go to break or dinner.'

Picking up blood-soaked swabs from the floor or anywhere else the surgeon flung them and carefully placing them on the swab rack was not Theresa's idea of nursing. Being under the eye of the senior sister made her feel, and act, awkward and clumsy. When she created a racket and havoc by walking into a sterile trolley and knocking a pile of stainless steel bowls on the floor she was relegated to the scrub room, to wash down the tiled walls. Although this was meant as a punishment it was a blessed relief for Theresa who set about the task with gusto. She was on her own and to fill the eerie silence she started to sing.

Farnton General employed not only ward and departmental sisters, staff nurses, cleaners and laundry workers, house officers and registrars but also Great Men who scrutinised all other staff from their elevated positions on high. One such Great Man had particular skills in arterial surgery. The surgeon prided himself on being a cultured man. He enjoyed opera, the theatre and was well read. A particular sport he enjoyed was ridiculing those below him in the hospital pecking order. In short he thought he was the Archangel Gabriel if not God incarnate. When he was operating the tension in theatre was palpable.

Theresa's syncopated imitation of the combined voices of a backing group *bobbodywoddybeepban* caused The Great Man to freeze. He painstakingly lifted his neck and turned his head tortoise fashion to look daggers at the senior sister assisting him.

Theresa paused in her scrubbing.

What the bloody hell was that - sounds like somebody stood on a cat?

She didn't understand a word the theatre sister yelled at her from the door of the scrub room but comprehended that she was now relegated to the out-house. She found herself in the company of a sawn off leg that was destined for the incinerator, drip stands and other odds and ends. Undeterred, she scrubbed away singing to herself. Another gaffe and she'd be scrubbing the car park.

Maggie, like Theresa, had dreaded theatre but once she understood the expectations and routines she found the work interesting. She concentrated hard to understand the workings of the autoclave, used to sterilise instruments and dressings. One of the staff nurses helped her draw a diagram of the process of using the complicated machine, with its valves and pressure gauges. Maggie's interest was noted and rewarded. She was invited to scrub up on a regular basis, usually to help the registrar in general surgery. She spent most of her time retracting the contents of the abdominal cavity. As he progressed with the operations, the young, overseas surgeon explained to Maggie the interaction of the various organs and the process of the disease that had landed the patient in hospital. Maggie was staggered when she was invited to step into the sisters' office at the end of her theatre allocation, to read her report. The report told her she was meticulous and thorough and strongly recommended that she consider work in theatre when she completed her training. She showed it to the registrar. He was seen to put his arm round her and give her a squeeze.

Theresa's report was less flattering.

# CHAPTER THIRTY-TWO

'We've been run off our feet all day,' Chris said when she crossed paths with Jenny and Sarah as they stowed their handbags in Thorpe linen cupboard, and she collected hers. 'I'll see you next week, after your nights off,' she called to them as they made their way into the office to receive the day report.

The ward was full to overflowing with three beds down the middle of the main room of the three-roomed ward. Two or more of the day's admissions were expected to die within the next few hours. Jenny and Sarah divided up the early jobs. Jenny got on with the milky drinks round while Sarah set about the hourly observations. Then, working together, they settled the patients for the night: giving bottles and bedpans, ensuring that false teeth were removed and in plastic cups and that sputum mugs were placed close to hand, drips monitored and cot sides in place.

They checked the more poorly patients as they scurried about their duties. The patient nearest the office was labouring with Cheyne Stokes breathing, signalling that he was very near the end of his life. Sarah and Jenny gently washed his face and tidied his bed. They pulled the screens round his bed so that he was shielded from the rest of the darkened ward. His relatives who had seen him at visiting time had chosen not to sit with him in his final hours. As his efforts to breath became more tortuous Sarah drew up a chair and sat with him as he took his final breaths.

'I'll contact the relatives and let them know about the death, then I'll see what I can do for Mr Murphy, his breathing is really strident,' said Sarah.

'Let me know if you need any help,' Jenny said.

Sarah made her way to one of the beds in the middle of the ward; Mr Murphy was gasping for breath, his arms stretched out grasping his bed table for support as he fought for air. His laboured breath was a mixture of shrill whistling and bird-like sounds. He gave Sarah a puzzled look.

'Please – little – girl – fetch – me – a – nurse,' he gasped.

'Try not to speak Mr Murphy, I am a nurse and I'm going to try and make you more comfortable.'

Sarah took two of the pillows from behind him and arranged them under his arms so that he could lean more comfortably on the bed table. He hugged the pillows and then settled his head against them. When Sarah arrived with folding screens to give him more privacy he lifted his head.

'Don't – bother – with – them – fancy – things.'

'I'm going to give you something to help with your breathing, Mr Murphy.'

'Thank Christ.'

'I need you to try and help me. I want you lie back and roll on your side,' Sarah eased the bed table from under his arms, 'and then I'm going to give you a suppository to help your breathing.'

'Are – you – bleedin' – stupid – little – girl? It's – my – chest – as – is – bad – not – my – arse.'

'Please trust me, Mr Murphy. I know it might sound daft but I promise it will work.'

With great difficulty Mr Murphy turned on his side gasping and cursing. Sarah inserted the bronchial-dilating suppository as high as she could in his rectum. She helped him roll back and resettle himself across the bed table.

When Sarah emerged from helping Jenny lay out the patient near the office she noticed Mr Murphy straightening up, his breathing less laboured. She rearranged his pillows against the backrest. He lay back slowly and closed his eyes.

Of the eight deaths that night, three of the patients who were on the ward at the start of the night duty died. Four of the six patients transferred from Casualty died within an hour of admission to Thorpe. Jenny and Sarah managed the ward together; there was no extra help or support, not even a night sisters' ward round. They were both too busy in Casualty.

'The miserable cow, fancy asking why we'd not set the tables for breakfast. All that she's good for is doing the flowers and smiling at visitors and not much else,' said Sarah, pulling a face at the back of an immaculately turned out third year nurse retreating up the ward.

'Come on, Mr Murphy's little angel, let's go and get some breakfast,' said Jenny.

Bone weary after her week on nights, Sarah dragged herself out of the now tepid bath water, dried herself and, resisting the lure of her bed, pulled on slacks and a jumper. She folded the clothes she would need for her five nights off, into her tote bag, pulled on her coat, and set off to trudge through Farnton's deserted Sunday streets to catch the bus to Stonelee.

When she stepped down from the bus she glanced up

the street toward her home.

That's odd. Where's my mum?

She dropped her bag on the pavement, checked her watch and looked down the street again. Although she resented her mother's usual stake out at the door, it was strange to arrive home and not be met. She let herself in the house, shoved the front door closed with her foot, then plonked her bag at the bottom of the stairs.

'I'm home, Mum. Where are you?' Sarah said.

'In the kitchen.'

Her mother sounded weary.

'What's wrong, Mum? Are you poorly?' Sarah said as she made her way from the hall toward the kitchen. 'Has something happened?'

Sarah and her mother had never been ones to embrace when they met. Quiet politeness ruled the house. When her mother turned from the sink to face her, potato peeler in one hand and potato in the other, Sarah saw disappointment and distaste play across her mother's face. Her mother had been crying, and for a long time. She looked like the grieving relatives at the hospital, the ones who kept the long bedside vigils.

'Yes, something has happened, something truly dreadful.' Mrs Green turned back to the sink.

'What? What is it?'

'Sarah? Sarah,' her mother turned from looking out of the kitchen window, 'how could you; after all I've done to try and help you?' Mrs Green reached into her pocket and pulled out a saturated handkerchief to dab away the tears set to add to the stains on her mottled face.

'Mum, I've no idea what you're talking about. What is it – what's upset you?'

Reaching into the drawer of the kitchenette Mrs Green pulled out a small pouch and held it out, her hands shaking.

Shit, Sarah thought. 'My Emko; I've been looking all over for that,' she reached out to take the pouch from her mother.

'How could you, Sarah? How could you?'

*I'm in for it now, good and proper. God, if you really do exist, help me, please.* Sarah's thoughts tumbled over each other as conflicting emotions raged. She pushed away a bubbling laugh as she blinked away tears. She longed for the cocoon darkness of her childhood refuge – the under-stairs cupboard.

'I'll put the kettle on,' she said. 'Why don't you go and sit down in the front room, Mum? I'll bring a tray through.'

A fresh stream of tears stalled further conversation. Mrs Green rubbed her face and dusted the tip of her dripping nose with the bottom of her apron. She tentatively gathered herself and headed for the front room.

'I blame myself, you know, for everything,' Mrs Green said.

'I don't understand, Mum,' Sarah handed her mother a cup and saucer. 'What do you mean – what are you talking about?'

'I've never told you this before Sarah, but it's my fault your father had that terrible accident, and now this. It's all my fault, all my fault.'

'Mum, I don't understand. How can Father's death have been your fault, it happened at the factory; it was an accident.'

'We should never have married. *I should never have married.*'

Jesus Christ! What's she going to tell me? Surely she's not queer, like Jenny's dad.

'Everybody expected it, you see. We'd been brought up together; we were related – distantly, like most folk in Stonelee. We'd played together in the fields and woods surrounding the village. We were in the church choir, the girls' and boys' brigades – all the village children were. It's what was expected. We did what was expected of us.'

'You keep saying that, Mum – about things being expected.'

'It's how it is – was. Your father proposed, I accepted. We were married, the church was full, the village turned out to watch the service. Then he was dead, and it was my fault.'

'But why was it your fault, Mum? I don't understand. What are you trying to tell me?' And what the bloody hell has it got to do with my Emko? Sarah thought.

Sarah watched her mother twist her wedding ring round and round her finger. She saw a deep blush suffuse her mother's face and neck.

'It was … It was the personal side of being together – being married.' She covered her face with her hands and rocked backwards and forwards. Racking sobs shook her body.

Sarah reached out to touch her mother, hesitated, unsure; she reached out again and awkwardly pulled her mother to her. They wept huddled together on the small settee.

'Are you saying you didn't like going to bed?' Sarah mumbled into her mother's hair.

'Yes.' Mrs Green raised her head and straightened up. 'It shocked me, frightened me. I hated it, felt it was dirty. I pushed your father away from me – forever. We never talked about it, me not wanting all that touching, that prodding. He was my friend, I trusted him – like a brother. He was kind and thoughtful, he moved into the back bedroom after that first night. Two months later I told him you were on the way. Three days later he was dead. Oh, I know they said it was the factory's fault, but I know…'

Sarah tentatively took her mother's hand.

'When you were born,' she held tight to Sarah's hand, 'I knew what it was to fall in love.' As tears fell onto their clasped hands, Sarah threw her arms around her mother's neck.

'Mum, there's something burning.'

'The chicken!'

They leapt up, dashed into the kitchen to find the oven belching smoke. Sarah grabbed a tea towel.

'Open the oven door, Mum.'

Sarah reached inside the oven, grabbed the roasting tin then threw it in the sink and turned on the cold water tap.

'Leave all this mess. Take two paracetamol and go and put your feet up. I'll let the smoke settle and then set to.'

'No, we'll do it together, after we've had another cup of tea.'

'Let's have a glass of sherry and leave the mess,' said Sarah.

'Sherry!'

'Yes, come on. Who's to know?'

Sarah wanted to ease her mother's discomfort yet at the same time she wanted to clarify the whirl of images and words that were fizzing and crackling round her head.

'Why did you always want me to be doing things – at church with the vicar and Mrs Evans, in the guides and at Sunday school?'

'I felt I owed it to Harold, to your father. It's difficult to explain. I didn't want you to be ordinary. I wanted you to have a good life with nice friends. I didn't want everybody to know all your business.'

'I have good friends, from school and at the hospital.'

'I know that dear, but it's my fault you see that you need that … that …'

'Birth control?'

Mrs Green took a swig of her sherry.

'Yes, dear. As I said, if I hadn't pushed you into training at the Infirmary you wouldn't have met Paul and he wouldn't be doing those things to you – before you were married.'

Sarah topped up the sherry glasses.

'We do them together, Mum.'

'As you like, dear. It's just that I expected you to be a vir… never mind. I'm feeling a little bit over-wrought.' She drained her glass. 'I think I will put my feet up, I feel a little woozy.' It took two or three attempts for Mrs Green to rise from the settee.

'That's fine, Mum. I'll come to evensong, if that's all right with you.' *I owe you one God.* Sarah cast her eyes toward the ceiling.

'That would be lovely dear. Oh, and, Sarah.'

'Yes, Mum.'

'The Reverend Evans says you can still have wreath and veil when you get married.'

Sarah sighed deeply.

'Go and lie down, Mum. I'll give you a shout when I've cleared up in the kitchen. We can have egg and chips for our tea.'

# CHAPTER THIRTY-THREE

Jenny stood at the Green's front door and waved until Dave's car had turned the corner by the Co-op. She stepped into the house and was immediately drawn into the preparations for her hen night.

Sarah was wandering about with a tea towel and a sherry glass, Maggie was spearing pineapple chunks and silver skin onions onto cocktail sticks and stabbing them into half an upturned grapefruit. Elizabeth was shaking a tea-towel to the beat of *Two For Tea and Tea For Two*. Theresa was slapping boiled ham onto uneven slices of a Hovis loaf.

'Where are your mum and Chris?' Jenny said, looking around.

'Mum's whisked Chris off to meet the vicar and Mrs Evans. Shift over Maggie, I need to get to the draining board to reach another glass.'

'Is there anything I can do?' said Jenny.

'No, this is your party. Why not take your case upstairs?' said Sarah.

Sarah and Jenny had insisted that Mrs Green join

them for the party rather than letting her follow her suggestion of reading upstairs. Initially the jokes and conversation were tempered by her presence. Inhibitions evaporated in inverse proportion to the amount of Babycham, Cherry B, cider and sherry drunk.

Jenny glanced at her watch.

'I want to say something, to say thank you, first of all, to Mrs Green. Sarah, please pass my handbag.' Jenny took the bag, reached inside and pulled out a small, expertly wrapped parcel. 'Mrs Green, you have been so very kind to me. Granny says you are my fairy godmother, making my and Sarah's dresses, giving me this lovely party and letting me be married from your home. Why do we cry when we are happy?' She gulped and paused to gather herself. 'Granny and I would like you to have this little gift.' Jenny strode over Theresa, sitting on the floor, to reach Mrs Green sitting queen-like on the settee next to Sarah. She bent and kissed her fairy godmother on the cheek.

'Thank you, dear. Thank you so much.'

'Open it, Mum.'

Mrs Green carefully undid the ribbon and rolled it up. She slid her finger under the sellotape and eased off the paper.

'Just rip it off, Mrs Green,' said Theresa.

'What is it, Mum?'

'The most beautiful cameo brooch. I don't know what to say.'

'Don't cry, Mrs Green. Granny chose it.'

'Is that it Jen, speech over?'

'No, Theresa. I need to thank all of you for, for being my friends. I don't know what I would do without you.'

'No presents for us then?'

'Come on, time to clear up,' said Sarah. 'Fred will be here any minute.'

'I do hope he'll have time for a cup of tea and a slice

of cake,' said Mrs Green, carefully closing the lid on her gift and holding it to her chest.

The young hairdresser tied the tapes at the back of Jenny's gown.

'Are you and your friend going somewhere nice?'

'Yes, to my wedding.' Jenny looked through the mirror toward Sarah flicking through a magazine. 'Sarah is my bridesmaid.'

Jenny enjoyed the feel of the hairdresser's strong hands massaging her head and coaxing the shampoo and conditioner into her tight curls. The worries she'd had about the wedding – being given away, where she would be married from, and not having guests on her side, seemed ages ago. Granny Ashford had been fabulous. She'd arrived at the Crown and Mitre on Wednesday and majestically assumed control of the final preparations. Visiting the dress on Thursday she declared to Mrs Green 'it is one of the finest wedding dresses I have ever seen, fit for the daughter of any member of the aristocracy'. She had read and approved the description of the dress Sarah had helped her mum compose for the local paper.

The bride wore a long sleeve, empire line dress, in satin, with an elegant train extending from the hem. The matching pill-box hat held a short pouf veil.

The dinner at the Crown and Mitre on Thursday night that Granny Ashford had insisted on giving for Dave and his mum and dad, young Brian, and Sarah and her mum had been great. Jenny had given her mother, and her little brothers, a fleeting thought that she quickly dismissed.

Jenny and Sarah paid the hairdresser then made their way to the bus stop to catch the bus to Stonelee. In three and a half hours she would be Mrs David Smithfield.

Fred indicated to the congregation that they should stand to welcome the bride. The rich soaring sound of Wagner's *Wedding March* from *Lohengrin* heralded the arrival of Jenny on the arm of her stately and gracious granny.

Jenny and Dave exchanged their vows. Jenny happy and relaxed, Dave nervous but gathering composure as the service progressed. As the new Mr and Mrs Smithfield made their way to the vestry to sign the register The Trinity Players left their seats on the bride's side of the church and formed a choir on the chancel steps. Brian had coached them well. The clarity of their rendering of Bach's *Jesu Joy of Man's Desiring* and Thomas Tallis's *If You Love Me Keep My Commandments* filled the church with glorious sounds. As the choir filed back to their seats Brian's assistant organist concluded the music for the singing of the register with *Air on a G string.* The vestry door opened and the *Wedding March* from Mendelssohn's *Midsummer Night's Dream* rang out. The wedding party made their way down the aisle and out into the early autumn sunshine. The photographer later commented to Granny Ashford that 'it's one of the happiest weddings I've been to in a long time.'

Paul and young Brian took charge of decorating Dave's car with empty tin cans, old shoes and balloons. Theresa helped by scrawling 'Just Married' on the back window with her lipstick.

Jenny emerged from the doors of the Crown and Mitre dressed in her going away outfit. She slid into the passenger seat, and after much kissing and many good luck wishes the couple finally drove away.

Glancing at Dave when he climbed back into the car after relieving it of its decorations, she was taken aback at the sight of a terrible rash on his face. On closer inspection it was lipstick deposited by their lady wedding guests.

It would take Jenny and Dave an hour to get to Knott End and their honeymoon.

# CHAPTER THIRTY-FOUR

Jenny kissed her husband goodbye and slid out of the car to make her way to the revolving doors at the entrance to the Infirmary. It was the first day of her theatre placement and her first day as a non-residential student nurse. It seemed ages since she'd last climbed up to the attic changing rooms as a cadet. Everything had changed; she was married, with a home of her own, she had a husband who loved her and friends who cared about her, she belonged, she was happy.

She swung her laundry bag onto the battered dressing table that sat under the grimy attic window and glanced around.

Ye Gods, I've not been allocated a locker, she thought as she hurriedly scanned the names on the green metal cupboards. I'm going to have to lug my coat and laundry bag to theatre with me.

'Hi Jenny, let's have a look at your ring.'

A bus load of living out students had arrived and set about the routine of putting on caps and aprons.

Jenny smiled and held out her left hand. Smithfield,

you twerp, not Hayes she thought. She cast around again and there, by the door, was a locker labelled 'J Smithfield'. Locker doors banged shut and padlocks snapped into place as the nurses on the early shift made their way, nattering and laughing, to report for duty.

'Wait for me, you two,' Jenny called to Chris and Sarah when she caught sight of them ahead of her in the corridor.

Chris stood on one side as Mrs Ashton, a state enrolled nurse, and Agnes, an auxiliary nurse, who staffed the 'middle rooms' of the theatre suite, greeted Jenny and Sarah with hugs.

'Two of our favourite cadets back with us. How grown up you both are,' said Mrs Ashton.

'Jenny's married now.' Sarah turned to her friend smiling.

'Well I never, when did all this happen?' said Agnes.

'Two weeks ago, I'll tell you all about it later – this is our friend Chris,' said Jenny.

'I'm sorry my dear, I didn't mean to leave you out but we enjoy seeing our cadets come back to us, well most of them. These two, well they were two of the best, even if they were always up to something,' said Mrs Ashton, smiling proprietorially.

Mrs Ashton and Agnes relied on cadets to support them with the mundane tasks of background theatre work: washing bloody gloves and mackintoshes, folding theatre clothes on their return from the laundry, packing drums with linen prior to sterilization and ensuring each surgeon and anaesthetist had the correct clothes and footwear.

Making 'tonsil bobs' had been Jenny's favourite afternoon job. Observing the white balls being used to stem the bleeding during the Saturday morning tonsillectomy operations, when cadets were used as 'runners' had made her feel she was doing more than marking time until she started her nurse training.

The theatre technician, wandering down the corridor in search of his morning coffee, joined in the bonhomie, telling Chris that it seemed only yesterday that he'd caught Jenny and her pals playing hide and seek behind the cupboards in the middle rooms and now here she was a married woman. Seeing Chris smiling he told her that Sarah had been no better. She'd experimented by holding a theatre glove under a tap in the wet room to see how much water it would hold before it burst.

'It took her ages to mop up when it exploded away from the tap, and she was wet through,' he said.

'Agnes, you're a pal,' said Sarah as two small sized dresses were handed to her.

'Jenny, you and your friend – Chris, isn't it – shouldn't have any trouble finding something to fit.'

'No, we'll be fine, Agnes. Come on Chris, I'll get you kitted out,' said Jenny leading Chris to the glass cupboard piled high with green dresses, trousers and tops.

'Yes, you'd best get a move on and report to the staff nurses. There'll be bother if you're still in your uniform dresses and caps when the sisters arrive,' said Mrs Ashton.

Theatre meant regular days with more frequent time off at weekends. Other than the tonsillectomy sessions on Saturday mornings, working weekends meant cleaning. The glass cabinets containing theatre instruments were emptied each week and washed out; the instruments carefully replaced in their allotted positions. The theatre tables and trolleys were disinfected; dressing packs were sterilized and stacked ready for the following week.

The theatre sisters were usually off duty over the weekend with staff nurses working to supervise the rigorous cleaning routines. The staff nurses had all qualified within the last year or two and while they were committed to maintaining high standards of cleanliness they were not averse to longer than usual breaks and catching up on gossip. The only dampener was that Matron, who had at one time been a theatre sister, had a tendency to pop in over the weekend to test the student nurses knowledge of the working of the autoclave. She was particularly keen on scrutinising headgear, on the look-out for rollers under theatre caps.

For Jenny the regular days on theatre at the start of her new, dual life as a wife with household responsibilities and a student nurse were a blessing. She quickly worked out a routine to manage the washing, ironing and cleaning. She delighted in wandering round the terraced house, standing in the doorway of each room then touching furniture, straightening cushions and tweaking curtains. She studiously read the manuals for the electrical appliances given to them as wedding presents. Granny Ashford had asked Jenny and Dave to choose between a washing machine and a refrigerator. A fridge didn't seem essential. The milkman delivered fresh milk early each morning; they both ate a main meal at work and made do with a substantial snack the evenings they were at home together. Jenny had mastered the eight-programme Hoover Keymatic. Even though the large machine took up more than its share of space in the small lean-to kitchen it had quickly become legend among the Smithfield women. Miffy had visited with a pillowcase full of washing to watch it work its magic without interference from Jenny or herself. The Kenwood Chef Mixer had yet to come into its own. Its inaugural use was planned for Sunday lunch, to say goodbye to young Brian before he set off to join his ship.

From the kitchen, Jenny heard Dave's key in the front door.

'Jenny, love, I'm home.'

Jenny appeared in the front room carrying a tray holding two mugs of Ovaltine and a biscuit barrel.

'I've missed you,' she said to a beaming Dave as he took the tray from her and lowered it to the floor.

'Come here, and let me look at you,' he said.

'Come on, the Ovaltine will be cold,' said Jenny with a deep sigh as she recovered from the reunion with her husband, who she hadn't seen for four hours.

'How was college?'

Dave picked up his mug and settled back into the settee.

'There's something we need to talk about,' he grinned.

'Mmm. It sounds like good news from the smile, but you're touching the side of your nose.'

'Am I?'

'Never mind – tell me, tell me. Who was it, what did they want?'

'Mr Brown, the head of department. He asked if I could spare a minute or two.'

'Is he like – the same as a matron?'

'No, that would be the principal. Anyway, to cut a long story short – he's asked me to apply for a full-time job.'

'I don't understand.'

'My old lecturer isn't coming back. The senior lecturer in the department has put in a good word for me and they want me to apply for the job when it's advertised internally – they think I'll be the only candidate. What do you think?'

'It's up to you of course, but I'm really proud of you. What are you going to do?'

'I've not stopped thinking about it. I only took the part-time job because of that bastard, George, but now, well, what a turn up. I expected to be at the engineering works for the rest of my life. I'm tempted, I really am, but it takes me ages to prepare two lessons a week. I was so nervous I told Mr Brown I wasn't sure I'd cope with preparing lessons for twenty or more hours a week. He was great, said he'd felt exactly the same when he first started teaching. He's suggested I go in during the day and talk to one of the full timers before I make my decision. I'm going in tomorrow – at lunchtime. Mr Brown is going to set me up to talk to a bloke who started in the department at the start of term.'

'We'd better be off to bed then, you'll need to get a good night's sleep,' said Jenny, looking saucily over her shoulder as she took the tray into the kitchen.

# CHAPTER THIRTY-FIVE

'What on earth made you apply to the Infirmary?' Theresa said to Elizabeth as they took their places at the tea table.

Theresa and Maggie had spent the afternoon in Farnton, trying on in Richard Shops and examining the new food section in Marks and Spencer. They'd had Horlicks and toasted teacakes at the Left Bank and then made their way to the Smithfields' for their tea.

'I didn't fancy you two bossing me about.'

'Us? Boss anybody about? Wait till you get to the Infirmary,' said Theresa with a smug nod. 'They keep their eye on you there. Matron sees you after every placement and the home sister checks your skirt lengths and the colour of your knickers if she passes you in the corridor.'

'You're kidding?'

'Just you wait and see,' said Maggie, nodding in unison with Theresa.

'Girls, girls, let's not talk about underwear at the table.'

'Sorry, Mr Smithfield. Did you enjoy the wedding?'

'Yes, luv, it were grand. Mrs Ashford did 'em proud; she can't be short of a bob or two.'

'Was that nervy looking woman in the front pew Jenny's mum?' Theresa said.

'Our Brian said it was when I asked him the same question.'

'Why did she leave the service when they went up to sign the register?' said Maggie.

'Summat or other to do with her husband not being invited, that is according to our Brian.'

As the three girls tackled the washing up they were free to share their views on Chris and Fred. Maggie and Elizabeth were careful not to say too much in front of their dad. They were well aware of his role in the church and his quasi-professional relationship with the vicar. Snores from the front room meant they were clear to gossip. However, Chris and Fred as a topic were soon exhausted and they moved on to Esther and Tommy.

Theresa was full of admiration for her brother and his wife. Esther had turned out to be bold and determined. She'd organised a secret flit from her parents. She and Tommy now lived over a butcher's. She was a student at the college and working part time at the butchers. The butcher's wife was something big in the darts league and was glad of a bit of time out of the shop.

'My mum's dead chuffed with Esther. She says she's making a man out of our Tommy and the off cuts of meat that the butcher says are "nowt but scrap" come in handy as well.'

'Does she still want to be a librarian?' Maggie said.

'Does she hell as like, she never did, it was all her dad's idea. She's got it all worked out; about how she can work in a solicitor's office and get qualifications.'

'What's her dad had to say about that? There was plenty said here, when our dad knew I was starting nursing,' Elizabeth said.

'He's tried to get his two penneth in but they've stood up to him. He waylaid our Tommy at the factory gates but Tommy said he let him rant on and then said "excuse me; my wife will be expecting me".'

'Gosh, that was brave,' said Elizabeth.

'He said he was shit scared and still shaking when he got home. I'll tell you what though, they've fallen on their feet with that butcher and his wife. That dad of Esther's barged in the shop shouting the odds and the butcher's wife stood up to him. She called him a "sanctimonious old sod" and told him to "bugger off" or she would be taking a "cleaver to his balls". Esther only saw the tail end of him. She'd been in the back shop washing the meat trays when she heard the commotion. All that was a fortnight ago and they haven't heard from him since.'

'Are they all right together, Tommy and Esther – getting on okay?' said Elizabeth.

'They're fine, holding hands all the time and kissing – makes you sick,' Theresa said, smiling.

'We're like three old maids; left on the shelf,' said Elizabeth.

'Yes, we'll probably end up living together like Matron and Sister Turnham,' said Maggie.

'I don't think so,' said Theresa, curling her lip and looking sideways at Maggie, 'they're lesbians.'

'Lesbian? What's a lesbian?'

Maggie turned the back door handle but the door wouldn't budge. She stepped back, stared at the door and tried again – it was always unlocked when she got home. Where was her mum? She went round to the front and rooted around at the bottom of her bag for her key. It was in there somewhere. She lifted her folders of notes out of her bag and plonked them on the doorstep. Where was the key? Finally she found it tucked in a redundant Mars Bar wrapper.

'Mum! Mum!' She looked in the front room. No sign. 'Mum!' In the kitchen she was disturbed to find the mixing bowl containing crumbled flour and lard and a puddle of water.

'Why's the front door wide open?' Elizabeth said, appearing behind Maggie in the kitchen. 'Where's Mum?'

'She's not here, something must have happened.'

'Did she leave the door open?'

'No, that was me.' Maggie, followed by Elizabeth, moved to into the hall to shut the door. 'Her coat's gone.'

'I'll get it.' Elizabeth turned to pick up the ringing phone from the hall table. 'Dave, what's up? Our Margaret? She's here. What's happened? Grandma! No, no, she can't be, here talk to Margaret.' Elizabeth held out the phone to Maggie and slumped down on the bottom stair.

'Dave! No, no, okay, we'll see you in quarter of an hour or so.' Maggie's hands shook as she attempted to place the phone back on its cradle. 'Shove up.' The sisters held each other and sobbed.

Maggie thought her legs would give way as she straightened up after scrambling out of the back of Dave's car. 'Come on, Thorpe's this way.' She led the way into the hospital, through the revolving doors and down the corridor. They were forced to slow their pace and follow the smell of the evening meal wafting out of the food trolley being pushed to the ward by a porter. At the ward door Maggie led her sister and cousin and dogged round the trolley.

'Is it all right for us to see our grandma? This is my sister and my cousin,' Maggie said to the sister who had emerged from the kitchen.

'Yes, of course. Are you from the General? I don't think I know you,' said the sister glancing at Maggie who was still dressed in her outdoor uniform. The sister indicated to the staff nurse to carry on serving suppers. 'Come into the office. What year are you?'

'Second year, Sister.'

Maggie took the proffered chair while Elizabeth and Dave stood awkwardly.

'Well then, Nurse Smithfield, as a second year I am sure you are aware of the implications of a myocardial infarction for a lady of Mrs Smithfield's age and overall medical condition. I am sure I have no need to tell you that your grandmother is gravely ill.' As tears welled in Maggie's eyes the sister looked at Elizabeth and Dave. 'You must expect your grandma to die within the next hour or so. I'll go and tell the Mr Smithfields that you are here. Last time I looked in on Mrs Smithfield she was able to understand who was with her, so try and be composed when you see her.'

Seeing the sadness and strain on the faces of her dad and uncle brought Maggie up short. It was true then, how could it be? How could her grandma die? She heard a sob and looking round realised it had come from herself.

'Mum, it's the children. Our Dave, with Elizabeth and Margaret,' Brian said softly to the tiny figure. She was very still and her eyes were closed.

Oh God, she's gone already, thought Maggie, clenching her fists.

As her Grandma's eyes flickered and then opened momentarily, Maggie's dad stood up.

'Come on Brian, let the children have a minute with Mam while we stretch our legs.'

'Hello Grandma, it's Margaret. Grandma, don't leave me …' Maggie choked on her whispered words. She stroked her Grandma's face and bent to kiss her. Elizabeth and Dave followed her example and bent to kiss their grandma.

Unable to stay away for long the two brothers returned to their mother's bedside and exchanged places with their children. As she made way for her dad to sit down Maggie heard the change in her grandma's breathing. Touching Elizabeth's arm and looking at her cousin she indicated that they should leave the bedside.

'I don't think it will be long, Sister,' Maggie said to the ward sister who was bringing the young houseman up to date in her office.

'Your mothers are waiting in the relatives' room. Why don't you join them and I'll send some tea down for you all.'

'I'm so sorry,' the houseman spluttered as the five faces turned toward him, 'the two Mr Smithfields are with their mother. I'm sure they'll be with you very soon.'


In the days following her Grandma's death, Maggie found the process of preparing to dispose of her grandma's body appalling. She left the front room in distress during the family's discussions with the undertaker. The need to choose the wood for the coffin, the coffin handles and the inscription for the small plaque was bad enough, but when the undertaker made suggestions based on how quickly the coffin would burn she was overcome. Before the undertaker had arrived Maggie had begged her dad and uncle to have her grandma buried. The thought of her grandma being destroyed by fire was intolerable.

As the family gathered for the funeral in the front room of her grandma's little bungalow Maggie reluctantly let her mum persuade her to go and say goodbye to her grandma who was lying in the open coffin in her bedroom. Pushing open the door Maggie was confronted by a plastic-looking version of her grandma lying with her hands folded across her chest. She backed out of the room stunned. When she had rejoined the rest of her family the undertaker respectfully knocked on the front room door. He glanced at the brothers.

'Should Mrs Smithfield's wedding ring be removed from her fingers before the lid is placed on the coffin?'

'No, Dad, no. Please no,' said Maggie, grabbing her dad's arm. 'She's never taken it off, not since the day Granddad put it there on their wedding day.'

'Please, give us a minute,' said Brian to the undertakers. Once they had absented themselves Brian put his arm around Maggie. 'What do you think will happen to grandma's ring if we leave it on her finger, love? I'm sure the men are honest enough but, less said, eh?'

Maggie nodded.

The service, conducted by the Reverend Fred in the familiar church, quietened Maggie's flickering thoughts. The committal at the crematorium was another matter. As the coffin began to slide slowly away and the curtains to glide silently around it she grasped her dad's hand. His answering squeeze saved her.

'Good-bye, Mum. God bless,' Maggie heard him whisper.

It had been the worst five days of her life.

# CHAPTER THIRTY-SIX

'I had nits when I was at primary school,' said Sarah. 'My mum went bonkers.'

'It's news in our house when one of the little uns doesn't have nits. There are so many kids in the classes at St Joe's the lice are on one long picnic. My mum's an expert with the nit comb, she squeezes the little buggers between her thumbnails, until they click, then she's sure they are good and dead.'

Theresa was relieved that the health visitor had emphasised that lice preferred clean heads. She joked about her family and their poverty but she was ashamed of her home. The vague smell of stale urine and fried food lingered despite her mum's valiant efforts with hot water and cheap bleach. Theresa's admiration for her parents and the battle they had to keep the home together and the children reasonably clean was soiled by her fear of being judged as disadvantaged – a poor Catholic family. Her friends would never be invited to visit – she envied Maggie and Sarah their clean, comfortable homes. Jenny and Paul's backgrounds overawed her, they were the type of people she had never expected to have as friends. How long would they remain her friends if they saw where she lived?

The health visitor and district nurse talks in preparation for the week 'on the district' had been lively and sometimes funny. The district nurse's apocryphal story of visiting an elderly man with chronic bronchitis who refused hospital treatment amused her audience. She enjoyed her visits, to check his condition and encourage him to eat nourishing foods and keep warm. He talked about his work in the coal mines and his love of choral music while they had a cup of tea. He insisted on offering her Brazil nuts; she accepted them, grateful for the snack. After several visits of indulging herself she protested that he should eat them himself – they would be good for him. He reassured her that she could have as many as she wanted. He didn't want them once he'd sucked the chocolate off.

The allocations to the Civic Centre in Farnton County Borough and to clinics in Lancashire County had been made, with arrangements for the initial meeting between the student nurses and their district nurse and health visitor colleagues sorted for the Monday morning.

'I hear you're with my mum next week,' Paul said to Theresa when he was sure he would be heard.

It was Saturday night and the Red Cat was full. The party of nine contributed their share to the volume.

'Yes, I'm looking forward to it,' said Theresa, attempting a sincere smile. 'Really looking forward to it.'

'Jenny has asked me to propose a toast,' said Fred, glancing round the table. 'To Dave, and his new career.'

'To Dave, and his new career.' Eight glasses were raised in salutation.

Dave leant over and kissed his wife on the cheek and then thanked them all for their best wishes and support.

Paul reached under the table and pulled out a large rectangular parcel.

'From all of us,' he said, stretching over Jenny to pass the gift to Dave.

'I never thought I'd own a brief case,' said Dave. 'Thank you everyone, thank you.'

'And now you own two,' Paul heard Jenny whisper. 'You can use it alternately with the one your mum and dad gave you yesterday.'

'Oh shit, that's my fault,' Paul muttered to Sarah. 'I should have listened to you when you suggested a pen and pencil set.'

Sarah smiled, Paul's voice drowned out by the background din.

'You look like a drowned rat,' said Theresa as she opened the door of Jenny's home and stood aside to let Sarah step into the small vestibule.

The rain was sluicing down. Theresa quickly pushed the front door closed and relieved Sarah of the useless umbrella she was carrying.

'This has seen its last downpour,' holding the dripping umbrella at arms-length, Theresa made to make her way into the kitchen. 'I'll chuck it in the bin when it stops raining.'

'No, don't. Let's wait until it's dry and see if we can bend it back the right way round. Miss Hines lent it to me and I have the feeling she's a bit of a stickler for doing-the-right-thing. I want to return it even though it might be fatally ill, if not dead.' She shrugged off her sodden uniform mac. 'What should I do with this, Jen?'

'Hang it on that peg on the back door.' Jenny carried on rolling pastry. 'Theresa, put that newspaper underneath it, to catch the drips.'

'Great, potato pie, just what I need to get warm.'

'You're soaked. Why don't you go upstairs, get out of those clothes and put on my dressing gown. I've just switched the immersion on, if you wait ten minutes or so you can have a nice hot bath.'

While Sarah was getting undressed she heard Chris and then Maggie arrive. Dave had his evening class so Jenny had suggested that she make tea for them all. She'd cooked the beef skirt and onions the previous evening as well as soaking the dried peas in boiling water with a teaspoon of bicarbonate of soda. The potatoes had been peeled that morning before she left to meet the health visitor she was shadowing. The pastry was now under way. She was in her own home, entertaining her friends and loving every minute of it.

'Maggie, why don't you put the kettle on and we'll have a cup of tea while we wait for Sarah,' said Jenny.

'This dressing gown drowns me,' said Sarah, curling up on the settee. 'Am I the only one walking?'

She was; the others were being driven around Lancashire and Farnton in an assortment of cars owned by the health visitors and district nurses they were with.

'I've been soaked all day. Not only does Miss Hines walk very slowly, she's about ten feet tall so her umbrella didn't protect me at all. She only decided to lend me that useless old thing this afternoon when we called in the Civic Centre to pick up a set of notes.'

Jenny heaped the dinner plates with pie and peas and they all tucked in. An unusual quiet settled over the kitchen table.

'Who taught you to cook, Jen?' Theresa said.

'Well, I suppose I learned from watching my mother cook for dinner parties, and the daily help cook the suppers for me and my brothers, but it was Miffy who showed me how to make potato pie. She says I've got to be taught all the Smithfield family recipes – sage and onion stuffing, flat cakes, Lancashire hotpot, and loads of others.'

'You are a bloody good cook if this is anything to go

by,' Theresa said, as she patted her abdomen. *That's what I've got to do now, watch and learn. If I want to get my future sorted I need to watch and learn.*

Theresa scanned the cars approaching the gates of the General. *I'd give anything for a fag. Trust me to get lumbered with a bloody consultant's wife, even if she is Paul's mum. I bet she's dead posh and knows stuff about books and poetry and all that. What the hell will we talk about all day, cooped up in a car? Bloody hell, this must be her.*

Theresa walked toward the car that had pulled into the kerb. The driver leant across the passenger seat bent forward, smiled and waved. *Here goes.*

'Hello Theresa, it's good to meet you at last,' said Rose, lifting a pile of case notes from the passenger seat. 'I've heard such a lot about you from Paul and Sarah. You don't mind having this lot on your knees do you?'

She doesn't talk posh.

'No, Mrs Thompson, that's fine.'

'Please, call me Rose when we're on our own. Mrs Thompson is all right in front of the families or in the clinic,' she smiled.

As they moved into the traffic, Rose gave Theresa a summary of the five visits they were to make during the morning.

'Mrs Taylor is an elderly primip who has been married for ten years and had given up hope of becoming pregnant. Her husband is a biology teacher at Farnton School who thinks he know everything about pregnancy and lactation. His views and mine do not necessarily coincide. It doesn't help that he was Paul's form teacher.' She glanced at Theresa and winked.

'He probably knows Jenny; one of my and Sarah's friends, she went to school with Paul.'

'I feel I know all your friends. Sarah tells me all

about you and what you get up too.'

Bloody hell, I hope not.

'Then we'll visit Mr Kelly on our way to a primary visit. I want to check that the home help service has started. His wife died a few weeks ago. The primary visit is to a girl who has been coming to my ante-natal talks. She is a lively soul, full of energy, which is as well given that her baby is huge; nine pounds, ten ounces, and she is intent on breast feeding.'

'Will she have trouble feeding because of the baby's size?'

'Not necessarily, it usually depends on how relaxed the mother is and her attitude to demand feeding. Then we'll visit two mums on the new estate, whose babies are due their six weeks assessments. How does that sound?'

'Great, interesting.' *When will we get a brew?*

When they climbed into the car after the final visit, Rose asked Theresa if she'd mind if they call in at her home.

'I can make us some lunch, that is, if you don't mind.'

'Yes, that's fine.' *Can't really say owt else.*

'I'm having period trouble and need to collect some supplies.'

*Aw, and she's so lovely.*

Theresa watched the changing streets as she listened to Rose summarise the final visit. She saw terraced cottages give way to large semi-detached houses. Rose took a fork in the road, drove past a church and the character of the houses changed again. Imposing detached houses surrounded by lawns, large trees and colourful bushes lined each side of the wide road. Rose indicated and turned into a drive.

*Bleedin' hell fire, I feel sick.*

'I hope you don't mind dogs, Theresa?'

'Err no. I'm fine.'

Theresa saw a large mutt bounding about at the back of the house. She took a deep breath. *Dear God, please let me keep my trap shut.* She followed Rose to the front door. Stepping inside the house she was aware she was gawping. She felt her spine tingle. She had seen the light – one day she intended to have a comfortable stylish home. Star struck, she trailed after Rose, into the kitchen.

'Do you like it, the kitchen? It's not long been fitted.'

'It's absolutely fab,' said Theresa.

Glancing round, she took in the sparkling white units with blue worktops, the white venetian blinds with the contrasting blue and white gingham curtains.

*Fancy having two lots of stuff at the window. I wish my mum could see this.*

'Come on, make yourself at home, sit at the table.' Rose handed cutlery and napkins to Theresa. 'I'll make us an omelette.'

*Jesus Christ, serviettes!*

Theresa didn't know where to feast her eyes. She wanted to watch Rose make the omelette but she also wanted to take in every nook and cranny of the kitchen. Rose made the decision for her by asking Theresa to grate cheese. The process of whisking four eggs and flashing the bowl of whipped eggs under the cold tap held Theresa's attention.

*Perhaps she's run out of milk. Although, I'm sure I saw some when she opened that fridge.*

'Is it okay if I watch?'

'Of course.'

Theresa peered into the fridge as Rose pulled out a butter dish.

*There's plenty of milk.*

Rose threw a knob of butter into the frying pan. When it was sizzling she poured in the egg mixture and proceeded to draw the sides of the egg to the centre of the pan.

Why doesn't she leave it to cook through?

When the egg had begun to set Rose added the cheese and with the mixture still runny flipped one side over and slid the omelette onto a waiting plate.

Christ, it's raw.

Rose sliced the thing in half pushed half onto another plate and handed it to Theresa. Reaching into the fridge she put a small bowl of salad onto the table.

'Left overs, from last night's meal.'

'Lovely.'

Over dinner Theresa found herself telling Rose about her family. As usual she made light of their circumstances.

Rose nodded and smiled.

She understands. How come? She's no snob.

The meal finished, Rose began to clear the table.

'Are you looking forward to the baby clinic this afternoon?'

'I am. Is it ok if I use the lav … toilet before we set off?'

'Help yourself, its upstairs, next to the bathroom.'

Theresa felt the spring in the thick pile of the fitted carpet. She made good use of her climb upstairs. From her vantage point she glimpsed the large sitting room with its squishy looking chairs and settee covered in cream loose covers. The curtains, with a pattern of leaves in mostly green with bits of cream and brown, were floor length. She'd have liked to take in more details to think about later, but she couldn't hang about on the stairs without looking suspicious.

God Almighty! Look at this bathroom. It's blue!

The basin was oval and held up by a pedestal that tapered to the floor. No toilet chains or newspaper in this house. Glancing into what she presumed was the main bedroom she saw matching dressing table and wardrobes, more matching long curtains, a fitted bedspread and bedhead in a pink and green flowery material.

I wonder where Sal sleeps.

The temptation to sneak a look behind closed doors nibbled.

*You wouldn't dare.*

Mesmerised, she made her way downstairs and into the hall.

'Are we ready for off?' said Rose.

'Yes, thank you for my din-lunch. I really enjoyed it.'

*How much water would I use for two eggs?*

# CHAPTER THIRTY-SEVEN

'How do we know that the job the health visitor does is worthwhile?' said Jenny, looking puzzled.

'Try and explain what you mean Nurse Ha... sorry, Nurse Smithfield,' said Miss Bolton.

'Well, it's something I've been thinking about since last week. I mean ... err, I mean,' Jenny looked toward the ceiling for inspiration, 'how do you measure something that's been prevented?'

Sniggers were audible in the lecture theatre.

'I'm not being funny,' she said turning to the miscreants, 'it's a serious question.'

'Indeed it is, Nurse Smithfield,' said Miss Bolton. 'Tell us what has led to your question.'

'Well, I enjoyed being on the district, particularly working with the health visitor who I was with. She only qualified last year, she is young and trendy. Sorry, I know that shouldn't matter it's just that she looks too young to be wearing that tweed uniform suit – it's like one my granny would wear.' Jenny waved her hands about. 'Anyway, she told me about the course, how she'd studied sociology, psychology and social policy and loads of other interesting stuff. Then she talked about the purpose of the job being,' Jenny paused trying to recall the phrase the health visitor had used, 'the detection and prevention of disease and handicap. So, I've been thinking. How does she know if she's succeeded? It isn't like changing a dressing is it – where you can see what you've done?'

'Did you ask your health visitor the question?'

'No, I didn't think about it until later.'

Miss Bolton took the unprecedented step of abandoning her lecture notes.

'Let us analyse the experiences you had with the health visitors and see if we are able to answer Nurse Smithfield's interesting question.' She hesitated, sucked her lips and glanced at the clock. 'Yes, I've got it – I know what we can do. Work in pairs and identify the activity, such as the advice given or the task undertaken by the health visitor, for example, the Scriver test.' She hesitated. 'And then next to it describe the effect on the patient, mother and baby or elderly person, and yes, I have it, and society as a whole.' She looked pleased with herself. 'Is everyone clear? Yes?' She cast her eyes around the lecture theatre. 'I'll come round and see how you are all getting on.'

'Well done Jen, you managed to give Beaky a kick up the arse. Her lesson was interesting, for once,' said Theresa as the group made their way into the reception area for the coffee break. 'What's up Sal?' She followed Sarah's exaggerated stare and on turning her head saw Miss Bolton marching off into the staff room.

'Oh bugger. Perhaps she didn't hear?' said Theresa, groaning.

# CHAPTER THIRTY-EIGHT

Jenny's attempts to get everyone together over Christmas were in vain. The cruel change list had sent the girls to five different surgical wards in the two hospitals. The likelihood of not getting together for two months was shrugged off as inevitable. Once more, Theresa and her belongings were on the move, across town, to the Infirmary.

'I was beginning to give you up for lost Nurse Booth, some of us have homes to go to you know.'

Theresa glanced at her watch.

'Sorry Sister, I thought I had to be here for dinner time.'

'Lunchtime, Nurse Booth, dinner is in the evening, but let's not argue the toss. It's good to have you back, you are nice and quiet and keep your room in good order. I like to welcome back nurses who are no trouble and don't have boyfriends ringing the doorbell ever two minutes.'

*Lunchtime, Theresa, not dinnertime; remember.*

'Same room as last time, Nurse Booth. I hope that's

all right. It's nice and quiet tucked away up there and you're near the bathroom.'

'Great. Fab. Thanks, Sister.'

'You know the rules about late passes and keys, you'll remember from the last time you were with us. Excuse me, Nurse. I'll just get that.'

The home sister couldn't resist picking up the pay phone. She liked to keep tabs on her girls. If it was one of the mothers she usually had a nice chat to bring the mother up to date with her daughter's activities, both professional and social. It wasn't unusual for mothers to run out of time and money without speaking to their offspring.

'Nurse Booth? Yes, she has only this minute arrived. Who should I say is calling? – Nurse Smithfield? Do I know you? You live out?' she sniffed and passed the phone to Theresa.

'Theresa, it's me.'

'Hello Mags, you've only just caught me. I'm going to dump my stuff and then go home for my tea.'

'I rang the General and they said you'd left. I knew you'd want to know, our Elizabeth got all her stuff for the start of her Introductory Block in today's post and guess what, they've taken geriatrics out of the ward allocations.'

'That's great news, tell her good luck; I don't suppose I'll see her before she starts. I need to dash Maggie, or I'll miss my bus, they're only every hour.'

Theresa had known about the change. Miss Bennet had told her when they had serendipitously met on the hospital corridor weeks ago. Theresa had been awed when Miss Bennet asked her to keep the news confidential as the ward sisters on geriatrics had yet to be told. Theresa wondered what their reaction would be. One of them had marched out of the meeting with the Hospital Management Committee right in the middle of her and Miss Bennet's presentation. The letter Theresa received from the chairman of the Management Committee thanked her for her valuable contribution to the debate, wished her all the best for her nursing career and apologised for his colleague's outburst. Apparently, there was now a ward sister vacancy on geriatrics.

Christmas came and went. Much to the student nurses' relief the requirement for them to work a thirteen-hour shift was abolished. They had a choice of Christmas Day or Boxing Day as an off-duty day, as long as there were enough staff to cover each day.

'Happy New Year,' Sarah whispered to the men who were still awake as she walked round the ward to check that all was well before she went to supper. She was looking forward to the week of nights: she'd have Theresa's company between shifts, odd that they'd become good friends. When they attended the tech as cadets Theresa had struck her as a bit common, a boorish joker. Somewhere along the way Theresa had begun to change. Okay, she was still far from quiet and liable to burst into the latest pop song without warning, but she was less aggressive in her clothes and attitude. Paul's mum had described her as 'a bright spark, a girl with something about her.' There'd been subtle changes in her appearance that Sarah had only noticed when she had seen Theresa, from a distance, at the nurses' Christmas dinner and dance. Her skirts, although still fashionably short, were more demure, her bust was no longer making a bid for freedom and she'd changed her going out makeup without discussing it with anyone. Her long hair was now cropped. Apart from the hair, the changes had been subtle. Of all of us she's the least settled, always restless, always moving. What's going to become of her? Sarah thought as she climbed the stairs to the dining room to meet her friend and wish her

Happy New Year.

In the middle of the week of nights Sarah met her mother in Farnton.

'Do you think Chris will want me to make her wedding dress; now that they've set a date?'

'Would you want to, Mum? I'll suggest it if you don't think it's too much work for you – with all the other sewing work you've got these days,' said Sarah.

'I'll make time, she's one of your friends and I do so admire the Reverend Fred.'

'Here comes our tea.' Sarah and her mother turned to see two waiters fetching loaded trays of tea pots, and stands holding sandwiches, savouries and cakes. It was Mrs Green's birthday and Sarah had arranged a surprise treat of afternoon tea at the Crown and Mitre.

'Should I pour, dear? I'm having Earl Grey and lemon, Mrs Ashford introduced me to it.'

'Are you enjoying your birthday, Mum?'

'I can't tell you how much. It is the best birthday I have ever had. As soon as I get home I will write and tell Mrs Ashford all about it. Did I mention I had a lovely letter from her only the other day?'

'Yes Mum, you have mentioned it.'

Sarah had to control a smile at the oft repeated phrase, 'my friend, Mrs Ashford'.

'When will Reverend Fred and Chris be married?' Mrs Green sipped her scalding tea. 'Is it all right to add sugar?'

'It is if you want to, Mum. You can call him Fred, he won't mind.'

'Oh dear me, I don't think so, no.' She heaped a spoonful of sugar into her tea. 'Thank you for the lovely surprise dear, I hope you have a quiet night duty tonight. I'll see you on Sunday. It's good of Paul to bring you to see me before he takes you to look after his mother. You are a good girl, Sarah. I am very proud of you.'

'Thank you, Mum, I'm looking forward to seeing you on Sunday. Come on, I'll walk you to the bus stop.'

Sarah had offered to arrange her off duty so that she could nurse Rose through the first days of her convalescence following her hysterectomy. When Sarah had suggested it, Hugh and Paul had jumped at the offer. As she walked back to the Infirmary Sarah rehearsed the conversation and the revelation that had explained so much.

'Sarah, it's too much to expect,' Rose said, shaking her head.

'No, honestly, I don't mind. I've talked about it with Paul and Hugh. They think it would be a Godsend. Don't you?'

'Do I find myself the subject of a conspiracy?' She'd smiled indulgently at the gang of three who were tucking into fish, chips and mushy peas chased down with a bottle of chianti. 'Pass the vinegar, Hugh; they never put enough on in that chippy.'

'Not like your mum and dad's chippy. The best fish and chips in the world bar none,' Hugh said turning to Sarah.

'Why? I don't understand?' Sarah was incredulous. 'Did your parents have a fish and chip shop?'

'They haven't had it for years, the hours got too much. They sold it and Dad got a job as a driver with the Co-op funeral service. Mum offered to help out, after my op, but her arthritis – well she couldn't have done much.'

Sarah choked on a chip.

'Back to your conspiracy theory, Mum.' Paul slapped Sarah on her back. 'You are right, as usual, especially since Sarah has already contacted Taylor, her next ward, and fixed up her off duty to make sure she's on nights the week before your likely discharge.' Paul shook more vinegar on his meal. 'So there's no going back now eh, Mum.'

Rose had finally accepted that she needed a hysterectomy and now that the decision was made she wanted it over and done as soon as possible. She was to be admitted the day after Boxing Day, which meant Sarah would need to start her week on nights on New Year's Eve.

'I have to say Sarah; your selfless offer has come as a huge relief to me. We are a registrar down and as the only consultant in radiology I am under enormous pressure. Rose and I will be forever in your debt. Won't we, darling?'

'We will. Thank you, dear, you are a real treasure. Pass me your hanky, Hugh. Forgive me, I'm overcome, it must be my hormones again.'

'I'm sorry I can't spend time with you, Mum, but term will have started,' said Paul.

'Sarah and I will be fine. Why don't you open another bottle, Hugh?'

# CHAPTER THIRTY-NINE

Theresa sniffed, then sniffed again as she ambled toward Sarah's bedroom. She'd shifted her stuff back to the General ready for the start of The Obstetric Nurse Training Course and was ready for a cup of tea and a catch up.

'I wondered what the pong was. Bloody hell! Are you dangerously ill, Sal?' Theresa cast her eyes around the room in wonderment. 'You can smell this lot in the corridor.'

The desk cum dressing table held two vases of flowers, with another one on the bedside table and yet another vase balanced on the narrow windowsill.

'That's bound to be knocked flying,' said Theresa, nodding toward the windowsill.

'Why don't you take it for your room?' Sarah retrieved the vase and held it out to Theresa.

'What's it all in aid of?'

'They're from Paul; we had a blazing row on Friday night. I walked out of a pub on the moors and then came back here. This lot arrived yesterday afternoon.'

'I presume you've made up?'

'More or less, although I think he still feels I'm being unreasonable.'

Theresa tucked her vase of flowers underneath the washbasin and then settled herself on the bed to hear Sarah's story.

'Come on, let's have the juicy bits.'

Sarah flopped into the armchair, shook her head at Theresa and folded her arms into her lap.

'We went to that pub on the moors, for chicken in a basket.'

'The one Jenny and Dave like?'

'Yes. Well, we were talking about going to the fun fair at Southport when he suddenly changed the subject and asked me if I didn't think it was time to find out about transferring to Manchester to finish my training.'

'What? Where the hell has that come from? You're surely ...'

'No, I've never thought about it. Anyway, I saw red. Do you know it's true you actually see red? I couldn't speak for a second or two and then I let rip. I told him he was selfish and thoughtless. He knows how hard I had to fight to get away from home, to live in. Then I well, I ...'

'Go on, Sal,' Theresa rubbed her hands together and wriggled to get more comfortable. 'Go on.'

'I told him he only wanted me nearby so that we could sleep together more often, and then I told him to bugger off. He looked a bit shocked then said he needed to go to the loo. While he was gone I walked out and came back here.'

'Bleedin' hell.' Theresa shook her fists, annoyed with herself. 'I'm not supposed to be swearing. How did you get back?'

'I hid in a ditch; my skirt's filthy – probably ruined, until he got in his car and drove away. It took him a while to give up looking for me, and then I hitched into town.'

'You – hitched, Christ!' Theresa nodded her head at the dressing table. 'I suppose, looking at this lot, that everything's sorted?'

'W-e-e-l-l, he understands I won't be going to Manchester, not until after I'm qualified. The other thing is,' she looked at her hands and shrugged her shoulders, 'I've agreed we'll get engaged on my birthday.'

'He can't make you, not if you don't want to.'

'I do, don't get me wrong, but I'm not ready to settle down and start planning a wedding, not yet.'

The next bride-to-be stuck her head round the door.

'It's only me. Good gracious.'

'A row,' said Sarah.


'Where the bloody hell is this classroom supposed to be?' said Theresa as she, Sarah and Chris wandered through the obstetric unit looking for the stairway leading to the first floor. A passing pupil midwife gave them directions.

'Good morning, I am Miss Nuttall, the new tutor in obstetrics; you are the first to arrive. Please, take a seat.'

'There's no way I'm sitting on the front row,' said Theresa, plonking her shoulder bag and file on a second row seat.

The classroom had been arranged in three rows of four seats. The introduction to obstetrics lecture given by Miss Bennet, in the last block, had interested Theresa enough that she wanted to be near the front of the classroom but it went against her ingrained principles to sit on the front row. Sarah and Chris took the two seats in front of Theresa.

The remainder of the group arrived, found seats, and set about the catching up on news.

'Don't you mind having a second-hand ring,' one

hoity-toity madam said to Chris.

'It's antique; it was Fred's mother's engagement ring.'

'Mmm, so whichever way you look at it, it's been used before.'

'She's another one that looks like Olive Oyl,' Maggie nodded toward Miss Nuttall's back while dragging her desk closer to Theresa's.

Miss Nuttall wandered around the classroom smiling and nodding at her students, she adjusted the models of the foetal skull and maternal pelvis on the top of the bookcase. At Maggie's desk she halted her progress, indicated to Maggie that she should stand and then tugged the desk back to its original position. As the large hand of the clock clicked onto twelve she banged the front desk with her right hand.

'She's definitely on the spinach,' said Maggie.

'Nurses, it is now nine o'clock. When you have introduced yourselves to me I will begin outlining the syllabus of this new addition to State Registered Nurse training. Shall we begin with you?' she pointed at Theresa.

'Nurse Booth.'

'Yes, I thought you might be.'

What the bloody hell does that mean? I bet Beaky's dropped me in it again.

'Miss Bennet has told me about your success with the Hospital Management Committee. I expect great things of you.'

'Really!'

'Shall we move on?' Miss Nuttall rewarded each nurse with a positive comment or asked a question so that by the time she was ready to start her introduction the nurses were settled and attentive.

'As you know, nurses, the Obstetric Course, as part of SRN training, is new; and I have to tell you not altogether welcomed by the more traditional midwifery sisters. It means that many of you who would perhaps have chosen to study for Part 1 of the State Certified Midwife qualification as a prerequisite …'

'A pre, what?' Maggie muttered.

'Nurse Booth,' Miss Nuttall looked expectantly at Theresa, 'I am sure you can extend your colleagues vocabulary by explaining the meaning of the term prerequisite?'

'It means …' Theresa paused. 'Something you need to do … or to achieve before you can do something else.'

'Like get married before you go to bed with a lad?'

Miss Nuttall massaged her right temple and sighed. 'As I was saying,' she gave Maggie a dismissive look, 'those of you intelligent enough to consider health visiting will no longer provide valuable staffing on the midwifery wards while working toward your Part I. The obstetric sisters' main objections, after concerns for staffing levels, are a reduction in standards. Therefore nurses, let me warn you I intend to set very high standards of nursing care, conduct and achievement. I will warn you now; the examinations will be rigorous and demanding. I have engaged the Consultant Paediatrician and Consultant Obstetrician and the most experienced of the ward sisters to lecture to you. Rigour is my watchword. Any questions?'

'Welcome to day two, nurses. Our speaker this morning is Sister Edwards. Her lecture will introduce us to the finer pints of breast-feeding,' said Miss Nuttall. She smiled at her colleague to indicate that she should begin.

Mavis Edwards, a single woman in her early fifties, had been born and bred in Farnton. She'd been a student nurse and a pupil midwife at the General. She lived three streets away from the hospital, with her widowed mother. She had a Farnton accent that she took no pains to hide. Sister Edwards had heard, many times, that a cup of tea was preferable to sex; she'd been a midwifery sister for more than twenty years with much of her professional life dedicated to dealing with the aftermath of the sexual act, so she had no doubt that virgo intacta was her preferred state. Two things in life she was sure about; Farnton Wanderers were by far the best football team in the world, her four older brothers had indoctrinated her at an early age. And the only way to nurture an infant was with the mother's own milk. She was convinced that she had invented the saying 'Breast is Best'.

'Well I've probably met most of you before; ow many of you cum from Farnton and District?' Ten hands were raised. 'About twenty years ago, by my reckonin', so fasten back your lugholes and let's get goin'.' Sister Edwards took a breath then with zealot-like enthusiasm went on. 'Let's have no messin' about – any mother can breast feed.' Lowering her voice and narrowing her eyes she continued. 'Young ladies, let me tell you, breasts are not, let me say again, not for young men to play with – they are to feed babies with.' She glanced at each nurse in turn. Her audience grimaced and squirmed. Jenny let out a quiet 'ooh' as Sister Edwards caught her eye. The products of that morning's lovemaking had squelched, warm and soggy, into her knickers. Sister Edwards continued, her audience rapt, the room quiet. 'There are four types of breast and they can all do the job.' She paused and with determination grasped her starched chest so that she held a breast in each hand. Releasing her chest she thrust her right hand in the air and demonstrated.

'Whoopers,
Doopers,
Droopers,

and
Dead dog's ears.'
Thirteen jaws dropped.

# CHAPTER FORTY

'We won't be long after you,' said Theresa as she Chris and Sarah turned away from Jenny and Maggie.

'Why? Where are you going? Why aren't you coming with us?' said Maggie.

'We're going to the home, to get changed into mufti,' said Sarah.

'Then I'll be the only one in uniform,' said Maggie.

'I can lend you something,' said Chris.

'No thanks, I think I'll go home.'

'Don't be soft, Mags. Go and help Jenny with the tea. If you two take your time and walk and we catch the bus we won't be long after you,' said Theresa. 'Come on you two, last to the home stinks.'

'We'll buy the food next time, won't we?' Chris said.

'Yes, you can't keep feeding us, Jenny,' said Sarah.

'This is only the second time you've been for a proper meal, and anyway, I enjoy it – the cooking, and you lot doing the washing up. And although I really, really love being married, I do miss our late night get-togethers.'

'Well, I feel more included now, I used to miss half the news, and you'd all think you'd told me stuff – like getting changed tonight.'

'Poor little diddums,' said Theresa, putting her arm round Maggie's shoulder, roughly pulling her close and giving her a noisy smacking kiss on the cheek. 'Poor little baby.'

'Gerroff.'

'Nurses, nurses, look at you tumbling about on the floor like a pair of puppy dogs. Is it any wonder the standard of nursing is in decline?' said Sarah.

'I was called worse than a puppy dog last night. That thug I went out with accused me of being a "prick tease." What do you think about that?'

'To be honest Theresa, it looks as though he had a good chew at you; it's ages since you had a love bite as big as that, so you must have got stuck in … if you know what I mean,' said Maggie.

'He did, we did – get stuck in. I admit it. I like that first bit, when you are closing in for the first snog and then settling in for a good necking.'

Maggie shivered.

'It sounds as though it went a bit further than necking,' said Jenny.

'Yes, well it moved on. We were sat on a bench in the park. He'd finished his ciggy. I was still smoking mine, there's no need to look like that Mags, I know I said I'd given up. Anyway, he took my cig from me, dead masterful, and ground it out with his foot. We looked at each other, time stood still, you know how it does, and then he pulled me to him and we started snogging. It was great at first and then his hands started wandering, then he tried to push me down on the bench and put his hand up my skirt. I gave him a shove, he landed on the ground. I gave him a kick and then ran off.'

'What if he'd come after you? What would you have done then, I really worry about you Theresa, I really do. Why don't you go for somebody who's clever and kind, somebody who cares about you?'

'Mags, thanks anyway, but I can look after myself, although I must admit I would like to meet a chap who'll see me and not just my chest.'

'Don't you mean your whoopers?' said Maggie, ducking out of Theresa's reach.

'Why yes, if you must be so crude, Nurse Smithfield, my rather exceptional whoopers.' She proudly straightened her back. 'I've decided, I'm going to change, become more refined and cultured. I mean it this time; I really do – perhaps then I'll meet a better class of snogger.'

'We like you as you are. Don't we?' said Chris.

'I'll tell you this though. No sperm is swimming up my parts. I wear knickers under and over my tights. The little buggers will have to be champion swimmers to get through that lot, and I'm going to stop swearing, I'll put sixpence in a jar every time I forget.'

'You'll be a millionaire by Easter,' said Maggie.

'Come on, dinner is served. Why don't you bring us up to date with you wedding plans, Chris?' said Jenny as the girls gathered round the table.

'Everything is fine with the wedding but, well, things have moved on with him – Harry Jones.'

'Has somebody kneed him in the balls?' Theresa said, shaking her left fist in the air. 'Bloody good for them, if they have.'

'Sixpence,' said Maggie and Sarah.

Getting up from the table, Jenny reached into the kitchenette, retrieved an empty jam jar and put it down in from of Theresa.

Chris hesitated.

'It won't affect the wedding will it, whatever it is?'

said Sarah.

'No, it makes things easier.'

'I need the toilet,' said Maggie, edging her way from her place at the table.

'Leave the door on its hinges, Mags.' Theresa called.

'I'm spoiling our evening, but I need to tell you. It's a long story but the upshot is my mum and grandma know about Harry Jones and his filthy habits.'

'How?' said Theresa.

'Well, some friend or other of my grandma's had a niece who worked for him. He's been touching her up. At first she though he'd brushed against her, but it kept happening and then one day he called her into his office, just as everyone was leaving for the day. He asked her to sit down and then went as though to get something out of a filing cabinet but instead locked the door.'

'Oh my God,' said Sarah, her hand covering her mouth. 'What happened.'

'Why didn't she do something?' said Jenny.

'At this stage she didn't know he'd locked the door. She genuinely thought he was at the filing cabinet. She didn't realize something was wrong until he put his hands over her shoulders and started to fondle her breasts. She jumped up, got hold of the chair and hit him with it. Apparently, he grabbed hold of her at the door but she managed to unlock it and ran out screaming. Her dad went to the office first thing the next morning but Harry Jones was nowhere to be seen. He didn't go home that night; he rang my mum and said he'd been called away on business. Soon after that my mum got an anonymous letter telling her that her husband was a pervert. It's been going on for years, that's why they can't keep office staff, according to my grandma's friend.'

'What's happening now, with your mum?' said Theresa.

'Well, last week she was determined to stay at the house, she had the locks changed but once I'd told her about what he did to me she packed her bags and moved to my grandma's. She's in a right state, blaming herself. She didn't go to work on Monday. My grandma is devastated.'

'What did Fred say?' said Sarah.

'He's been marvellous with them both; they spent all day on Sunday at the vicarage.'

'You've been a long time, Mags. You missed Chris's story …'

'Did I?'

'So, what about the wedding? Jenny said.

'Well, as you know, Theresa has graciously agreed to be my bridesmaid. Fred's sons, Charles and Michael, are jointly acting as best men. Sarah's mum is making the dresses and my mum will give me away …'

'My mum will have to give me away. Aren't we an odd bunch?' Sarah said.

'…the reception is being provided by the mother's union, guides and … oh, you know, all Fred's followers.'

Chris cleared the table and folded the cloth. Sarah and Theresa washed and dried the pots and pans. Maggie brewed the tea.

'What's going to happen with you and Paul, when do you plan to get married?' Chris said as Sarah draped the tea towel over the edge of the draining board.

'In a year or two. I said three but, as I thought, my mum, and Rose and Hugh, have ganged up on me and want it to be sooner, so we'll see.'

'Don't let them push you into anything,' said Theresa.

'I won't. But I do want the chance to be on my own. I know we tease you Theresa, about trying to change, but I think I know how you feel about wanting to find out who you are and what you want from life. I want to see … oh, I don't know … a bit of life without someone always seeming to peer over my shoulder. Does all this make sense?'

'It does to me. Through Dave I've changed, become a different person, he's set me free and … Oh, I'm sorry.' She wiped her eyes with the heels of her hands. 'I'm so happy, it's my period, ignore me.'

As they settled in the front room Sarah made herself comfortable on the floor. Undoing her tote bag she pulled out her knitting.

'What's that you're making?' said Maggie.

'A bedspread for my bottom drawer. It's a joint effort between Paul's mum and me. She's challenged me to knit at least five squares a week. So far she's in the lead, but she is convalescing. Hugh says her knitting has become more an obsession than a hobby. I'll be glad when she goes back to work – then I'll have a chance to catch up.'

# CHAPTER FORTY-ONE

Miss Nuttall took her students through a review of the week's introduction to obstetrics; she outlined the requirements of the case study that formed part of the assessment for the course. She went on to give the dates of the written examination and viva and sent her students off to get their off duty for the following week.

The following eleven weeks were amongst the most carefree of the three-year training. There was no night duty, and therefore no unsupervised responsibility for patients. The cry of 'we're at the end of our second year' when the obstetric students were asked if they knew how to take blood pressure readings or carry out basic observations, was unheeded by the staff midwives and sisters on the maternity wards and departments. They were accustomed to working with pupil midwives who despite being State Registered Nurses and experienced staff nurses on the general wards were nevertheless novices in working with mothers and new born babies. House officers, qualified junior doctors, on their obstetric rotation, were a bunch who had a tendency to think they were God's gift despite their lack of skills and experience. Youngsters without qualifications were not likely to be taken too seriously, albeit they were good at making beds, serving meals and wielding a razor – allowing the real midwives to deliver babies and supervise pupil midwives and junior doctors.

Maggie told her mum, dad and Elizabeth that working in the ante-natal clinic was 'like watching *The Nun's Story*'. She had watched the women; well dressed, or careworn, posh or with broad Farnton accents, as they metamorphosed from ordinary women who were fit and well, but pregnant, as they stepped into the cubicles running the length of the ante-natal clinic. Once in the small space the women changed from their street clothes into the clean hospital gown hung behind the second door of the cubicle. With their status now reduced to that of the ubiquitous patient they entered the consulting room when a knock indicated that they should step forward to meet the obstetrician and his team.

At the end of the sixty-two hour placement in the ante-natal clinic, the students were confident enough to palpate a mother's abdomen and correctly determine the difference between the skull and buttocks of the foetus and therefore identify its lie in the maternal pelvis. They were also proficient in the use of a foetal trumpet to count the heartbeat of the unborn child.

'How many deliveries have you observed so far?' Chris said to Theresa.

'Six down, six to go. Hopefully I'll get another one in this evening.'

Chris was working on Sister Edwards's lying-in ward. She was impressed with the skills of the blunt, forthright woman. Sister Edwards's approach to the new mothers was no nonsense yet kind and encouraging. She was prepared to sit patiently and help the infant and mother get the hang of breastfeeding. The majority of women who started breastfeeding as in-patients left the ward after eight days or so still feeding their babies. If a mother chose not to breastfeed, Sister Edwards left the heretic in the care of her junior sister or staff nurse.

'Do you fancy coming into town with me this afternoon?' Theresa said, giving Chris a sideways look.

'Yes, I can do. Is something wrong?'

'Erm, well no but I could do with some moral support. Ah, support, that's a good one.'

'Theresa, what on earth are you rambling on about?'

'Mrs Green noticed the wheals on my shoulders and suggested I might benefit from a brassiere fitting …'

'Why does she do that; pull a funny face and mee-maw?'

'I don't know, perhaps she's embarrassed, she's lovely though. I don't know why Sal goes on about her.'

'Good evening, Nurse Booth. I trust you've returned to us refreshed.'

'Yes, Sister.'

'Just as well, because you and staff will have your work cut out tonight. We've an elderly primip been admitted and she's had next to no ante-natal care. She might not deliver until after your shift is due to end,' said Sister Almond, raising her eyebrows.

'That's fine, Sister. I'll stay on duty.'

'Good girl, believe me that patient will definitely need extra support.'

The patient was in her late thirties and had been astounded to find herself pregnant after eighteen years of marriage. She'd supposed she was 'on the change'. Visiting her family doctor because of a persistent cold and sore throat she'd mentioned her increased weight and the absence of her 'monthly friend'.

'Hello, I'm Nurse Booth. I'm going to be helping to look after you until your baby comes.'

'That's nice. My name's Mrs Marshall, Jean

Marshall. How long will it be before I get my baby?'

'A while yet. I'm going to start getting you ready for the delivery. I'll go and collect everything I need and then I'll shave you, OK?'

'Should I take my teeth out?'

Theresa chortled to herself and made her way to the sisters' office.

'Oh ye God's, it's difficult to believe that in 1968 there are still women who don't know that the baby comes out of the same door it went in. I'll go and break the news of what lies ahead, when I've finished giving staff nurse the report. Thanks for telling me, Nurse Booth.'

By the time Theresa had collected her equipment together and returned to her patient the sister was holding Jean's hand and carefully explaining the process of labour and birth to the astounded mother-to-be.

# CHAPTER FORTY-TWO

It was Sarah's birthday and more or less all of the obstetric group were going to the coffee bar in Farnton. It would only be the jukebox but they could have a dance and help her celebrate the actual day of her birthday. The engagement celebration was planned for Saturday. Rose had suggested a dinner party to include Paul and Sarah with Mrs Green and herself and Hugh. 'It will be a lovely opportunity for us all to get to know each other,' she'd said to Sarah.

While Sarah stood waiting for Paul at the entrance to the nurses' home on the Saturday evening of the dinner party, she tried not to feel let down. Having made the decision to become engaged she'd warmed to the idea and become quietly excited about an engagement and birthday party. Now here she was all dressed up and facing a night when she'd be on pins hoping her mum wouldn't put her foot in it with Rose and Hugh. Paul had never mentioned buying a ring. The girls had disappeared earlier in the afternoon without mentioning the engagement party. Theresa had said she needed to go home for one thing or another. Chris had gone to the vicarage, something about Fred being concerned about the aftermath of Michael's parents evening. Jenny and Maggie she'd not seen since the outing to the coffee bar. To make matters worse Paul was now ten minutes late; no doubt he'd been playing football and gone for a swift one after the match. Sod him. He'd have got her mum worked up, waiting for him to pick her up on his journey home to Farnton from the university.

'Paul's been held up, so I've been sent to fetch you,' said Hugh as he leapt out of his car and chivalrously ran round the bonnet of his car to hold open the passenger door for Sarah.

I'll bet he has, thought Sarah, blinking back tears; she pressed her lips together and balled her fists. She was seething. Her birthday bash had been fine, she hadn't expected anything else, but this, well, she was beginning to wish she hadn't agreed to get engaged.

Sarah jumped as the car horn interrupted her reverie. They'd arrived in the Thompson drive.

'Oops, clumsy old me,' said Hugh.

'Paul's managed to get here, then?' Sarah said, nodding towards his car parked further along the drive.

Hugh once more dashed round his car and taking Sarah's arm led her to the front door.

'You're here at last,' said Paul as Sarah stepped into the hall. 'Come here my darling.' Sarah thought about resisting as she was pulled into Paul's arms but he was kissing her and well, it had probably been the traffic coming out of Manchester that had delayed him. As they came up for air Paul reached into his trouser pocket and pulled out a small maroon box.

Taking out a diamond solitaire he slipped the ring on Sarah's finger and brought her hand to his lips.

'Let's go and meet our guests,' he said.

Sarah and Chris were comparing rings when Theresa pushed open Sarah's bedroom door with her bottom, she backed into the room carrying a tray with three mugs of Ovaltine.

'It was a fab party and I managed to have a good nosey around the rooms I'd not been in last time I was at the house,' Theresa said, handing out the drinks. 'Had you really no idea?'

'No, none whatsoever. To be honest I was a bit peeved that nobody seemed interested, none of you had said good luck or all the best before you all disappeared.'

'It was brilliantly organised, I didn't know your mum and Paul's mum got on so well,' said Chris.

'I didn't know they'd met, let alone been to each other's houses, and arranged all this behind my back.'

'Nothing romantic will ever happen to me,' said Theresa with an exaggerated sigh.

'It will, it will happen when you least expect it,' said Chris. 'One thing I didn't understand was why Maggie said it had happened to her. She hasn't been engaged has she?'

'Mags? You must be joking. No, she means the surprise party her mum and dad gave her before we started our training. Go on Sal.'

When Sarah had recovered from her surprise and shown off her ring, the plot emerged. After the incident on the moors Paul had visited Mrs Green to ask for Sarah's hand in marriage. He'd taken his mum so that the two mothers could meet. Rose had waited in the car and then been invited in for a small sweet sherry. Mrs Green had changed into her going-into-town clothes and the three of them had gone to Blackburn's jewellers. The two mothers had helped Paul narrow down his options and then wandered around the shop whilst he made his final choice. They'd only seen the ring for the first time after it was placed on Sarah's finger.

'My mum's been at Paul's all day helping Rose with the buffet. I still can't get over how relaxed she was and what a wonderfully deceitful lot of friends I've got.'

'Fred thinks your mum is lovely, he spent quite a bit of time talking to her about his problems with Michael,' said Chris.

'Oh dear, what's wrong?'

'Let's not spoil your lovely evening Sarah, it can wait until tomorrow.'

'Is everything all right at home, Theresa?'

'It is; everything's going great with the Booth Brigade. Sorry Sarah, I confess it was a pack of lies I was in town with Maggie and then round at her house to get changed for the party.'

'I'm off to bed, see you both tomorrow,' said Chris.

'There won't be many more nights like this, putting the world to rights before we go to bed. Just me and you left living in, Theresa, once Chris is married,' Sarah said.

'Let's make the best of it then, go on Sal, tell us about your day.'

The district midwife had taken Sarah to visit a home on one of the less salubrious council estates in Farnton. Sarah had recoiled at the state of the house. The internal doors had been removed and most of the skirting boards had been hacked off the wall to provide fuel for the open fire. Nappies lay in the hearth, drying in front of the fire. They hadn't been washed, just taken off the infant and left to dry. The electricity was illegally connected and there was faeces smeared on the wall of the front room.

'All the mother was concerned about was that the midwife should remove her stitches, she told us that they were getting in her husband's way – scratching him.'

'I think the whole business about sex is really confusing. I keep thinking about that poor patient on

2E.'

'Why, what happened?' said Sarah.

'She's the one I told you about, the one who asked if she needed to take her teeth out. Well I called in to see her on my way off duty. She was glad to see me; she was wobbling about on a ring.'

'Get on with it Theresa, we're all agog.'

'And so you should be; you're going to learn a thing or two about married life Chris, just listen to this. "How are you getting on with feeding your baby?" I said to her. "He's on the bottle," she said. Wait till you hear the next bit; she said she told that bad tempered old battle-axe, she meant Sister Edwards, to bugger off because she tried to make her get her titties out. She said she told Sister Edwards that she couldn't have her titties on show. Here it comes Chris, the marital advice because …' Theresa paused and winked, 'her husband has never seen her undressed and he wouldn't want the little lad doing that … sucking at her.'

'Theresa Booth, you've made that up,' Sarah said.

'I have not Sal, cross my heart and hope to die, I have not. Though I do admit it's added to my confusion about sex and all that.'

'Why? What confusion?' Chris said.

'Well it's supposed to be beautiful and full of meaning and all that, especially if you read something like *Lady Chatterley's Lover*. Which is all well and good until you look at the Church, well the Roman Catholic Church which preaches that sex is as a duty to make babies, for married people only, I might add, and look what that's done to my mum.' With a short pause for breath she continued, 'It's almost impossible to get birth control if you're an unmarried girl, and if you're not married sex is dirty and a sin. Is it any wonder older women like that patient are in the dark about how their bodies work and where babies come from?'

'Theresa, relax,' said Sarah.

'Relax! I'm confused. I tell you free love's still a long way to travel before it reaches Farnton. You and Paul have a long time to go before your wedding, Sal, let's hope you don't get caught.'

Sarah and Chris looked at each other and shook their heads. Once Theresa latched on to an idea she worried it to death.

# CHAPTER FORTY-THREE

'I think we revised all the right stuff,' said Maggie. The group were gathering up their belongings at the end of the three-hour written paper.

'I hope I get the foetal skull in the oral tomorrow,' said Jenny.

'Why? You seemed confident when we were revising last night,' said Sarah.

'It seems easier to describe than the maternal pelvis.'

'Let's have a cup of tea and then revise for an hour before supper,' said Theresa.

Jenny and Maggie were staying at the hospital for supper so that they could revise with Theresa, Chris and Sarah for the oral examinations before making their way home. Miss Nuttall caught up with the five students as they sauntered over to the nurses' home.

'How was the paper?'

'It was fine, we think we revised all the right topics,' said Chris smiling at Miss Nuttall.

That's what I've just said – trust her to butter up to Miss Nuttall, thought Maggie grizzling to herself.

'Try and relax as well as revising this evening,' said their teacher.

Taking Miss Nuttall's advice they discussed anything but the oral. Chris and Fred's wedding was only two weeks away and plans were well advanced. Chris was worried about Fred and the impact that Michael's poor progress at school was having on his enjoyment of preparing for their wedding. Michael's attendance at school had been sporadic and his achievements limited. At the head teacher's request Fred had visited the school and been informed that unless his son's attendance improved by the May half term Michael would not have a place in the upper sixth. Slamming doors and swearing were the outcome of Fred trying to be simultaneously firm and supportive.

'Is he rude to you?' Theresa said.

'He isn't really anything to me. It's as though I'm just one more person who comes and goes through the vicarage. He grunts at me when I say hello and if I've made a meal he mutters under his breath, takes his plate and cutlery and goes to his room to eat.'

'When does Charles come home?' Sarah said.

'Early next week, so maybe he'll be able to talk to Michael,' said Chris without conviction.

'What's this got to do with our exam?' Maggie said. 'I'm going home to revise on my own.'

Despite being asked to describe the finer points of the maternal pelvis as part of her oral, Jenny gained the highest marks in the examinations at the end of the Obstetric Nurse Training Course. She was chuffed with the results. George Hayes had done a good and enduring job in undermining her confidence. She knew she was a good nurse; her ward reports were consistently complimentary and indicated that she knew when to ask for help and guidance from senior staff, while being able to use her initiative as well as work calmly under pressure. The hospital finals were during the next block, so to build on her success, Jenny was determined to use any free time she had to study. Even though her life had changed, so much for the better, she still believed that it was going to come crashing down; exam or any other sort of failure, and the thought of George gloating chafed her happiness. Jenny was hesitant to disturb her new life. Dave, now settled in his lecturing post, was keen to move to a better area of Farnton but Jenny argued that it would be too much upheaval in her final year of training. She agreed that they should start house hunting once she'd had the results of her finals, providing she passed her examinations the first time.

Theresa lifted up her arms in an attempt to allow the still air to cool her armpits. She glanced under her arms and saw the pale blue satin stained with sweat marks.

It's bloody boiling in here. I have to get out for a breath of air or I'll pass out.

She stepped out of the French windows in the vicarage dining room and wandered into the garden. Groups of wedding guests stood about on the lawn. To avoid them, and attempt to clear her head, she cut round the side of the house and decided to explore the out-houses she could see. She sniffed the air and sniffed again – cigarette smoke. The enticing smell led her round the back of a substantial looking shed.

A fag would go down a treat.

She closed her eyes and imagined the relaxing effect of the nicotine as she pictured herself pulling on a cigarette.

'Sorry, I didn't mean to disturb you.'

'What?'

'Don't put it out, enjoy it.'

'Are you sure?'

'Yes, course I am. You don't happen to have a spare

one, do you? I'm Theresa, by the way.'

'You said,' Michael extricated a packet of ten Benson and Hedges and a box of matches from his trouser pocket, 'when the photographs were being taken.'

'Ooh, that tastes good. I've given up – supposedly. The wedding was lovely, wasn't it?'

Michael turned his head away from Theresa as he exhaled.

'You don't swallow then?'

'What's it to you?'

'Nothing, nothing at all. I'm trying to be friendly. Your dad's married one of my best friends and well … never mind, thanks for the fag and all that.'

'Don't go. I'm sorry I don't mean to be rude. It's just that I don't give a shit about all this.'

'Why?'

'You're a nosey cow aren't you,' he smiled half-heartedly. 'If you must know, I've got a headache. I guzzled a load of sherry and then had a whiskey or two, behind the old man's back.' He slid to the floor and sat on his jacket. 'And, I want my mum.'

*Jesus Christ, what the bloody hell is all this about?*

Theresa watched as the boy slid to the flags and curled into himself, resting his forehead onto his knees. Lifting up her bridesmaid dress, she wasn't risking a telling off from Mrs Green, Theresa lowered herself down beside him; the slab of stone was hard and uncomfortable against her bum. She reached out and then pulled her arm back, not sure whether to hug him. She settled for resting her hand on his shoulder.

*Keep calm, and sit it out.*

Michael changed position, lifted his body, pulled his jacket from under him and wiped his nose down his jacket sleeve. Theresa looked askance at the line of silvery snot.

That'll need sponging down.

'Sorry, you must think I'm a tosser; that stuff about my mum.'

'Is that what all the bother's been about, you wagging it?'

'How do you know?'

Theresa told Michael that Chris had been worried about both him and his dad and that she had shared her concerns with her friends.

'Are you bothered about your dad getting married again? Chris would never try to replace your mum. She's not old enough, for one thing.'

'No, in my own way I'm pleased the old man has picked up a nice bit of skirt,' he glanced at Theresa. 'He expects me to be like Charles – brainy. And I'm not. Mum understood ...'

'Let's have another fag, but if you don't mind I need to stand up; my bum's gone dead and my frock's getting creased.'

Theresa watched Michael find the cigs and matches.

'I'm close to my mum, she understands how I feel about things – the church, my holier than thou sister and other stuff. She's the only person, well grown up, who lets me be myself, well her and one of my tutors,' said Theresa.

Theresa drew a cigarette from the packet Michael proffered.

'No one talks about her, it's as though she never existed. The do-gooders have taken over the garden. We used to work on it together.'

With prodding and probing Theresa discovered that the first Mrs Cummings had been a talented amateur gardener, winning prizes locally. Once she became ill Michael had been her helpmate, digging, pruning and weeding, at her instructions. After her death the garden was taken over by well-meaning parishioners. Over the years Michael had watched his and his mother's work disappear.

'Mum and I talked about me becoming a gardener, a proper one, with qualifications. That's what I want to do, not waste my time at that bloody school.'

'Theresa, Theresa, where are you? Come out, come out wherever you are.'

'Coming, Sal,' Theresa peered out from round the side of the outbuilding. 'Come on Michael, it's Chris and your dad; they're getting ready to leave. Let's wave them off and then find a proper drink and have another fag.'

'Where've you been? We've looked all over for you.' Maggie looked beyond Theresa to the figure dawdling across the lawn. 'You've surely not, don't tell me, you can't have been snogging with Michael!'

Following the departure of the newly-weds Theresa took two of the bottles of beer she'd found in the kitchen and climbed the stairs to Michael's attic bedroom. In answer to her knock Michael peered round the door. The smell of sweat and stale air caught her as he stepped out of the room and closed the door. He'd spruced himself up a bit; his hair was brushed and he'd changed out of his suit into grey trousers, blue check shirt and a plain blue tie.

'Have you still got some ciggies?'

'One or two.'

'They hunkered down on the top step, smoking and swigging beer from the bottle.

'How do you feel?' said Theresa.

'Same as before, like I'll always feel. Trapped – in this bloody vicarage and that friggin' school.'

'Esther, my sister-in-law, was like you; trapped.'

'Don't tell me she had a marvellous experience – a miracle, and now she's found salvation. Save it. I've heard all that guff before, from my dad, you know; The Vicar.'

'You really are a sarky little bugger.' Theresa glowered at Michael. 'For your information, she was pregnant at sixteen, had a shotgun wedding, lost the baby and then did a moonlight flit from her bloody awful parents' house. She now lives with my brother – over a butcher's shop. She enrolled at the local college for her A levels, works in the butchers part-time and nips over and helps my mum with our little uns. She's her own salvation; she didn't need your or anybody else's God to save her. You need to stop feeling sorry for yourself, get shifted and sort yourself out.' Theresa let out a heavy sigh. 'Well, like I said …'

'Sorry,' Michael muttered into his chest.

'Michael, it's up to you.'

'Will you help me?'

*Theresa, when will you learn to keep your gob shut?*

'Where is he now?' said Paul.

'Gone to the Crown and Mitre, for a meal with Charles, and some of Fred's relatives.'

Paul and Sarah had taken a triumphant Mrs Green home, she was sure of at least one more wedding dress commission as a result of the day's proceedings, and then made their way to Jenny and Dave's to meet Theresa, Maggie and Elizabeth for the evening. Theresa gave an 'I said' and 'he said' recount of her time with Michael.

'I remember him as a little boy, he was always smiling and chattering and yes, when I think about it now, I remember him being in the vicarage garden with his mother,' said Elizabeth.

'Why didn't you say no? Look what happened last time you took on somebody else's problems,' said Maggie.

'What are you going on about, Mags, somebody else's problems? I don't understand.' Theresa flashed a glance at Sarah and Jenny.

'Chris Warrington; trailing about after us and spoiling everything and now she's gone and married our vicar.'

'What!' Theresa said.

'Margaret, that's enough.' Elizabeth forced a smile at the friends gathered round the tea table. 'She's been drinking Cherry B all afternoon.'

'Who'd like another cup of tea,' said Jenny, catching Dave's eye, 'and another piece of cake?'

'What happens next?' said Dave with a furtive glance at Maggie.

'I've arranged to meet him outside the tech at half nine on Monday morning. I'm supposed to be going home to help our Tommy paint their bedroom but an hour or two won't make any difference.'

'Wouldn't it be better to wait until Fred and Chris get home?' said Sarah.

'See, Sarah agrees with me. Don't you?' Maggie stuck her tongue out at Elizabeth.

'He says he's getting it sorted,' Theresa said, shaking her head at Maggie and her daft talk.

'The college library is the best place to go, that is, if he turns up at the college and takes your advice to do what Esther did. Would it help if I had a word with the librarian when I get in on Monday? She's really helpful.'

'Thanks Dave that would be great.'

*Perhaps I should have told him to hang on until his Dad gets back.*

# THIRD YEAR

## CHAPTER FORTY-FOUR

The third year of training started with allocations to the outpatient departments at the two hospitals. The Infirmary had clinics in the main Out Patient Department and the Fracture Clinic as well as a daily dressing clinic in Casualty. Paediatrics, psychiatry and gynaecology outpatients attended clinics at the General. The allocation of student nurses to provide support to patients and departmental staff was essential if the exigencies of the various outpatients departments were to be met. Six weeks working with outpatients meant regular days, no night duty and, best of all, weekends off.

The third week back on duty after the holidays Chris offered to host the now established if-we-are-all-off-duty-let's-get-together Thursday evenings. With Sarah and Theresa the only ones now living-in these meetings replaced the late night gossips in the nurses' home – and Maggie was included.

Jenny, Sarah and Chris walked the short distance from the Infirmary to the vicarage. Chris settled Jenny and Sarah with a cup of tea and the proofs of the wedding photographs while she got on with the meal and they waited for Maggie and Theresa to arrive from the General.

'Where's Theresa? Isn't she with you?' said Sarah glancing up at Maggie's arrival.

'She's with the vic... I mean Fred; he asked her to step into his study. I warned her to keep her nose out ...'

'Come and sit down and look at the photographs.' Jenny hutched up and made a space on the settee. 'These are the ones we've seen.'

Sarah glanced at her watch.

'I hope everything's all right. I'll go and see if Chris nee...' Sarah sat back down, as the sitting room door opened and Chris and Fred appeared. 'What ...'

'Don't be alarmed, Sarah dear, everything is ...' said Fred.

A door banged and Michael appeared carrying a huge bouquet of flowers. He thrust them at Theresa who immediately burst into tears. Fred pulled Theresa toward him, crushing her and the flowers.

'Please explain to our friends,' he said to Chris as he fumbled for a handkerchief.

Chris who by now was also looking teary suggested that they all move into the dining room so that they could talk over supper.

'Michael, I think it would be better if you explained what you, Charles and Theresa have been up to while we were on our honeymoon,' said Chris quietly as they moved across the hallway into the dining room.

Fred's grace included thanks for loyal and supportive friends and family. He particularly thanked God for interceding, through Theresa, and returning his beloved son to him. Theresa blew her nose, before she tucked into the cold meat salad and new potatoes.

'I've not stopped smoking and drinking though,

Dad,' said Michael.

'With Theresa as your saviour you are not likely to, either,' said his stepmother, smiling at her friend.

'I've given up smoking – again, in my quest for refinement,' said Theresa.

Dave's faith in the college librarian had been well founded. By the time Michael and Theresa had arrived she'd not only found information about colleges offering horticultural courses but had contacted a college in the Lancashire countryside. She had obtained details of vacancies for the college year starting in the September. Charles had driven Michael to the college, to meet the tutor responsible for horticultural courses. All that stood between Michael and his enrolment was Fred's permission, which had been given without hesitation. To top it all, Michael had taken it upon himself to visit the Civic Centre and persist until he had found the correct person to speak to. He now had a temporary job with the Parks and Cemeteries Department.

'The Cummings now have a team approach to funerals, Dad comforts the relatives and conducts the service and I dig the grave.'

'Funerals apart, come on everyone let's sit down and have our meal. Oops, please start I just need to excuse myself.' Chris hurriedly left the dining table.

'Hello, is it all right if I come in?' Chris put her head round the door of Fred's study. 'Have you finished your sermon?'

'Yes, all done. Did you enjoy your walk?'

'I did.' Chris paused. 'Although, it wasn't a walk as such … I've been to the surgery; they've got a Saturday morning surgery for people who can't get in …'

'The surgery!' Fred looked aghast. He caught his hip on the corner of his desk in his haste to reach Chris. 'Why?'

'I'm not poorly love, don't look so worried. I'm, I'm pregnant.'

'Chris, Chris, Chris,' he said. 'I can't believe it. When?' Fred threw his arms around his wife.

Once she'd calmed her husband down with a cup of tea and left him in quiet prayer Chris rang and left a message for Theresa to ring her when she got back to the home.

'Holy Trinity Vicarage, Mrs Cummings speaking. That's good, you got my message.'

'There's nothing wrong, is there?'

'It's just that I … Well we've got some news, I'm pregnant.'

'Bloody hell!'

'I forgot to take the Emko out of my suitcase and well …'

Chris told Theresa that after the boys she and Fred wanted her to be the first to know. She intended to see or leave messages for Sarah and Jenny the next day.

'What about Maggie, do you want me to tell her?' said Theresa.

'Perhaps not, Fred will tell the Bishop tomorrow, and then he'll let the parish know later in the week. I'll try and speak to Elizabeth after Mr Smithfield has been told officially. Somehow, I don't think Maggie will be interested.'

'I don't know what's up with her these days? One minute she's herself and then she's moody and then you see her and she's smiling; all secret and dreamy,' Theresa said.

For Maggie, dealing with death on the wards was an ongoing burden. Her grandma's death was the single tragic event of her life. It had brought the realisation of mortality. She dwelt on her own death; imagining the piercing cold of lying in the mortuary fridge. The images she retained from the crematorium, cold and sterile with the final grandiose swishing close of the curtain haunted her daydreams, and at times, disturbed her nights. She kept her morbid fears and thoughts to herself. Her friends' taunts about her limited understanding of sex in its different forms were bad enough. She didn't want them to know she was in a tizz about death and dying. Besides, they weren't the only friends she had at the hospitals. The shifts during the sixteen weeks of medicine and surgery left her to her own devices; she rarely saw any of the others. Her dad ferried her backwards and forwards at the end of her shifts. Her split shifts and her days off she spent with her new friends, in their rooms. She found she enjoyed getting to know new people, people who were interested in her, who didn't tease her and treat her like a spare part. Grown up people who didn't care about the length of her skirts, or make-up or weddings or recipes. So what if she wasn't supposed to be in their rooms, it was nice to make people from overseas welcome and to learn about their different countries, and one of them always watched out to make sure no one saw her sneaking in and out. Now it was back to study block where she'd be shoved to one side in favour of that stuck up Chris Warrington. It would be Fred this and Fred that and look at me, aren't I clever getting pregnant.

Theresa had been angry and disappointed, but not surprised, when her mum had waited until everyone else was either in bed or out of the house and then told her and Win she was expecting again. Win had crossed herself and uttered *Deo Gratias* while Theresa had determined to 'kill that bloody priest'. Her mum wasn't sure of the date of her last period. She admitted to her daughters that she felt tired and 'out of sorts'. When Theresa asked if she could see her mother's maternity cooperation card she discovered that her mum hadn't seen her family doctor, which meant she hadn't had any ante-natal care or booked in at a hospital or maternity home for the delivery.

Theresa went home on the middle Saturday of her two week block to see her family and keep her promise to help Win, who had completed her Introductory Block and was set to leave home, as Theresa had done, and move into the nurses' home. The sisters had bumped into each other in the School of Nursing and in a moment of sisterly generosity Theresa had offered to help Win shift her stuff to the home before she started her first ward the following day. Theresa's fervent hope was that the off duty would never put her and Win together on the same ward. Although they had both always wanted to be nurses Theresa thought Win was in for a nasty surprise when the reality of life as a student nurse hit her.

When her dad got home from the bookies Theresa pleaded with him to call an ambulance but he refused to go against his wife's wishes saying he would call the family doctor on Monday morning if necessary.

The appearance of the priest at the back door accelerated Theresa's departure back to the hospital. Win was left to move on her own.

Theresa was deep into outlining the nursing care of an elderly woman admitted to hospital with pneumonia, as part of her hospital final examination, when she felt a tap on her shoulder.

'Nurse Booth, leave that; you need to step outside,' Miss Bennet whispered.

Theresa looked up, disorientated. 'I don't underst…'

'Come with me, I'll explain in the corridor.'

Theresa looked around the classroom. Blank faces looked at her, pens poised over exam papers.

'Nurse Booth, it is imperative we hurry.'

Dazed, Theresa stumbled after Miss Bennet.

'Ah, your sister has arrived.'

'What's the matter, why?'

'I am sorry to have to tell you …' as Miss Bennet hesitated Theresa staggered against Win, 'your mother; she is very poorly.'

'Theresa, what's wrong?' Win grasped Theresa's arm. 'Tell me what's wrong.'

'Come on Win, come on.' Theresa grabbed Win's hand.

'Nurses, calm down. I will come with you.'

Theresa wanted to run, to get to her mum, to see her. *Dear God, whoever and wherever you are I'll do anything you want, you name it I'll do it but please don't let her die. You can have the baby; keep it for your own. Is that what you want, a pure little soul? Take it, we won't miss it. But please, please, leave my mum with us.*

The familiar corridor blurred, Theresa was only dimly aware of the wards, pharmacy, the turn off to the dining suite and the WVS shop.

'I'll leave them with you now,' Miss Bennet said to the junior sister.

Theresa gasped when saw the almost imperceptible shake of the head the sister gave Miss Bennet before she turned and led her and Win into a side ward.

'My God, no, please no.' Theresa pushed in front of the priest to retrieve her mother's hand from his. Her dad was rocking slowly back and forth in a chair on the opposite side of the bed.

'What's he doing here?'

Theresa nodded at the priest as she sank to her knees at the side of the bed. Win stood at her sister's shoulder.

'What's happened, Dad?' Win looked beseechingly between the priest and her dad. 'I don't understand.'

'I found her, on the settee. She couldn't talk to me. I ran to the phone box … dear God, and, when I came back she, I don't know, I couldn't rouse her …'

'It's time, I think,' said the priest.

'Time? Time for what? Bloody hell, NO.' Theresa glared at the vulture hovering at the foot of the bed. 'Keep you bloody hands of her; its all your fault you bloody hypocrite.'

'Theresa!'

'Don't you dare Theresa me, Win. You're as much to blame as he is. Our Mum is going to die because of you, him and your self-righteous friggin' church.' Theresa bent to kiss her mother. 'I'm sorry, Dad. I'll come back when he's finished his mumbo jumbo.' Keeping her eyes on her mother's face, Theresa edged her way past her Dad, then the priest and through the ward door. She was enveloped into the arms of the plump little figure in maroon waiting in the corridor.

# CHAPTER FORTY-FIVE

Theresa stayed with Tommy and Esther, sleeping on their living room floor. She used the excuse of the arrival of her aunty and nana from Ireland, and the major shuffle of sleeping accommodation, to get out of the family home. The visits of the priest once or twice a day tested her patience as well as her tongue. She, Win and Tommy had been at home to support their dad when the undertaker called to make the funeral arrangements. The idea of a requiem mass was repugnant to her, but she accepted that it would be, as the last rites had been, what her mum would have wanted. The cost of the funeral was prohibitive but her dad and Tommy's mates had organised a whip round and Nana had arrived with a bundle of notes in her handbag.

'Tom, that's the front door,' said Esther. The young couple froze. Visitors were rare and those who visited regularly used the key on the string that was attached to the screw holding the letter box in place.

'It can't be your mum and dad, not after all this time. Can it?' said Tom.

'I'll go,' said Theresa, 'they don't scare me.'

The rat-a-tat-tat continued.

'No, I'll go they've no hold over me now,' said Esther.

Theresa and Tom listened intently.

'Theresa, it's your priest at the door, he's asking for you,' said Esther.

'What the bloody hell does he want?' She threw down the tea towel she was using to wipe the pots. 'Why has he followed me here?'

'I don't know, but I've left him standing at the door. Should I invite him up, or will you go down and see him?'

'I'll go down, you don't want that bastard up here, contaminating the place.' Theresa clomped down the stairs, snorting; her breathing heavy, her eyes wide.

'What do you want?'

'Theresa, won't you let me come up and pray with you before your dear Bernadette's funeral tomorrow? I know it is what she would want.'

'What my mother would want is to be alive, with her family. How do you think my dad and our little uns are going to cope without her? It's because of you, you and that bigoted, sanctimonious bloody church that she is dead. Now, shift your arse and bugger off.'

Theresa went to the funeral. She cared too much about her dad and her brothers and sisters not to. She took no part in the Mass; instead she fastened her eyes on the coffin and systematically recalled her life with her mum.

Once the pots were washed from the funeral tea and the little ones were in bed, Win announced that she was off to catch the bus to return to the hospital. Theresa, who couldn't stand the thought of an hour's frozen silence on the journey with Win, excused herself to return to

Tommy and Esther's to collect her bag. She had a bottle of cider with them and left to catch the last bus back to the hospital.

She stepped from the bus, dropped her bag in the bus shelter and slid down the back wall until her bottom landed on the soft bag. She stared out into the autumn night.

'Hello Miss, are you all right,' said a male voice.

Startled awake, Theresa shook her head to focus on a policeman towering over her.

'Yes, yes, I think so.' Cold and stiff she struggled to stand. 'What time is it?'

'Nearly midnight.'

'Is she drunk?' said a second voice.

'No I am not, I've had two glasses of cider – you cheeky bugger.'

'Watch who you're calling a cheeky bugger, Miss. Let's get her to medical emergency,' said the second voice.

'Leave me alone. I live here, in the nurses' home. I've come from my mum's funeral.' She started to cry. Her pent up anger had kept her tears at bay during the funeral and the pitiful wake. She felt lonely and bereft. 'I haven't slept properly since it all happened; please leave me, I'll walk up the drive.'

'Come on love, get in the car and we'll run you up to the home,' said the first policeman. He picked up her bag. 'It's a fair walk; I was up there last week for a burglary.'

'I'll need to call in and see the night sister and ask her to let me in, just drop me at the main door of the hospital.' Theresa, struggling to move her feet and legs, hobbled toward the police car.

'I'll come in with you and explain. My name is Graham, by the way. What's yours?'

As the police car swung round the drive in front of

the home Theresa looked up and saw Sister Smith peering out the kitchen window on the sisters' corridor. She thought she saw Miss Bennet hovering in the background.

'Come on, Nurse Booth love, I'm sure I saw Bea Bennet at the window.' The night sister unlocked the front door. 'We'll get her to make you a warm drink and see you tucked up in your room.'

'I told you Bennet, it is that trollop Booth. Who else would it be; being brought home in a police car at this time? I ask you?' Theresa heard the voices before she saw the two figures in night clothes and curlers. 'She isn't a trollop, she is a dear child who has just lost her mother in childbirth.'

Theresa and the night sister watched the two figures descend the stairs.

'Thank God you're still up, Bea. It's poor Nurse Booth. Will you be able to see her to bed with a hot drink and two paracetamol? We're pulled out and I need to get back.'

After a ragged sleep Theresa found the strength to drag herself out of bed and across to the School of Nursing. Everything had happened so quickly; her mum died on Monday, the funeral was yesterday – Thursday, and here she was back in block.


'Come on Theresa, you should know we're not going to leave you on your own, not so soon after your mum's funeral. It's our last ever study block and there's little chance of us all being together until the 21st birthdays in the New Year,' said Jenny. 'Honestly, it's no trouble, I enjoy cooking and Paul and Dave will be there.'

'Yes, come on Theresa. It won't be the same without you will it, Maggie?' said Sarah.

'You can tell us all about the funeral, what they did with the baby and everything.'

'Maggie!' said Sarah.

'Where's Chris?' Theresa looked around.

'What are you bothering about her for? You've enough on your plate.'

'Maggie,' said Jenny, touching Maggie's elbow and shaking her head. 'Theresa, take a deep breath; she's at home resting in bed, she's got high blood pressure – she's having twins.'

Dear God no, not again, please don't let her be like my mum.

'How is she?'

'Fine, don't worry. She's just resting. The family doctor and the midwife are visiting regularly.' Jenny put her arm round Theresa. 'It won't be like your mum, promise.'

'You're very quiet, Maggie. You're not upset about Chris are you?' Jenny said.

'Why would I be bothered about her? I'm fine. I won't be there tonight, by the way.'

The evening had been a blur. Theresa excused herself and left Jenny and Dave's early, insisting she walk back to the nurses' home. She was relieved to be on her own and back at the home.

'Hey, Booth, I'm sorry about your mum. You didn't hear me the first time, I said aren't you going to pick up those flowers and take them to your room?' An anonymous body traipsing down the corridor peered from underneath a towel she was using to dry her hair. Theresa glanced round and saw a large bouquet of flowers in a bucket at the side of the table in the entrance hall. She read the card and made her way to the telephone booth.

'That bobby sent me flowers,' she said to Jenny.

'Let me tell Sarah everything's all right, she's worried something might have happened.' Theresa heard mutterings. 'What does the card say?'

'He wants me to go to the Free Trade Hall in Manchester with him on Saturday, to a Gershwin concert.'

'Sarah says stay up until she gets back.'

'I'll have a bath and wait for her. I can't go, I've nothing to wear and it seems wrong; it's too soon.'

'Sarah will see you later, and we can talk about clothes tomorrow because you are definitely going, even if I have to come and get you ready myself. Sleep tight.'

Theresa was ready, standing in the entrance hall of the home waiting for Graham Evans to take her to a concert of American music – Gershwin, who she had heard of, and Aaron Copeland, who nobody had heard of. Followed by 'a bite to eat' at the Danish Food Centre, whatever and wherever that was.

*Wait till I tell my Mu... Bloody hell, don't cry Theresa, your mascara'll run, and that'll be his car's just turned the corner.*

# FINALS

## CHAPTER FORTY-SIX

The hospital final results were with each of the matrons. At the Infirmary, Matron had arranged the dark green petersham belts and epaulets, each labelled with the potential owner's name, in an order to coincide with the appointment time of individual nurses. It was Matron's custom to hold a simple ceremony where the sludge green belt and epaulettes were removed and the new, darker green belt fastened around the waist and epaulettes hooked onto the shoulders. The procedure might be simple for Matron, but not for the potential hospital finalist. The correct fitting of the apron; no rolling the skirt over or pulling the waist tight and fastening with safety pins, was essential. Given that the nurses were now well into their third year and the twelve aprons had been worn and worn again the majority of the finalists had spent the previous evening searching for long lost apron buttons and sewing them back into place.

Sarah arrived outside Matron's office five minutes before her appointed time of 9.20. She glanced down at her chest and checked her watch. Had the fingers moved? She checked again.

'Good luck, Nurse Green,' the home sister said as she waddled past, 'although, I doubt you need it.'

'Thank you, Sister.'

'I thought you'd have gone in by now?' said Jenny as she walked toward Sarah.

'So did I, it's twenty five past. Are you nervous?'

'A bit. We did enough revision. Didn't we?'

'God forbid, she's failed again,' Sarah said as the door opened and a figure fled out of Matron's office and ran down the corridor.

'Nurse Green?' Matron stood, unsmiling, at the door of her office.

'Do take a seat, Nurse.'

In her nervousness Sarah made the mistake of perching on the edge of the cushion sitting innocuously on the polished chair; she found herself sliding toward Matron's knees.

'Well Nurse Green, congratulations are in order.' Matron turned and reached for a dark green bundle. 'Am I correct in understanding that you wish to staff on Jones ward?' Matron, looking doubtful, tapped the side of her right eye. 'Since I became matron, I have never known such a request.'

'Yes, Matron, I enjoy the variety of work in ophthalmics.'

Matron grimaced. 'Shall we get on?'

Sarah unhooked her epaulettes and handed them over. As she unbuttoned her belt she watched Matron give her the once over and nod.

'Do you intend to take the ophthalmic nursing certificate? I understand you are engaged to Rose Threlfall ... sorry, Thompson's son and he is at Manchester, as was Jerr... Dr Thompson?'

'Yes. I mean yes, I am engaged to Paul Thompson but no, I won't be doing the ONC. I'm more interested in thinking about health visiting, in the long run, but I want to concentrate on my state finals before I make any decisions about the future.'

'Very wise, Nurse. Very wise indeed. Please give my regards to Doctor,' Matron's chest heaved as she sighed, 'and Mrs. Thompson.'

'Thank you, Matron.' What the hell was all that about? Sarah thought.

Jenny requested that she be allocated to staff on Thorpe.

At the General, Maggie opted for theatre, and although Theresa toyed with the idea of paediatrics she rejected it. Paediatrics wouldn't fit in the long term plan she was developing, based on her admiration of Miss Bennet; she requested gynaecology. Chris, at home on bed rest, telephoned Matron to be told she was a successful hospital finalist. The hospital finals completed meant Sarah, Jenny, Maggie and Theresa were set to face their state final examinations. Chris was to defer to a later date. Fred and Theresa ganged up on Chris. Theresa scrutinised her cooperation card after each antenatal appointment and translated the numbers and abbreviations for Fred.

'I can explain the abbreviations myself. I was on the same obstetric course as Theresa.'

'I know, my love, but Theresa is still in the shadow of her mother's death and we are both very anxious about you. I think it helps her to be involved with our babies, keeps her grounded. People can behave quite strangely when they experience sudden loss and penetrating grief.'

'You are a lovely man Fred Cummings, help pull me up.' Chris eased herself off the bed, slipped her feet into her shoes and lumbered slowly down stairs. 'I'll get lazy resting on the bed half the day.'

'Let me get that,' said Fred as the letterbox rattled. 'If

you bend down we'll need a crane to get the three of you up again.' Fred emerged from the vestibule leafing through a clutch of letters. 'One for you, love.'

'It's Theresa's writing.' Chris walked into Fred's study to borrow his paper knife and deftly split open the envelope.'

'Ye God's Fred, what did you say about behaving strangely? It's Theresa – she's eloped with Graham, the policeman.'

'Jenny, Jenny, come and read this.' Sarah was standing in front of the pigeon holes in the Infirmary nurses' dining room. She handed over a letter.

'I'm flabbergasted, bloody hell,' said Jenny.

'What's made her do that, without telling us?'

'God only knows. Although, when we went out with them, when you were on nights, they couldn't keep their eyes off each other. Or their hands come to think of it.'

'He's just what she needed, don't you think? The way he treats her, as though she might break.'

'You're an old romantic Sarah Green, and if he thinks she's fragile then Graham the Gentle Giant had better watch out.'

Theresa went to find her during her coffee break.

'Maggie, Maggie, I'm married,' Theresa held out her left hand, 'to Graham; we eloped.'

'So, what do you want me to do about it?' Maggie shrugged. 'You'd better go. Sister's in a shitty mood.' Maggie turned to retreat back down the theatre corridor.

'Maggie, Maggie, please don't be like that.' Theresa checked the time. *Bugger I need to get back, I haven't time to get changed to go into theatre.* 'Come back and talk to me.'

Theresa watched Maggie disappear into the theatre preparation room.

# CHAPTER FORTY-SEVEN

Marianne and Alice Cummings were born on the 16 January 1969. The babies were good weights at five pounds twelve ounces and six pounds two ounces. Chris was adamant she was not breastfeeding. Sister Edwards might be very good at the theory but she needed to have a go at living in the real world. The thought of having her breasts exposed with a baby tucked under each arm and feeding simultaneously made Chris shudder. She had become a wife, mistress of the vicarage, stepmother and now mother in a whirlwind.

The constant calls to the vicarage, at the door and over the telephone, had abated slightly, particularly from the members of the inner sanctum of the coven. Even so, calls were unpredictable and not conducive to the demand breastfeeding of twins Chris informed the district midwife, who handed over to the health visitor, who harrumphed and complained to the family doctor, who shrugged his shoulders.

The beginning of January to the end of April was a time of twenty-first birthday parties. Theresa's party was combined with a wedding celebration and house warming.

Theresa and Graham moved into a police house after renting a furnished stone cottage for two months. For the move to the house they bought a double-bed and put-you-up settee using interest free higher purchase. On their days off they scoured second hand shops in Farnton and neighbouring towns to find sturdy furniture which included; a utility dressing table, a matching wardrobe, dressing table and bedding box and four bentwood dining chairs and a double leaf dining table. Graham borrowed a van from a police colleague and huffing and puffing and stopping for much needed kisses, he and Theresa hauled their motley furniture collection into their marital home. A search of the local bookshop had been rewarded and with frequent consultations with the book the couple were developing expertise in sanding and re-varnishing. The previous occupants of the house had been so made up with the elevation of their status to Inspector and Mrs they left decent carpets in the hall, stairs and landing.

Sarah and Paul offered to pay for the material for front room curtains as a combined wedding and twenty-first present; the gift included Sarah making up the curtains. Theresa and Sarah had wandered round the market and found an orange and yellow check fabric that would contrast with the dark turquoise of the put-you-up. When Sarah had arrived to hang the curtains she brought a gift from her mother, one orange and two yellow cushions.

Bricks and planks were introduced to each other to form makeshift bookcases. An electric cooker was on rental from the Electricity Board. Theresa and Graham had a home they could call their own and to which they had invited their friends and family for the triple celebration.

'Would you please raise your glasses to Tessa, my beautiful wife, on the occasion of her twenty-first birthday party?'

'Tessa?' Elizabeth raised her eyebrows at her sister.

'It's what he thought he heard her say when he found her in the bus shelter,' said Maggie, curling her lip. 'She goes along with it, like she goes along with everything she thinks will better her.'

'What are you blathering about?'

'Her, and her hoity-toity friends. Anyway, I'm going now, I'm meeting my own friends.'

'Which friends? Does Dad know?'

Maggie picked up her handbag. 'Anyway, I don't give a monkey's, and they'll see I get home.'

Elizabeth watched her sister leave the room and made her way over to Jenny.

'Jenny?'

'Hello Elizabeth, is something wrong? Where's your Maggie going?'

'She says she's going to meet some other friends.'

'What other friends?'

'Precisely. There's something funny going on. I'm going to have it out with her once and for all when we get home.'

'Let me know if I can help, we've all been concerned about her for a while now. She won't let any of us near her, she avoids us … hello.' Jenny turned to greet a tall, attractive bohemian looking woman who was hovering close by.

'Hello, I'm Nell Evans, Tessa's mother-in-law. You must be her nursing friends; she's very fond of you all.'

'Yes, I'm Jenny; this is Elizabeth who is also my cousin-in-law. Her sister, Maggie has had to …. well,' Jenny and Elizabeth glanced at each other and glanced away, 'err well, she isn't here just now. Our other friend is Chris, she was here a minute ago, I expect she has gone to see to her babies, her husband is the vicar over there in the corner. He's talking to Sarah and Paul ...'

'Graham is very lucky to have found such a live wire as Tessa. He's very quiet himself, and you are such a charming group of friends.'

'Are you on your own?' Jenny scanned the room.

'I'm afraid so. My three elder sons are tied up and my husband doesn't travel very well – he's not having a very good retirement, health wise. I'm sorry to say Graham missed out; we were older when he arrived – he was a surprise. Oh dear, forgive me,' she cast a furtive glance at Fred, 'I'm forever speaking out of turn.'

'Fred? I've forgotten he's older, he's just one of us now,' said Jenny.

'Who are the young couple? Surely she can't be wearing a wedding ring. What an interesting bunch you are.'


Sarah's protestations that she'd had a big party the previous year to celebrate her engagement fell on deaf ears. Her mum and Rose compromised with a cheese and wine party to be at the Greens' home, in Stonelee, for ladies only. They invited Sarah's school and nursing friends and the vicar's wife, in lieu of her husband. Mrs Ashford sent her apologies; she would be visiting later in the month for Jenny's twenty-first when she hoped to spend time with 'dear Mrs Green and Sarah'.

'The new fridge is coming in useful, Mum.' Sarah crouched down in front of the open door of the gleaming white bulk. 'Where would we have stored this lot?' She shuffled plates to make room for a cheese dip.

'I can't believe you managed all these years without one, Marjorie,' said Rose.

'Neither can I, it's marvellous for storing left overs.' Sarah smiled at her mum's face as she incredulously watched Rose dump bread, left over from making harlequin sandwiches, onto the pile of rubbish being stashed for the dustbin. 'They look pretty, the sandwiches with a brown and white slice,' Mrs Green's voice squeaked as it rose.

Sarah gave her mother a loving glance; her mum had changed since their set to about the Emko. When she smiled, which she did much more frequently, her eyes lit up. Sarah had heard her humming along to *Housewives' Choice*. The long talks Sarah and Rose had shared during Rose's convalescence were thought provoking; they had prompted Sarah to consider life from her mum's standpoint.

The telephone and fridge had been items of serious discussion between Sarah and Mrs Green. Her mum had never spent so much money and had felt faint and dizzy in the Electricity Board showroom when it was time to pay. She told Sarah 'it's an awful lot of money but Rose and Mrs Ashford say a fridge is essential for entertaining.'

'Thank you, both of you, for a brilliant party.' Sarah kissed her mum on the cheek as they closed the front door on the last guest; she stepped toward Rose and planted a kiss on her cheek. 'It was really great to have all my friends here.'

'Where was that quiet girl? You know, Elizabeth's sister?' said Rose.

'Maggie. She couldn't change her off duty, strange really, when she's in theatre and they work regular days,' said Sarah.

'I don't know about you two but I'm ready for a cup of tea after all that wine. Do you know the twelve of us went through three bottles of wine, what was it – Blue Nun?' Mrs Green said, making for the kitchen.

Jenny and Maggie had a joint party in traditional Smithfield style. The guest list included local family as well as Granny Ashford, who had made the journey from Devon, Marjorie Green, and Tommy and Esther, who joined girls from the hospital and their boyfriends, or in some cases husbands. One or two more recent friends had been asked to come along and join in with the fun.

'It's good to see you enjoying yourself, Margaret.'

'Why wouldn't I be, Dad?'

'No reason luv, well other than your mum and our Elizabeth keep going on about you being upset about summat or other.'

'Take no notice, Dad. They don't know what they are talking about.'

'Where's yon lad from?'

'India.'

'Mrs Ashford said she thought he was, and she should know with her dad having been out there.'

'I need to get back to him, Dad.'

'Right oh luv, I'll come and say hello later. It's good of you to have invited him to your party, with him being so far away from home.'

Maggie sauntered across the room beaming at the man holding out his arms to her.

'You may turn over your question paper and begin the morning examination,' Miss Bennet said.

Maggie could feel sweat under her arms, between her legs and running down her back. The smell of new-mown grass wafted through the open windows. She looked round the old classroom at the green shoulders of the girls around her as they scribbled away. She sat back in her chair and unfastened her collar stud. She reached out for the question paper folded it in half and fanned herself. She glanced at the clock; two hours and fifty minutes to go and then another three hours in the afternoon.

Three days later it was practicals day. Strict chaperoning of the student nurses ensured that those candidates yet to meet their inquisitors did not meet those who had emerged from the ordeal. Miss Bolton supervised the students as they arrived at the School of Nursing and before they entered the practical rooms. Uniforms were pristine, well they were by the time the candidates met the examiners. Miss Bolton had six cards of white hair grips and two tins of Cherry Blossom brown polish and associated dusters as well as a pair of nail scissors. Mr Bradshaw kept a strict eye on the time, ensuring that each nurse had exactly thirty minutes with the examiners. Miss Bennet was stationed in the old classroom holding captive those who had completed the practical and were intent on pouncing on each set of candidates as they emerged from their inquisitions and working them into lather as they dissected questions and answers.

The captive students and Miss Bennet turned toward the door. It was too early for the next group to emerge.

'Nurse Booth, Evans, I mean, come here – quickly.' Miss Bolton stood in the doorway. Theresa looked quickly at Miss Bennet who nodded her permission for Theresa to leave the room.

'Nurse Smithfield felt faint and dizzy during the practical. Go and sit with her in reception and remember, do not speak to other candidates.'

Maggie was slouched in an armchair, gazing into space.

'What's up Mags? You look like death warmed up.'

Maggie stared at Theresa and shrugged her shoulders.

'What's it to you?'

'Maggie, why are you being like this? What the bloody hell has got into you?'

'I said – what's it to you?'

Theresa perched on the edge of the armchair next to

Maggie's. 'What's up Maggie, are you poorly?' Theresa bent forward to try and catch Maggie's eye.

Maggie gave her a fleeting glance and brought her hand together to rest on her abdomen.

Theresa looked and looked again.

'What! Bleedin' hell, Maggie. I don't, I can't believe it. What are you trying to tell me?'

Maggie shrugged and turned her head away.

'Is everything all right, nurses?'

'Nurse Smithfield needs to go home; I'll go with her, if that's all right, Miss Bolton.'

The bus journey into town and then out of town to the Smithfields' home dragged by. Theresa gave up asking questions; Maggie's stock reply of 'what's it to you?' and her refusal to make eye contact added to the strain of the journey.

'You can go now,' Maggie said as Theresa pushed open the garden gate. 'Go back to your fancy husband and friends and tell them the news; how stupid, daft Maggie's got herself up the duff. You can all have another good laugh at me. I wish you were dead, I wish I were dead.'

'Margaret? Theresa? What's the matter?' Mrs Smithfield emerged from the side of the house and hurried down the path.

'Mum, I need to talk to you.' Maggie started to cry. She grabbed at her mother's arm. 'I'm pregnant.'

'Good lord, no!' Mrs Smithfield glanced down at her daughter's abdomen. 'I thought you might be. You're not, are you? How can you be?'

Maggie trudged toward the house followed by her mother.

Theresa turned to make her way back toward the bus stop.

*How the bloody hell has all that happened?*

# CHAPTER FORTY-EIGHT

On the 21st of July 1969 man landed on the moon and the State Registered Nurse final examination results were out. The finalists formed orderly queues outside the two matrons' offices. Of the twenty-four student nurses who entered training in May 1966, eleven had taken the final examinations. They were joined by those who had queued for results before, some of them three or four times, with one unfortunate for the fifth and final time, no matter what the result.

The door of Matron's office opened and Sarah came out beaming, wearing red epaulettes and a red belt.

'I'll hang on and wait for you,' she said as Jenny walked quickly through the opened door of Matron's office.

Jenny emerged.

'We've done it, Sarah, we've done it.' Jenny grabbed Sarah's hands and twirled her round. 'Do you think I've time to ring Dave before I go back to the ward?'

Theresa adjusted her red belt as she waited for Maggie to emerge from Matron's office. In the six weeks since the practical examination news of Maggie's pregnancy had spread. Jokes about immaculate conceptions alternated between speculations as to the name of the father.

Despite Maggie's continued rejection of her, Theresa was intent on waiting for her friend and walking with her, back to theatre.

The door of Matron's office opened and Maggie emerged, the dark green still in place on her shoulders and waist.

'Come on Mags; ignore that lot,' Theresa said marching past the queue. 'Do you want me to let Jenny, Sarah and Chris know how you've gone on?'

'Please yourself Theresa, just like you always did, always do and always will do. Bugger off and leave me alone. It would all have been all right, but for her.'

'Who?'

'Chris Warrington. She spoiled everything.'

'What, I don't understand.'

Theresa stood and watched Maggie slouch down the corridor.

'Maggie wait, you can't go on like this.'

'Like what?'

'Being a daft bugger and shutting me – us – out. What's up Mags, come on tell me. I thought I was supposed to be your friend.'

'You were. But then I, well, I proved you right in the end, didn't I?'

Maggie leaned against the wall and turned her head away from Theresa.

'Come on, Mags, you can't go back to theatre in this state. Let's get some fresh air. Theresa hustled Maggie outside where she guided her to a bench outside the main entrance.

'Can you remember the first day we were here, when I was drenched?'

'Theresa, I need to … our Elizabeth says I have to tell you …'

'Mags, spit it out. Please, I want to help you …'

'You were right, Theresa, and I'm like you said I was – daft; a daft kid. Look at me.' Maggie looked down at her distended abdomen. 'I thought you didn't want me; that you wanted to be with Chris all the time. Our Elizabeth said its because I lived out and you lot … I'm so tired Theresa.'

'Maggie, you daft bugger, come here.'

'Are you all right, nurses?' said a passing porter.

Theresa wiped her eyes, and released her grip on Maggie.

'Thanks, we're fine. Final results and all that,' said Theresa.

'Mags, your Elizabeth is worried to death about you. She told me about how you managed to get …' Theresa patted Maggie's abdomen. 'Honestly, you're as bad as Tommy and Esther messing about and not … well you know what I mean. Why didn't you tell him before he went back to his own country?'

'He has a wife … and children.'

'I know luv, Elizabeth told me. But you've got me and the others, as well as Elizabeth and your mum and dad. Elizabeth says your dad's all right now he's got over the shock.'

Maggie sniffled and nodded. 'It was horrible at first. He kept crying and wouldn't look at me…'

'I've missed you, Mags. What with losing my mum, and our Win; I don't think me and her will ever speak to each other again. I need you, Mags, I always have and I always will. I wish you'd let me help you, but well, I'm here with you now and that's what matters. I'm going to make sure you bloody well pass next time. You wait and see.'

Theresa nudged Maggie then reached out to stroke

her friend's abdomen. Maggie fastened her hand on top of Theresa's.

'I've missed you too,' Maggie said. 'Have you got a dry hanky I can borrow?'

# A NURSE'S LIFE BY JANE GRANT

*Heart-warming and humorous tales from a 1950s student nurse*

In this warm and witty book, Jane Grant recounts her life as a trainee nurse in a busy 1940s London teaching hospital.

Jane, and her friends Mary and Phyllis, discover that both happiness and heartache can be found on the wards of St. Bernard's Hospital. Before long they realise it takes determination and a sense of humour to deal with the colourful characters of hospital life – and that goes for the staff as well as the patients.

The young nurses gain their medical training under the watchful eyes of strict, but generally fair, sisters and matrons. They meet patients who are facing the biggest challenges of their lives, and share with them moments of bravery and fear. There are times of laughter, but also of tears.

There is romance too, as Jane and her fellow student nurses enjoy the attentions of the hospital's handsome young doctors, falling in and out of love for the first time.

*A Nurse's Life* is a moving and amusing account of a bygone era, brought vividly to life. Also available in this series, there is more from Jane and her friends and family in *More From a Nurse's Life, A Sister's Life and A Country Life.*

*A Nurse's Life* and the rest of the Jane Grant series are available as ebooks from Amazon.

Printed in Great Britain
by Amazon